BROAD STREET

A Novel

Christine Weiser

PS BOOKS

Regional Publishing, National Voice
A division of Philadelphia Stories

Regional Publishing, National Voice
A division of Philadelphia Stories

2021 S. 11th Street
Philadelphia, PA 19148
www.psbookspublishing.org

ISBN: 978-0-9793350-1-3 (0-9793350-1-9)
SAN: 856-2156

Published by PS Books, a division of Philadelphia Stories, Inc.
Philadelphia, PA
© 2008 by Philadelphia Stories, Inc.
All rights reserved

Design by Derek Carnegie

All proceeds for the sale of PS Books titles go to support *Philadelphia Stories*, a free nonprofit literary magazine publishing writers and artists from the Delaware Valley.

Cover Image: "Blue Tressed and Dressed"
by Marlise Tkaczuk © 2008

To Carla Spataro,
for helping me find my voice.

CHAPTER

Noelle called me and said it was time to put the breakup behind me. Three weeks was long enough, she said.

I took a deep breath. This party would be fine. He probably wouldn't be there. He probably wouldn't bring her. I covered the dark circles under my eyes with makeup. I pulled bright red lipstick across my lips. I twisted my curly brown hair into a ponytail. It was just another party, I repeated. But I knew it was really the first of many attempts to avoid the ex in the small circle of our Philadelphia friends. Our friends. That wasn't quite true. They were Dale's friends, mostly musicians he'd met through his band. They accepted me when I was attached to him. I wasn't sure how well I would fare now that I'd been amputated.

I walked to the large open suitcase that served as my makeshift closet, my clunky boots echoing cruelly in the empty room. After the breakup, I had moved my few belongings from Dale's apartment to this tiny house in a dark pocket of South Philadelphia. I couldn't bring myself to settle in. It would be too final.

I selected a bright miniskirt from the suitcase pile and wiggled it over my hips. I picked through a pile of shirts, trying to find one relic that didn't remind me of Dale. Sweet, charming, funny, cheating, Dale. I settled on a sleeveless black turtleneck, pulled it on, then collapsed on the bed. I was already exhausted.

I have to get back to my life.

I took a deep breath, pulled myself up, and descended the stairs to the small living room. Two folding chairs stood unused in one corner. A trash-picked sofa sat in another, draped in the blanket cocoon I wrapped myself in nightly after work, basking in the blue glow of bad television. Pathetic.

As I walked toward the front door, I was startled by my reflection in the living-room window. Who was that girl? She looked braver than I felt.

I took the subway to the party in Center City. I walked from the stop down a quiet street in the business district, where merchandise peeked out from behind thick steel gates. As I approached the address of the old brownstone, I heard the muffled sound of voices and the latest Nirvana album. I felt a wash of panic. I could be back home and under my blanket in twenty minutes; but my feet kept moving forward. I found the appropriate apartment number, rang the bell, and was buzzed in without question.

The party was a crowded gathering of hipsters. I scanned the room for familiar faces, feeling stupid. The few I recognized looked at me, then quickly turned away. Finally, I spotted Noelle.

"Hey Kit," she smiled. Her sandy hair hung neatly around a tiny, plain face. "How are you?"

She gave me a hug. Noelle would be one of many mutual friends walking the tightrope between the fallen couple. I tried to balance her with a forced smile.

"Hi Noelle," I said. "Thanks for inviting me. Who's having this party, anyway?"

"Pete and his girlfriend, Margo." She nodded toward a guy talking to a group of people. "Pete's in that band, Smarmy."

I had seen them play a few times with Dale. I remembered Pete as the junkie-thin lead singer bobbing back and forth to a turgid wall of guitar noise.

"And that's Margo over there," Noelle pointed to another corner.

My eyes followed her finger to the corner of the room. Margo was tall and curvy, her long black hair shining with streaks of midnight blue. Her full lips were accented with bright scarlet lipstick; her blue eyes painted with a swish of black eyeliner. She wore a low-cut red satin dress that hugged her figure, and held a martini and cigarette gracefully in one hand as she smiled at a chatting male guest. I felt flat-chested and plain.

"I'll introduce you."

My heart thudded noisily as I followed Noelle closer to this intimidating creature.

"Hey Margo," Noelle said. "This is my friend, Kit."

Margo moved her cool smile away from the guy to fix her eyes on me. She inhaled deeply from her cigarette; her pool-blue eyes bored through me. I felt like a frog pinned down to a board, a scalpel dangling above me.

"Don't you go out with Dale?" she asked.

Noelle gasped.

"I used to," I said, attempting my cheeriest tone.

"Oh. Sorry," she said, looking over my shoulder at the rest of the crowd.

"It's all right," I mumbled.

Margo's eyes continued to scan the room. I fiddled nervously with the clasp of my purse as I awaited further instructions from our hostess. After a moment, she looked back at Noelle and me.

"So," she said in a bored tone. "Can I get you guys a drink?"

"I'm going to go grab a beer outside," Noelle said.

Just as I was about to follow Noelle's lead, Margo turned her piercing gaze toward me, and smiled with aloof politeness.

"How about you, Kate, would you like a martini?"

"It's Kit, and…sure."

I followed Margo to a table that sparkled with a liquor rainbow. She poured with expert precision, first filling a chrome shaker with ice, then using both hands to tip in a clear stream of vodka, then a splash of vermouth. She snapped on the lid, spun the shaker, then filled the triangular glass until the martini almost kissed the rim. Dropping a sword of olives in the drink, she turned and handed it to me.

"You've done that before," I said, trying to sound charming.

She laughed. "A few times."

We both took long sips of the grown-up drink. Margo continued to smile politely, but kept her eyes moving around the room.

"What do you do, Kit?" she asked indifferently.

"I'm a proofreader." I took another sip from the smooth glass. The vodka was already massaging my anxiety with its warm fingers. "How about you?"

Margo waved her hand as if shooing an invisible insect.

"Oh, I do PR for an insurance company. It's selling out, I know, but it's decent money." She turned her gaze from the crowd back to me and leaned closer, crowding the air between us with musky perfume. "Sorry about mentioning Dale. I didn't know."

"That's okay." I took another sip. "We just had a different definition of monogamy."

Her eyebrow lifted slightly as she smiled.

"Really? I can relate to that." She nodded toward the corner at Pete, who was flirting with an attractive hipster. She lifted the plastic sword out of her empty glass and pulled off three olives in one bite. Her lipstick remained perfect. "Let's get another drink."

I wondered why this beautiful girl would put up with someone like Pete. I also wondered why she was ignoring her other guests to spend so much time with me, a stranger.

"So," Margo began, pulling another cigarette from a silver case. "Last time I saw Dale he was playing at The Barbary with the Electric Love Muffin. I don't remember meeting you there."

"I don't think I was at that show."

But I did remember that night. We'd had a huge fight and he stormed out. Toward the end, he started a lot of arguments before his gigs. I realized later it probably had something to do with a third party.

"Probably a good thing." Margo took a drag from her cigarette. "They were pretty bad that night. I stopped going to Pete's shows. I thought it was fun for a while, but then I just got tired of being ignored." She paused to glare in Pete's direction, then took a sip from her martini.

"I know," I said. "Dale was really different in college."

I was hit with a quick, painful memory of the first night he had serenaded me on his acoustic guitar. I had met him at the college radio station; we both lived on the periphery of our conservative school. A conversation at a frat party about music evolved into six amazing months. And then we graduated, and moved to Philadelphia.

"He wasn't in a band in college," I said.

"A band is just their excuse for getting drunk with their buddies. They don't even know how to write a decent song."

She was right. I had played so many strong women musicians when I was a college radio DJ: Chrissie Hynde, Debbie Harry, L7. These women controlled their universes. Their lyrics captured the confidence I craved: dumping their guys, seducing their guys, not even thinking about guys. For two hours a week, I considered myself a missionary to all women. But when I moved in with Dale, I found my opinion melding with his. The bands we listened to grew angrier and louder. I stopped listening to my music and convinced myself that his screeching atonal bands were just as appealing.

"What kind of music do you listen to?" I asked.

"Oh, I like the old stuff, like Wanda Jackson, The Collins Kids. It's real simple, it has a hook, not like the crap these guys play."

She lifted her glass to her lips, then realized it was empty.

"This is a problem. Looks like you could use one, too."

She took my glass from my hand and refilled them both from the tall silver shaker she'd left on the table. I didn't normally drink hard liquor, and could feel myself disappearing a little, but I was immensely grateful for the company. I hadn't really talked to anyone about Dale. My parents didn't want to upset me, so they acted like we'd never dated. My kid sister was wrapped up in her own little college clique. I wanted to tell these things to Margo, not just because we had things in common, but I really wanted her to like me. We sat on the couch and smoked cigarettes and swirled martini after martini, my intimidation dwindling with each new glass.

"I never knew what I would find when I came home from work," I slurred slightly. "Sometimes Dale would just be sitting around smoking with guys from his band, and I'd walk in all corporate and they'd look at me like I was someone's mother."

Margo nodded her head sympathetically.

"Some days Dale wouldn't even be there when I got home," I continued. "I never knew where he was, and if I asked he'd say I shouldn't be so paranoid. Some nights he didn't come home at all."

"What an ass," Margo said. "Pete's the same way. He's a bartender, so he sleeps in and stays up late and listens to music when I'm trying to get to sleep so I can get up the next morning and make some decent money to pay our bills. All he cares about is 'the band' and his friends."

"Exactly."

We both stared at the tattooed people in the room.

"You know," Margo said, "these people work in comic book stores and coffee shops and they feel so superior to people like us who have the nerve to get a nine-to-five job." She shook her head in disgust. "Just because they can wear an eyebrow ring to work they think they're fucking artists. What gives them the corner on creativity?"

"Don't forget record stores," I said, "with their superior fucking attitude. God forbid if you pick up the wrong fucking CD—they look at you like you just voted for Orrin Hatch."

"Please," Margo rolled her eyes and took a long sip of her drink.

We stared, hurling invisible daggers at the clueless gathering.

"I know I could write a better song than most of the people in this room," Margo said. "I play a little guitar. It's not that hard."

"Really?" My already high opinion of Margo escalated. I had always wanted to try playing. "Have you ever played with a band?"

"Nah. I just mess around on one of Pete's acoustic guitars. How about you—do you play?"

"Actually, I kind of know how to play bass. Dale gave me one, and I took it with me when I moved because I knew he wanted it back, but felt too guilty to ask for it."

"Really?" Margo said, taking a drag off her cigarette. "Maybe we should get together. See what happens."

"I'd like that," I said.

Margo glanced over at Pete. Two guys who looked just like him stood at his sides. They were passing a joint and laughing. She turned back to me, her cheeks flushed.

"I can definitely get an electric guitar from Pete. He has, like, a dozen of them. I'm sure he can spare one."

The buzz of the martinis accentuated my enthusiasm. Thoughts of parties and gigs and new friends clouded my blurry vision.

"We can play at my house," I said. "I have plenty of room."

"And I've got a ton of song ideas. Real simple stuff. I could bring some CDs over." Margo fell back into the couch and grinned. "This is great. What better way to get back at these guys than to piss on their precious territory? Let's do it."

Margo lifted her martini in the air and we clinked glasses, the bond as strong as a blood oath.

My head was pounding. When I opened my eyes to take a quick inventory of the dead weight below my neck, I saw a full party wardrobe, boots and all. How did I get here? I found hazy memories of taking a cab home, of talking with Margo. How much had I confessed about my Dale debacle? I looked at the clock. 11:30. Who cares, I rolled myself into the comforter and closed my eyes again. There was no one to judge me today.

The phone rang about an hour later. The piercing bell sliced through my empty house. It was probably my parents. It was their Sunday ritual to ask hopeful questions about my miserable life. It might be Dale, calling to apologize, to beg for my forgiveness and promise me eternal commitment. Or not. Soon, it stopped, and my world returned to silence.

The next time I opened my eyes it was 3:30. My body still felt poisoned, but I was ready to feed it something greasy.

I rotated myself slowly until my legs were hanging off the bed. Carefully, I sat up. My head thudded rebelliously in this new position. I managed to stand up, put on a less-rumpled wardrobe, and pull myself together enough to head to Burger King. Before I left, I paused to check my messages. There were two. The first voice made me wince.

"Hey, it's me." Dale's voice, low, soothing. "Just wanted to see how you're doing. Give me a call if you feel like it."

Must have been from last night. Not exactly the begging-to-take-me back tone. Asshole. Then another voice spoke.

"Hi Kit, it's Margo. I feel like shit today, but I had a great time hanging out last night. I wanted to see if you were still into getting together today. Is it okay to do it at your place? Give me a call. My number's 215…"

Getting together? I scanned the hazy clips of my long dialog with Margo. Plenty of male bashing, I remember that. What else had I promised? A band. In my drunken stupor I had agreed to start a band.

When I rescued Dale's bass from the back of the closet, I was reminded of the day he had given it to me. We were still in the bubble of college life, and he had shown up at my dorm room with a guitar case.

"I want you to have this," he told me, kissing me softly on the cheek. "Bass isn't that hard, and I think with a little practice you could be good. You have a good instinct about music." He handed me a Surfer Rosa CD by The Pixies. "Play along with this. Kim Deal is a great rock bassist."

I thought that gift was the beginning, a symbol of his commitment. My damp eyes stung as I ran my fingers over the cool surface of the instrument. Margo would be here any minute, and I wasn't sure I was up to it. What would I say to her? Dale had always been the greeter, the one to make people feel comfortable. I was content to be the vicarious host.

There was a knock on the door. I dried my eyes against my sleeve, and took a quick glance in the mirror. A hangover would explain the glassy eyes. I forced a smile onto my weary face that made my cheeks quiver.

"Hi!" I said, too enthusiastically.

"Hey," she grunted as she pulled the equipment through the door.

"So," I asked, "what does Pete think about this idea?"

"He is totally stewing," she said, smiling. "I mentioned it to him this afternoon— when he finally rolled out of bed—and I don't think he took me seriously at first. But, when I was getting ready to leave tonight, he definitely seemed freaked out. He kept asking me who you were, and what kind of music we were going to play, and that kind of stuff. It was great. And, he gave me this."

She leaned down to prop up a hard leather guitar case, unbuckled the locks, and popped it open. In it, cushioned by a plush red bed, was a black Fender guitar. Its hour-glass body glistened, accented by a silver pick guard. This guitar had been loved. I did not think we should be playing a guitar this beautiful.

"Wow," I said stupidly. "I can't believe he lent this to you."

"Yeah," Margo said. "I'm always giving him shit about spending too much time playing, so he couldn't exactly say no."

We stared at the guitar as an awkward silence hung in the air. The acidic taste of anxiety burned at the back of my throat as I scrambled for something interesting to say.

"Want a beer?" I asked.

She snapped the case closed, then looked up and smiled. "Yes!"

I had found our glue.

Relieved, I brought two beers out to the living room, then pulled together my two lone folding chairs. I leaned Dale's bass against one. I didn't have an amplifier, so I would have to pluck it acoustically.

Margo pulled the guitar from safety and leaned it against the other folding chair. A black cord rested in a center compartment of the case. She plugged the cord into the guitar, then the tuner, and tuned each string.

"Can you give me a hand with this?" she asked. "I have no idea how to work this thing."

She pulled a small amp over to her chair and we struggled to set it up, doing our best to match the right plugs with the right receptors. The AC was easy to figure out. Margo followed the three-pronged plug that snaked out the back of the amp and shoved it into the outlet. I flicked the switch marked "power," and was delighted when a red light began to glow. The guitar, though, was not so easy. The cord slipped into the body of Pete's guitar, but the other end needed to attach to the amp and there were several holes that seemed to be the right size.

"Let's try this one," I suggested.

I stuck the other end of the guitar cord into one of the amp receptors. Instantly, the amp loudly squealed like a speeding car braking to avoid collision.

"Oh shit."

I yanked the cord out of the amp.

"Oh my god," Margo said softly. "Pete will kill me if I fuck this up."

We leaned closer to the amp, hoping it would whisper its secrets to us. I scanned my tired brain for memories of the hundreds of times I had watched Dale play guitar. I knew that one knob on the guitar body was volume, the other treble/bass. I turned them both counter-clockwise, nervous. If I killed Pete's amp, that would certainly be the end of our little experiment, and any chance at a new life.

"Let's try this," I said.

My hand shook slightly as I forced the metal plug into another receptor on the amp. Nothing.

"Maybe try turning it up again."

I turned the knob on the amp. The guitar slowly began to hum. It wasn't pretty, but we had volume.

"Excellent," Margo said, strumming the open strings.

Margo pulled a Mel Bay Guitar Book out of her large bag and opened to a page that illustrated chords.

"This book is great," she said. "I know the basics, E, A, D, G—they're in just about every basic rock song—but I'm still a little new to the minors and diminisheds."

Margo strummed some sloppy chords while I tried to find accompanying notes on the bass. I had never played with another live human being, and the inability to pause and rewind was a little frustrating. Still, it was a new sensation. Connection. I couldn't describe it any other way. We chugged out careful chords like tiny birds clambering out of the nest.

After an hour, we agreed that we were too hungover to learn much more.

"Do you want to get together next week sometime?" Margo asked as she packed up the guitar.

I had passed the test.

"Sure. How about Friday night?"

"Hmm. I can't on Friday"

Oh right. Most people have plans on Friday nights.

"How about Thursday night?" she said.

"Perfect."

The next day, I called about an ad in the local paper that listed a cheap amp for sale. It was a primitive handmade monster that entombed a 12-inch speaker in a plywood box. The equally unkempt owner, a disheveled teen attempting the costume of a rock star, was thrilled to hand me this package for fifty dollars.

For the next few weeks, Margo interrupted my lonely nights and rote work life every Thursday. She brought over 60s garage and Wanda Jackson CDs, music I'd never heard before. We played along with the CD tracks. Margo did her best to imitate Jackson's bad little girl vocals that screeched about jail riots and wild parties while we both struggled to duplicate the simple chords on our guitars. We played Jackson's "Fujiyama Mama" over and over until I was sure we had driven my neighbors insane. We also played along to no-hit wonders like The Vectors, Rocky and the Riddlers, The

Keggs, Sir Winston and the Commons, and The Golden Catalinas—all featuring catchy songs through the mud of poor production. As we sat and listened to the thirty-odd songs squashed on the murky Back from the Grave CD, I could almost forget about Dale in three-minute increments.

One night, Margo showed up with some good news.

"I found a drummer," she said.

"Really? Who?"

"It's a friend of this guy Joe who hangs out with Pete. He was over the other night and was talking about this girl who had just quit some all-girl band and was looking for a new project. Pete was so pissed when Joe gave me her number. It was great. She lives near here in a warehouse space off of Broad Street ..." And then she stopped, and smiled. "That's it."

"What?"

"Broad Street! How fucking cool a name is that for a band?"

I thought about this, feeling a slight tug on my feminist upbringing. My parents had spent many hours dishing out the importance of equal rights to my sister and me. I wasn't sure they would agree that this was a fucking cool name. But this was different, I rationalized. This was just a tongue-in-cheek poke at the gender of our band.

"I like it."

"I think it's awesome," Margo laughed. "Broad Street. That's hysterical."

"We can practice at this cheap place where Pete used to rehearse. It's called, like, Fishtown Studios or something. Anyway, it's only ten bucks an hour and it has all the mics and drums and stuff all set up. I'll call Linda tonight to set something up. Check out her name—Linda Licht. Isn't that perfect?"

Linda Licht. She had the name of a porn star and experience. She was in.

CHAPTER

Soon after this announcement, I decided to brave a trip home. It was about a 30-minute drive to my parents' home in Swarthmore, a Kodak-moment suburb outside of Philadelphia. I rolled down the windows to breathe in the morning air, sweet with the smell of fresh-cut grass. I drove my rusting Toyota past BMWs, Mercedes, palatial stone houses, impeccably manicured lawns, a lifestyle I would never afford as a single proofreader.

I pulled into my parents' driveway. Their house was a comparatively modest, two-story stone home on a small plot of land. A rocking chair and wooden bench invited guests to the front porch to relax, greet the neighbors, discuss the current headlines. This house was one of the few places I felt good with Dale. Surrounded by family, rather than pierced musicians, Dale was calmer, more attentive. He held my hand; he opened doors; he gave me gentle kisses.

But this day I wanted to remember only bad things about Dale.

My mother was bent over her favorite distraction—the garden. She was a horticultural artist, painting new colors and shapes all year-round. Today's canvas showcased small, deep purple irises, framing a backdrop of tall daylilies in pinks and oranges. She stood to greet me, rubbing her muddy jeans with muddy blue gardening gloves. She was still beautiful—a small, slightly graying brunette with milky white skin and a hint of pink in her cheeks. Her deep brown eyes lit up as she smiled.

"Well, hello!" She walked toward me, arms outstretched. I walked into them, let them embrace me. For just a moment, these small arms could protect me from anything.

"Hi mom."

Parting, she took my hand and scanned me head to toe.

"How are you?"

"I'm okay."

I swallowed the intense desire to cry.

She smiled. "You look good."

I knew she was lying. I'd lost weight, circles shadowed my eyes, my hair hadn't cooperated for weeks. I was grateful for her effort.

"Let's go find your father."

As I crossed the porch and walked through the squeaky door, I was reminded of the aroma of childhood—cool, musty, with the slightest hint of baking bread. A wooden staircase climbed to our bedrooms. A long mahogany table took up most of the rarely used dining room; deep rust-colored walls were dotted with old family photos. To the left was the living room, home to a potpourri of mismatched plaid love seats and an overstuffed chair, all bordering a coffee table littered with newspapers, New Yorkers, half-read fiction. Dusted light spilled through the windows and onto the emerald green walls, illuminating colorful abstract prints from a neighborhood artist. My father sat in a faded armchair, the *New York Times Book Review* in his lap. Seeing me, he smiled and tossed the review on the coffee table.

"Hi Dad."

He pulled the glasses from the end of his nose and smiled.

"Kittimany."

He was the only one to ever call by my full name, something he borrowed from his years as an English professor. He grunted dramatically as he pushed himself out of the chair. My father was twelve years older than my mother and loved to grumble about his decaying body. Despite his thick white hair and beard and watery blue eyes, he was still the same fiery person who seemed continually disappointed in me.

He walked over and hugged me. He smelled slightly of cigarettes, which he insisted he gave up. I chose to ignore it.

"How are you, Dad?"

"Bored."

Since retiring from Swarthmore College three years ago, this had become a standard answer. He had been passionate about his work as a professor, devouring literature like candy. But with no students to impress, life was less interesting for him. Plus, it was another thing to complain about.

"Why don't you do something?"

He looked at me and smiled, as if tolerating the naiveté of youth, when life still could get better. He sat back in his chair and I sat in the loveseat next to him, ready for the interrogation.

"How's work?" he asked.

"The same."

"I just read an interesting piece in the *Times*," my father said, leaning back in his chair and crossing his legs. "It said teaching is one of the fastest growing professions around."

I had long ago realized that the *Times* was merely a nom de plume for my father's opinion. He wanted me to go back to school and get a PhD and follow in his perfect footsteps, and was not afraid to embellish his plan for me with fictitious references.

"I don't want to be a teacher, Dad. You know that."

He let out a sigh that turned into a phlegmy cough. After it subsided, he continued.

"I was just telling you about a piece I read, that's all."

"Yes, I know, Dad. It's always an innocent comment."

We sat in silence for a minute.

"So what's new?" he asked.

I grasped for some redemption in my current life, and found only one.

Trying to sound casual, I said, "Not much. I started a band."

This was not quite the truth, since two mediocre musicians sitting in my empty room was hardly the Rolling Stones. But I wanted him to see a whisper of strength in me, even if I didn't actually feel it. He looked at me quizzically.

"A band? I didn't even know you could play an instrument."

"It's just electric bass. It's not that hard to play rock."

"I thought you hated Dale's band," he said.

There. He'd said it. He brought to life the name that had lurked beneath most of his questions lately.

"I did. But it's just for fun. I'm not quitting my job or anything."

Of course, if we happened to get signed by a label—a fantasy term Dale used to toss around with his band buddies—I wouldn't think twice about walking away from proofreading medical articles.

"Do you really think that's the best use of your spare time? What about joining a book club, or volunteering for a homeless shelter? You might meet some interesting people."

"Dad, in all the volunteer work you had me do as a kid, the only people I met were other dorky kids. I'm tired of hanging out with dorks."

He leaned forward in an angry scowl.

"You know how much we sacrificed fighting for the rights of people who couldn't fight themselves."

"Yes, Dad, I know. You've been espousing the holy virtues of the 60s my entire life. But, unfortunately, this is the 90s where there are more than two causes. There are too many things to fight for now."

"That doesn't mean you shouldn't fight for anything."

I rolled my eyes.

"I'm just having fun," I said. "I'll save the world later."

We sat in silence, contemplating my being a disappointment as a daughter until my mother rescued me with two glasses of iced tea.

"Do you want to sit outside?" she asked.

"Gladly."

I got up and walked away, trying to ignore the heavy sigh released from my father. I followed my mother through the screen door and sat beside her, rocking slowly in our chairs like two old ladies. I sipped at the tea—homebrewed, of course, with just enough sugar and fresh mint.

"How's work?" she asked.

"It's all right. My boss still gives me a hard time, but it's not too bad."

"How are you?"

"I'm okay."

"Your father and I worry about you living alone."

"Please. Dad isn't worried. He's disappointed."

She stopped rocking.

"That's not true. He's very proud of you." She paused. "I know he comes across a little strong, but that's just because he doesn't want you and your sister to sell yourselves short. It's not as bad as when I was young, but I think it's still tough for women. But you're strong enough to handle it."

"Sometimes I don't feel very strong."

She reached her hand over to mine.

"You are. Give it time."

"Dana!"

My father's voice called from behind us. My mother snapped her head around, then pushed herself out of the chair and walked quickly toward the house. The porch door creaked open and banged shut, thus reminding me of our household irony. My liberated mother could never quite apply her ideals to her relationship with my father.

When he called, she always ran.

I heard them talking through the screen door behind me. My father apparently had misplaced a certain pair of reading glasses and only my mother could be trusted to search the house for them. I continued to rock, wishing for something stronger than iced tea.

A red Cabriolet pulled into the driveway. My sister.

Nikki hopped out of the car. Her bleached white hair was shaved down to slightly longer than a peach. Her face, eyebrows and ears sparkled with silver hoops. Bright green eyeliner highlighted her light brown eyes; her small frame was encased in its usual tight black jeans and tank top. She was a junior at Moore College of Art, learning how to design Web sites for the masses. My mother returned to the porch and we both greeted Nikki with hugs.

"How are you, honey?" she asked.

"I'm great. I just had an interview with Spirit, and I think they may offer me a summer job."

Spirit was only the hippest ad agency in Philadelphia. Things always worked out that way for Nikki.

"Really?" my mother stood and gave her a hug. "That's great, honey."

Nikki pulled over a chair.

"Yeah, I met with the owner today. Really nice guy. Cute too. I showed him my portfolio and he seemed impressed. They're going to call me this week. The money's not great, but it would be a good experience. Maybe they'll hire me next year after graduation." Nikki turned to me. "So what's new with you, Kit?"

I used the only ammo I had in my arsenal.

"I started a band."

They both turned toward me, surprised.

"Really?" Nikki looked at me skeptically. "Do you sing?"

"Mostly I play bass."

"Since when can you play the bass?"

"It's not that hard. We're doing a really simple garage-rockabilly-punk thing. This girl I met, Margo, plays guitar."

"You planning to play out?" Nikki asked.

"Soon. We still have to try out a drummer."

"Hmm," Nikki said. "Interesting."

My mother reverted to safe terrain.

"You two hungry? Dinner's about ready."

CHAPTER

Margo picked me up on a Saturday afternoon to drive us to our first practice as a real band. It was a beautiful day—just what I needed after the previous weekend with my parents. The sun baked the car with approving warmth; we blasted PJ Harvey. She told me about her conversation with Linda earlier that week. Linda had been in an all-girl band called The Pussy Willows, and complained about how their lead singer completely monopolized the band, telling every band member exactly what to play and not allowing anyone else to introduce new ideas.

"I told her there was no danger of that with us!" Margo said loud enough to be heard over the music and wind gushing through the open car windows. "I said we weren't looking to make a living at this. We're just having some fun."

This surprised me. In the past few weeks, as we started to write our own material and our set list grew, I grew increasingly committed to the idea of a band. I fantasized about my family's face when I told them I had just been signed to a major label. All of their doubts and cynicism would be swallowed by a big fat check. I had hoped Margo might have these fantasies, too.

When we arrived at the studio, it was dumpier than I expected. It was basically a beaten row home squashed between other beaten row homes. When I stepped inside, we were greeted by its owner, a towering figure with the physique of an aging basketball player.

"Hi, I'm Frank."

He thrust out his hand for each of us to shake.

"Hi," I let him envelop my hand. "I'm Kit. There's another girl coming, too. She should be here shortly."

"Great. You gals are on the second floor."

I carried my bass and accessory makeup case up a narrow stairwell and into a small, dark room. I winced at the stale stench of cigarettes and body odor that hung in the air, and walked past a battered drum kit that sat in the corner on a riser. I dropped my equipment in front of the army of amps that lined two walls. In another corner, a P.A. dotted with red and green lights glowed like a bizarre Christmas decoration. Beside that, a halogen light bloomed to the ceiling, where a dark slow burn had formed above it. The moss green carpeting was worn with large brown stains and cigarette burns. Rock was certainly not a tidy pastime.

Margo and I went through our routine—set up our instruments, open beers. When Linda walked in, Margo was all smiles and charm.

"Hi!" she chirped. "I'm Margo."

She walked over and shook Linda's hand.

"I'm Linda," she said, smiling politely.

Linda was tall and lanky with long blond hair. She wore faded jeans and a maroon T-shirt spotted with bleach stains. Her flat, gray eyes stared out over a hooked nose. She wore no makeup. She made no attempt to paint her pale face, to hide its imperfections. I admired her confidence to be so publicly naked.

"I'm Kit." I squeezed her fishy grip too tightly. "Would you like a beer?"

"No thanks, I don't drink."

Margo and I looked at each other. This was a problem.

"Oh, and," Linda continued, "I'm sorry."

Margo looked up as she placed a cigarette between her lips and poised the lighter beneath the tip.

"I have asthma. Would you guys mind smoking outside?"

Of course I knew that resenting someone who merely wanted to keep their lungs pink was selfish and immature. But I did. I enjoyed these pleasures. Now I felt guilty for wanting a beer and a cigarette. I felt guilty for resenting Linda.

"No problem," I forced a smile onto my lips and looked over at Margo, who rolled her eyes.

Linda sat down at the beat-up drum kit and tuned it with expert precision. We began with a Wanda Jackson cover, "Riot in Cell Block #9." Once we started playing, the awkward beginning began to fade. We clicked. Linda was not a great drummer, but she breathed new energy into the songs that they never had in my living room. Margo's strong voice captured Wanda's energy as I shrieked background responses, doing my best impression of a jail-house riot. I loved playing this song. It used my favorite four chords (nothing diminished here). I had a chance to scream, turn up my bass, and let the volume envelop me in a wall of rock.

And then the wall caved in. Linda stopped playing.

"Margo, are you in tune?"

For an experienced guitar player, this may be a simple question. But to a new guitar player, this could be interpreted as: "Margo, do you know what you're doing?"

Tension closed around my throat.

Margo replied with a snip, "Well, I did just tune, Linda, but I'll do it again."

She yanked the cord out of her amp, let out a heavy sigh, and plugged the end into her electronic tuner. The silence was thick and heavy.

Linda didn't seem to notice. I watched in amazement as she used the break to pull out her drum key and methodically twist tuning rods, tapping each head with her sticks as she adjusted the pitch.

The rest of the practice dragged on painfully. Margo barely lifted her head to sing the lifeless words. Linda blindly played along as acid poured into my stomach.

After the longest two hours of my life, we packed up. Margo gathered her equipment with quiet anger. Linda threw her sticks in a bag, handed me her portion of the fee for the practice place, and cheerfully asked, "Same time next week?"

"Yeah, sure," I answered quickly. Margo didn't say a word.

We grabbed handfuls of equipment, I paid Frank, and we walked out together.

"See you later," I said with all the enthusiasm I could muster.

"See ya!" Linda replied as she climbed into a small white car. As we watched her pull away, Margo looked over at me.

"Who does she think she is telling me I'm out of tune? She can barely keep time."

The idea of a successful band dangled before me, a cruel carrot. Without it, I would go back to a string of quiet nights, with nothing to do but dissect my pathetic life. I needed to fix this.

"I really don't think she meant anything by it," I said, careful not to seem like I was taking sides. "She probably just doesn't think before she says stuff. I really don't think she meant to hurt your feelings."

Margo popped open her car trunk and threw in her guitar. I put in my bass and makeup case and she slammed the trunk lid closed. She lit a cigarette and rounded the car to open the driver side door. We both climbed in silently. I waited for her next reaction as she started the engine.

"I suck," she said quietly.

"You don't suck."

"Yes I do."

"Margo, you've only been playing guitar for two months. You've made amazing progress in a very short time. Don't let Linda get to you. Aren't you having fun with this?"

"Yes."

"We're just getting started. You're a great singer, and you should feel good about your guitar playing. It takes some people years to play bar chords, and you can already do that. And the more we practice, the better you'll get. Let's give Linda another chance. If it doesn't work, we can always get another drummer. This is our project, nobody else's."

I hoped this new script didn't sound too forced. I was in unfamiliar terrain here; it was usually my frail ego that needed stroking.

"You're right," she said.

She popped in a tape and we drove home, emboldened by the shrill strength of Patti Smith's *Horses* filling the car. But I knew it would not be over so easily. It would take very little to set Margo off again. We were doomed.

As I wrestled my keys into the front door, balancing my bass under one arm, makeup case under the other, I heard the phone ring. I burst through the door, dropping my stuff, and ran to it.

"Hello?"

"It's me." It was Dale.

"Hi." I tried to sound positive, healthy, healed.

"How are you?" He whispered in his usual sexy purr.

Deep breath.

"I'm really good, thanks."

"Really good?"

"Yeah. I actually started a band with this girl Margo."

"Pete's girlfriend?"

"Yeah, do you know her?"

"Oh, yeah. Most people do."

What did that mean? I wasn't going to take the bait.

"Anyway, we just practiced tonight with the drummer from The Pussy Willows."

"Linda? I heard she got kicked out."

"What do you want?"

He paused dramatically.

"I just miss you. I was thinking maybe we could get together for a drink sometime."

Oh God. Be strong, Kit. Remember what he's done to you. Remember that girl. Remember the lies. As hard as I forced these mantras through my head, I kept remembering the gentle kisses on my parents' porch.

"I miss you, too," I said.

"Kit, I am so sorry about everything. I know I fucked up. And you were right to move out. We probably needed some time apart. But I really miss you. When can we get together?"

He was saying all the right things, like he always did. He always knew he fucked up. He always knew he was wrong. But how many mistakes was I expected to forgive?

Then, a stranger's voice came out of my mouth.

"I really don't think that's a good idea."

"Oh, come on, just a beer." There was a hint of anger in Dale's voice. "I'd just like to hang out with you for a little bit. That's all."

"I don't think so."

Another pause. I could almost see his confused expression.

"I have to go," I said. "I'll talk to you later."

I stared at the phone receiver, back on its cradle, silent. After some time elapsed—five minutes? An hour?—I stopped staring and walked to my stereo. Liz Phair's *Exile in Guyville* was still in the CD player. I pressed play, turned up the volume and crawled into my cocoon. Her words washed over me. Despite all of the ugly things her guy had done to her, she kept standing tall. Would I ever be this strong?

CHAPTER

The next morning, the alarm clock buzzed to life with an out-of-tune Spanish radio station. Opening my swollen eyes, I stared at my stained ceiling, then turned my head to the window. I was glad to see it was gray and rainy.

After pulling myself from the bed, I began my routine. Turn off the radio. Turn on Good Morning America on my small bedroom television set. Take a shower. Stick my hair in a ponytail. Half-heartedly apply some makeup. Throw on some jeans and a short-sleeve blouse (casual Friday!). Walk to the subway. Take the subway two stops to City Hall. Walk two blocks to my office. Ride up the old elevator to the 14th Floor (really the 13th). Walk into the hermetically sealed office.

"Morning Kit."

Our current receptionist was a matronly woman with gray hair, wire-rim glasses, a plain gray suit that she seemed to wear every day, and an open wound on the back of her head. There were many speculations about this wound, but we mostly tried to pretend it wasn't there.

"Morning," I said as I shuffled quickly by her to my office.

I stopped remembering their names after the fifth receptionist. I just remembered their aspirations: the writer, the actress, the animator, the graduate student. This seemed to be the first one who wanted to be a receptionist. I would probably have to avoid that wound for years.

I first went to our small lunchroom to pour myself a cup of coffee. Our little Catholic-school-girl intern sat at the lunch table painting her nails with her feet propped up on another chair. She was a junior in high school and proudly wore the sheen of her tough neighborhood. She smacked gum and smoked cigarettes and rolled her skirt up far above Catholic code. She was here to make photocopies and run errands, but we all quietly feared her. I made my own copies.

I walked back to my office. It used to be the storage closet, but the custodian found it too small, so it was given to me. It was just wide enough to put a desk across the back of the room and a chair in front of it. I had to pull myself tight against the desk in order to shut my door, which I did this morning to avoid engaging in small talk. It didn't work.

"Morning!" Rachel said, pushing my door open as much as she could.

Rachel was another proofreader at the medical publishing house. She was short and plump, with gigantic round glasses that shrunk her eyes to tiny blue dots. She had thick, prematurely graying dark hair that she kept short. Our friendship started over lunches, during which we commiserated over the morbidly dull copy we were required to read every day. She always seemed to be in a good mood, despite being here two years longer than me. What especially struck me was her complete confidence. She was not attractive, not dynamic, not especially engaging or funny, but she just didn't give a shit what anyone thought of her. She was engaged to an easygoing guy she met through a synagogue event. She ate dinner at her parents' house every weekend, along with her fiancé, younger brother, and racist grandmother. I envied her.

"Hey Rachel," I said.

"How was the drummer last night?"

"Oh, I don't know. She seemed pretty good, but I'm a little worried about her and Margo."

"Why?"

"Well, Linda—the new drummer—told Margo she was out of tune, and Margo got upset."

"Was she out of tune?"

"Well, yes, but I think Linda could have been a little more sensitive."

Rachel wrinkled her forehead.

"I would think you might need thicker skin than that to perform music."

I felt a surge of defensiveness. Rachel had never played an instrument. How would she know what it was like?

"I know it sounds over dramatic," I continued, "but it can be a little intimidating playing an instrument in front of a new person."

"Oh."

She was right, of course. Margo was overreacting, and this would be a major handicap to getting anywhere. What would happen when we played in front of an audience? When we got our first dose of criticism? I wasn't sure I could handle that any better than Margo.

My phone rang.

I turned toward it and saw it was an internal call from my boss.

"Gotta go," I said. "The beast is calling."

"Good luck," Rachel said, closing the door behind her. I picked up the phone.

"Kit, we have a problem." This was not an unusual greeting from my boss. Still, her voice made my stomach drop. "Could you come into my office for a minute?"

I took a deep breath, grabbed a notebook and pen, and proceeded down the dead man's alley that led to Jean Zimmerman's office. She sat at her huge mahogany desk, dramatically backlit by the Philadelphia skyline. She was a tall, hard woman eternally clad in masculine power suits. Her short, frosted brown hair and expensive designer glasses amplified her steel-gray eyes. Looking up from a stack of papers on her desk, she turned these weapons on me.

"Sit down."

I obeyed.

"Kit, I just got a call from Dr. De Medio. Apparently there was a mistake in the LES-relaxing medication table that appeared in Risk for Esophageal Adenocarcinoma. Instead of 2.47, there is an equation that reads 24.7. This is a crucial mistake. Do you have any idea how that could have happened?"

I read four or five manuscripts a day. I edited this one over three months ago. It was one big esophageal blur.

"I'd have to check my notes."

Her eyes burned with anger. I guessed this wasn't the right answer.

"Do you have any idea what this does to our reputation? Dr. De Medio is furious."

She paused, inviting me to contemplate my ineptitude.

"I'm sorry. I'll check my notes."

She stared at me for what seemed like a very long time.

"Get back to me later today."

"Okay."

As I walked back down the hallway, I waited for a knife to pierce my back. But I made it back to my desk, pulled the file on the job and tried to piece together an excuse. There were usually three doctors reviewing every manuscript. It was my job to ensure that their corrections were accurately made in the final copy. I pulled the final manuscript and the last proofs from Drs. Saunders, Li, and De Medio, and flipped to the controversial table. There it was, magnified by hindsight: Dr. De Medio's red marker changing a 24.7 to 2.47. Shit.

I walked back to Jean's office. She looked up at me.

"I missed it."

"Sit down."

I could still waitress. I could pursue a career more in line with my father's definition of success. Or, I could devote myself to a bohemian life of music. I would meet new people, maybe a nice guy. Yeah. It would be great.

"Kit. Your work here has always been good. And we all make mistakes." I couldn't recall Jean ever saying this to me before. "But it just seems that lately your mind has been elsewhere."

Tears welled up in my eyes. I was completely unprepared for them.

"I know. I'm sorry." And then I was sobbing, and incredibly embarrassed, but I couldn't seem to stop. "I'm just going through a bit of a personal thing."

Jean fidgeted in her chair. Finally, she pulled a tissue from a box on her desk and handed it to me.

"All right. All right. It's not the end of the world. You need to be more careful. I have to put this down as a warning, but I'm sure you'll try harder from now on. Right?"

I nodded my head and got up from her desk, futilely trying to cover my puffy face and red eyes as I walked back toward my office. All eyes watched me pass, the rumors beginning to hatch. I made it back to my desk, shut the door and sighed. The reality was, I desperately needed this job; I couldn't move back home with my tail between my legs. So, until our big record deal came in, I would keep pulling pink files and attempt to be more careful.

CHAPTER

$B$and practices were a roller coaster. Sometimes two hours would go by smoothly; even bordering on fun. More often, Linda spewed an unfiltered comment toward Margo and tension filled the room. These practices were always followed by a phone call from Margo, followed by my new role as cheerleader.

Despite this, we got better. We added more songs, some originals, some covers, and before long we had enough to play a 30-minute set. Where Dale's band had tended toward testosterone-filled loud sonic dirges with masturbatory guitar leads, light on melody and heavy on distortion, our songs had verses, choruses, structure. Although we didn't have the crutch of a second guitar or a keyboard, we used vocals to patch any acoustic holes. Margo had the strongest voice, so she sang most of the leads; I harmonized background vocals.

After one of the good practices, we decided it was time to set up a show. Margo proposed an idea.

"I was thinking, Kit," Margo said. "Your place would be perfect for a party. We could invite a bunch of friends and try out our material before a safe audience. We can split any costs and help you set up."

I doubted my place was perfect. I wasn't ready for a post-Dale coming out party, and I resented Margo for forcing me into it.

"I don't know," I said feebly. "What about your place?"

Margo cocked her head and pursed her lips.

"You've been to my place. There's no way I can fit a band in there. Besides, my landlord would never put up with the noise."

"I'm not sure how my neighbors will feel about the noise either."

Margo smiled, but I could see she was getting annoyed.

"We won't be that loud. You have a row house. I have a small apartment. Think about it. It just makes more sense at your place. If you're worried about a mess, don't. We'll help you out. Right, Linda?"

Linda looked up from tuning the drums.

"Sure," she said.

We set a date, just three weeks away.

As the evening approached, I was flooded by a tidal wave of emotions. Would people like us? Could I do this without Dale? Would I be evicted? Would I die alone? Everyone would be there. Not just our close friends, but also Dale's and Pete's friends—hip scenesters who occupied the dark corners of Philly rock clubs. I was convinced they would hate us. We lacked the bitter sheen of these overeducated, white, middle-class Bohemians. Our music was far too perky to touch such cynicism.

Still, I ordered the keg. I rented microphones, monitors, cables, stands. Margo took care of the invitations. As the number of guests grew, I became increasingly anxious. Margo continued to assure me that I wouldn't be alone. This would be a shared effort.

When the evening arrived, I was as ready as I could be. The instruments were set up; the beer was chilling; bowls of salted snacks and ashtrays were placed strategically throughout the house. I sat at my kitchen table, drumming my fingers. The clock clicked slowly toward the witching hour, and just when I thought I couldn't stand one more second of tortured waiting, the first knock came.

It was Noelle and a girlfriend, a safe beginning. Next to arrive was Nikki, wearing a midriff-baring tank top and tiny black miniskirt. She brought two friends who obviously shopped at the same store. Then, plain Linda with a plain guy who helped her carry miscellaneous drum pieces. She walked over to me.

"Hey Kit," she said quietly. This is Gino." Boyfriend? Roommate? I couldn't tell.

"Ready for tonight?" I asked Linda.

"Of course," she said.

"Aren't you nervous?" I asked.

She gave me a patronizing look.

"I've played live before, Kit. I was in The Pussy Willows, remember?"

"Oh. Margo mentioned you were in another band."

"Yes. We put out two CDs and played dozens of shows. So, I think I can handle a living room."

I smiled at her as my hand clenched into a fist. I hadn't realized she thought she was too good for us.

"Super," I said. "Excuse me."

A stream of eclectic faces of varying familiarity continued to swim through my door, most of them people I'd never seen before. I pointed them to the keg and watched the door intently, trying to will Margo to walk through it. But the party evolved without my assistance, and soon the white noise of banal conversation competed with the stereo. I hid in the kitchen, pretending to do little chores.

When Margo finally arrived with Pete, she looked gorgeous in a clingy black dress and leopard heels. She made her way through the crowd, tossing an indifferent greeting toward Linda, and eventually finding me in the corner.

"Where've you been?" I asked.

"I feel sick," she whispered. "I had diarrhea before I left the house. I can't eat. I think I'm going to puke."

"Maybe you need to eat something," I said.

"I need a beer."

I followed her as she wound her way to the keg and filled two cups. I heard the door open again.

"Hey, Dale!"

Margo and I looked at each other.

"What's he doing here?" she asked.

"I don't know." I was simultaneously furious, amazed, curious. How dare he stride so callously into my solo debut?

I swallowed a gulp of beer and walked out to the living room to see Dale work his usual charm. His tall, slender frame slithered through the party. He swung his dark curly hair back in big, sincere laughs. He wasn't particularly handsome, but he emoted the essence of cool, sprinkling it like pixie dust on the crowd, lighting up pockets of the room as he passed through them. As he leaned in to charm a new follower, he turned his eyes to me.

"Excuse me," I saw him mouth, and he walked through the crowd until he towered before me.

"Hey Kit," he said softly. "I hope it's okay that I came."

"You don't leave me much choice."

"Look, I know I fucked up. And I know I have no right to ask you for another chance. But I just… I don't know. I miss you."

I looked over at Margo, who was watching me with concern.

"Now is really not the time for this conversation," I said. "You did fuck up. And I'm not just going to forget that. Excuse me."

As I turned away, my body fought me with cruel memories. But I took a deep breath, and walked over to Margo.

"He's gotta lot of balls showing up here," she said. "Are you all right?"

I turned back to see Dale staring at me, eyes ablaze. Then he turned to flirt with one of the unfamiliar faces, bending forward seductively to whisper in her ear. This stranger giggled and blushed.

"What an asshole," Margo said.

"Yeah." I lit a cigarette, my hands were shaking.

I let Margo introduce me to people I didn't know and I tried to appear unaffected by Dale's presence. I watched him from the corner of the room as he started talking with Pete, then looked over at us.

After fortifying myself with heavy refills of beer, I turned to Margo.

"We should start," I said.

She looked at me pleadingly. "Already?"

"We have to start sometime. It'll be over before you know it."

"I have to go to the bathroom."

She squeezed up the crowded stairs, pushing her way to the front of the line.

I started setting up the equipment, turning on microphones, amps, tuning my bass. I felt the eyes in the room on me. Was I going to be sick?

Linda soon followed my lead and sat behind her drum kit, twisting knobs and tapping her drums exactly as she had done before. I realized she never deviated from her routine. Tune the snare drum first, starting with the nut farthest from her. Move methodically clockwise around the snare. Apply the exact principles to the tom-tom. Twist, tap, twist, tap. How could she be so calm? I admired her. I hated her.

I looked into the room. Most were watching us sideways without interrupting their drunken conversations. Pete talked with one of his bandmates. Noelle smiled at me maternally. Then I saw Dale. Tucked into the far corner of the living room, he leaned one arm against the wall in a subtle embrace around my sister. Nikki leaned against the wall, laughing. Her tiny black miniskirt exposed milky, legs elongated by black platform shoes. Her tight black tank top exposed her perfectly flat midriff, accented by a silver belly ring. What the fuck were they doing? She was talking now, tilting her head just right so her eyes seemed bigger, doe-like. Dale listened intently, then smiled.

Suddenly, the white noise in the room began to slow, like a record turned off as the needle still licked the grooves. My breath was forced through an invisible straw; I inhaled, but only in short gasps. The light around the room dimmed to a spotlight on the new couple.

"I just puked."

Margo's voice pulled me back to reality. I looked over at her, dazed for a minute, then my breath seemed to come back slowly.

"You ready?" she asked.

I forced a shaky smile.

"Yeah."

"Great. Let's do it."

I picked up my bass, slung it over my shoulder, and waited. Margo walked up to the microphone.

"Good evening everyone," she cooed. The crowd turned, polite but apathetic. "We're Broad Street, and we're here to rock your world." She turned to me and smiled. "Ready girls?"

Four clicks of the drum sticks, and we were off. Margo strummed her guitar like a pro, swinging her hips with the beat. Linda perked up behind the drums, keeping the rhythm moving. I tried desperately to keep up. I stared at the once familiar set list, my mind searching for answers. What notes did I play here? When was the change? I felt the audience's eyes bore through me. When I didn't have to sing background vocals, I slanted away from the crowd. I slowly turned my volume down.

The audience didn't seem to notice. Our accessible pop bounced around the room in a cacophony that hid our imperfections. Each song wrapped around the simple framework of the E, A, D, and G chords. One song used these chords for a surf instrumental. Another song rumbled over a primitive African rhythm to proclaim, "never pick a man who's prettier than you are." Our songs were about living out repressed post-feminist fantasies in glorious ass-kicking frenzy. No more dick rock. Enter three girlie feminists not afraid to wear a dress, makeup, heels. What the fuck was wrong with being a chick?

I began to breathe again. The light began to brighten. Maybe I could do this.

After we finished, the room exploded. Our friends, Linda's friends, Pete's friends, everyone applauded and cheered with genuine enthusiasm. I felt beautiful, talented, capable.

It wasn't until after I started packing up my equipment, after swallowing dozens of compliments, that I realized Dale and Nikki were gone.

My head was pounding, again.

With each step down the stairs to my living room, the air ripened with the smell of cigarettes and stale beer, setting fire to my frail stomach. I stopped halfway down the steps to sit and look through the banister at the disaster before me. Half-full plastic cups of beer occupied every flat surface of the room, most of the charcoal gray liquid had cigarette butts floating like life preservers. Musical equipment was squashed in the corner of the room, no cables wrapped, no guitars returned to their cases, no microphones saved from the drunken crowd. Only the drums were missing, a fact I credited to Linda's chronic sobriety. She would probably wake early, happy to be alive. She would eat a sensible breakfast of fresh fruit and herbal tea, then off to volunteer at the Y. After that, a five-mile run along the river, then back home to read a thick book with thicker words. I rubbed my temples, feeling completely defeated by my home, by myself.

By my sister.

I went to the answering machine. Six unheard messages.

I listened to each one impatiently, quietly hoping one would be Dale telling me how much he enjoyed our show, that my kid sister seemed pretty drunk so he gave her a ride home to protect me from any unnecessary heartache, how much he respected the new me and would value it forever.

Instead, message after message spoke from the past. Voices asking for directions to the party, wondering if they could bring anything, what time the band started. None of the messages was from Dale or Nikki. No calls from Margo or Linda offering to clean up, either.

I replaced the phone and walked through my destroyed living room into the apocalypse of my kitchen. Sticky shot glasses filled plastic bowls that once held snacks. Most of these snacks seemed to have ended up on the floor in crushed sandy piles. My sink overflowed with glasses and plates. Closer inspection revealed not all of them survived the weight of poor balance. The keg sat in the middle of the room, a dark halo on the wooden floor beneath it. Maybe I'll move. But first I would go back to bed.

As I headed back toward the stairs, the phone rang. I didn't have the energy for a conversation, but curiosity made me answer it.

"Hello?"

"Hey Kit. How you feeling today?" Nikki asked.

"Like shit."

"Me too. Great party last night, though. You guys sounded awesome."

"Thanks."

"Sorry I couldn't stick around. I told Sandy I'd meet up with her at the Khyber at 11:30 and you looked like you were having so much fun after the gig that I didn't want to interrupt."

"How'd you get down there? I thought you came with Lisa."

"Um…" a pause, "Actually, Dale gave me a ride."

"That was nice," I sneered.

"Come on, Kit, don't be mad. I'm sorry. He was going to the show anyway and he offered and I needed a ride. It was no big deal."

"You two looked pretty chummy at the party."

"Oh, that's just Dale. He's just a flirt. It doesn't mean anything."

The more she defended him, the more convinced I became that they had slept together.

"Whatever." Rage tapped behind my eyes. "I have to go clean up this mess."

"Do you need help?"

She definitely slept with him.

"No, thanks. I'll talk to you later."

She hesitated. "Okay. I'll see you."

The high road was exhausting. I might just nap for a few days.

CHAPTER

A week after the party, I got a call from someone named Ben offering us our first real show. I vaguely remembered his band Lava Dance as Dead-like and psychedelic, with Ben as the smarmy lead singer. He told me he got my name from a friend who had heard us at our party. The gig would be in two weeks in Downingtown, about 45 minutes from Philadelphia, at a new club called Caper's. I played the conversation with as much cool as my anxiety could muster, then called Margo, my head buzzing with adrenaline.

"Shit," she mumbled. "If we play in Downingtown, my parents will be there."

"So?"

"So, my parents are insane. They had this little hit in the late 70s and they will never, ever let me forget it. If they're even remotely near a stage they turn into, like, Captain and Tennille. Not that they're not neurotic anyway. It just makes them worse."

This surprised me. Margo never said much about her parents, and this information would certainly have been at the top of my list.

"What was their hit?"

"Ugh."

"Tell me!"

"Okay. It was called 'Can't Fake that Smile.' It was a sappy little love song that got some minor airplay and they act like it was 'I Want to Hold Your Hand.'"

I laughed. "What were the called?"

"Parallel."

"What the hell does that mean?" I kept laughing, but could tell Margo was not as amused.

"Beats the fuck out of me."

"Oh my god, that is so awesome. Why didn't you tell me?"

"Because I've spent my entire life trying to forget it."

"Why? We wouldn't have much material if it weren't for one-hit wonders."

"True. But it's just, well, kind of pathetic. You can't understand until you meet them."

"They must love that you're in a band."

"They don't exactly know yet."

"What?"

"I don't know. The last thing I want them to think is that I'm following in their footsteps. I'm telling you, these people are nuts."

"Margo, you have to tell them. They would be so proud of you."

"I know."

"So are we taking this gig, or what?"

There was a long pause on the other end.

"Sure."

The night of the gig, I wore the shiniest, girliest thing I could find. As I examined myself in the mirror, I knew exactly what my father would think. I looked like a slut. He wouldn't understand it was just entertainment. His performance attire as a teacher was just as cliché—tattered sweaters, jackets with elbow patches. These were the roles we played. Margo was lucky to have parents who understood.

Margo showed up looking amazing as always. She wrapped her tall, shapely figure into tight black jeans and a shimmering gold top. Linda chose to celebrate her sexuality in a more refined manner—jeans, T-shirt, no makeup. The excitement seemed to have created a truce between Margo and Linda for the night. They ignored each other.

We squashed ourselves into Margo's car among amps, drums, guitars, stands, cymbals. I pressed myself against the dash to pull the seat forward while Linda pretzeled her body around equipment. Margo and I chirped excitedly in the front seat like two teens off for their first date.

"I hope I remember that song."

"Do you like this dress?"

And then I asked the wrong question.

"Is Pete coming tonight?"

Margo's face drained of enthusiasm. "I don't want to talk about Pete. He's being an asshole."

"Okay, sorry." I changed the subject to the set list we would play that night.

When we got to Downingtown, I read Margo the directions. Right on Union. Left on Main. There was a shopping center and a parking lot on the right. Turn into the parking lot.

A shopping center? As we pulled into the lot, we simultaneously realized that our first real gig would be in a strip mall. Silence enveloped the car as we gaped at the neon Caper's sign sandwiched between a laundromat and dollar store. We popped the car doors open and poured ourselves out of the car.

"This won't be bad," Margo said, attempting conviction. "We're gonna have a blast."

I pulled out my bass rig, carrying it to the club in my high-heeled boots. This was not an easy task. As I followed Margo and Linda into the club, I was surprised that Caper's was bigger than I expected. The door opened into a small room. A few hard-looking men lined a wooden bar, each parallel to a pint of beer, burning cigarette, and a shot. In the back of the room, an open doorway lead into a large warehouse space. There, a stage loomed ominously along one wall, empty bars bordered the other three walls of the room.

We continued to load our stuff into the club, trying to mimic the confidence of seasoned musicians. After we were almost done, a rotund man waddled over to us. His thinning black hair was slicked back; a cigarette dangled from his stained, chubby fingers.

"I'm Johnny," he spat over his chewing gum. "I run this place. If anyone gives you girls a hard time, you come see me."

Why would anyone give us a hard time? What kind of place was this?

We thanked our new friend and he waddled away. Once he was out of earshot, we snickered. He was obviously showing off in front of three young women. We could handle this.

Linda climbed on stage and pulled her drums to the back, unzipping bags and pulling pieces out. Margo and I were starting to lift our equipment onto the stage when a piercing voice interrupted us.

"Maggie!"

"Oh, Jesus," Margo groaned, turning to face the shrieking woman. "Hi Mom," she said, forcing a smile to her lips.

"Maggie, oh my god, you look fabulous!"

Margo's mother ran toward her and embraced her dramatically. Her hair, dyed the color of champagne, was teased into a high helmet. This contrasted with her too-tan skin, which clung tightly to her bony arms and chiseled cheekbones. She wore bright pink leather pants and matching pink heels that accentuated her long, thin legs. Her short-sleeved white shirt was tied up to reveal a flat brown stomach. Glimmering rhinestones accented her long pink nails. I stifled the urge to grin.

"Thanks, Mom," Margo said glumly, turning her eyes toward me with a grimace.

Margo's mother let go, and held her back for further inspection.

"I love that top!" she exuded. "Your boobs look fabulous in it!"

She turned toward me.

"I don't know where she gets her figure," she said. "I wasn't blessed like she was. This body cost me plenty of overtime at the WalMart!"

"Mom, this is Kit."

"Hi, sweetie! I've heard so many great things about you." I found this odd, since Margo only recently revealed her band secret to her parents. "I'm Vincenza Bevilacqua. But please, call me Vinnie."

She embraced my hand tightly.

"Nice to meet you, Vinnie." I was too frightened to say anything else.

"That's our drummer, Linda, up there," Margo, said pointing.

"Hi Linda!" Vinnie called to her. Linda interrupted her intense concentration on a drum to lift a stick in quick greeting. Vinnie turned back to us.

"My husband should be here shortly. He's out parking the car. Oh, there he is. Orlando, Honey! Over here!"

An equally tan man walked toward us. He wore a bright blue Hawaiian shirt, open at the neck to unleash a gold chain hidden in a jungle of hair. His tight, pale blue jeans capped off a pair of pristine white sneakers.

"Honey, you look terrific," he exclaimed, giving Margo a big hug. "Look at that outfit. Wow! Are you gonna be able to maneuver in those tight pants?"

"Dad!"

"Orlando," Vinnie smacked her husband's arm, jangling an armory of bracelets. "Leave her alone. Honey, meet Kate."

"Kit," I carefully corrected her, doing my best to keep smiling.

"Oh, sweetie, I'm sorry. Kit. Orlando, this is Maggie's friend Kit."

"Orlando Bevilacqua," he said, pumping my arm up and down vigorously. "This is an exciting night for our little girl! I'm sure Maggie's told you we had a little bit of music success ourselves."

Margo rolled her eyes.

"Yes, Maggie's mentioned it," I said, feeling Margo shoot me a glare. "That must have been exciting."

"Oh, yeah, yeah. Went to number three in Lexington! Good times, good times. Maggie, did I tell you 'Smile' is being considered for an Allstate commercial? Ricky called us the other day. We just have to jump through a few legal hoops and then sit back and watch those royalty checks roll in! She's a mean old bitch, this entertainment biz. Anyway, what the hell am I going on for? This is your night. You gals must be so excited! Well, go ahead, don't let us old farts hold you up—get up there and do your thing!"

"We're not playing for a little while, Dad," Margo said quietly. "Why don't you and mom go get a drink while we get set up?"

"Great idea, Honey!" Orlando said. "Come on, Pumpkin," he said, slapping Vinnie on the ass. "I'm thirsty!"

"Oh, you are so naughty!" Vinnie squealed, then turned to me. "But you know that's how I like my men."

"Ain't no other man like me," he slapped again. "Let's go, baby."

We watched them walk out toward the front bar. I could see the drunks at the bar part to let the couple squeeze through. Orlando called to the bartender, snapping his fingers in the air. The young woman sauntered over to him glumly. He leaned over the bar to say something. I waited for her to slap him, or walk away angrily, but instead she laughed. Vinnie, too, was dazzling a grizzled man on a bar stool next to her, and soon he was smiling, too.

"They're interesting," I said.

"Welcome to my world," Margo said, turning away to grab her amp and carry it up the small stairs that led to the stage. When I leaned slightly forward to pick up my amp and bass, I felt a tap on my shoulder and turned toward an attractive guy. He was obviously not one of the regulars.

"Hey, Kit," he said. "I don't know if you remember me. I'm Ben."

Ben was taller than I remembered. His dark brown hair spiked up to platinum peaks, accenting dark green eyes. He wore a Sex Pistols T-shirt and worn jeans. I found myself quietly attracted to him, a sensation I hadn't felt since Dale.

"Yeah, I remember you. How you doing?"

"I'm great now. You look awesome."

Blood unexpectedly rushed to my cheeks.

"Thanks. You, too."

I fiddled with my hands, not sure what to do with them.

"We're looking forward to playing with you guys tonight," I smiled, hoping I didn't have anything in my teeth.

"Me, too. Come here, I want to introduce you to the sound guy."

He touched my bare arm. His hand was rough, calloused from what I assumed was years of playing guitar. I followed behind him as he walked toward a tall figure standing in a lighted booth.

"Hey Gary, this is Kit from"—he turned to me—"I'm sorry, what's the name of your band again?"

"Broad Street."

He laughed. "Kit from Broad Street."

I reached out and shook Gary's hand, making sure to squeeze with a little confidence.

"Nice to meet you," I said.

"Same here. Can you guys get set up for sound check in about twenty minutes?"

His question implied I knew what I was doing.

"No problem." I turned toward Ben and smiled. "I'll talk to you later."

"Yes you will," he smiled.

I walked away, feeling his eyes on my ass. I tried to move seductively, but wobbled in my high heels. I picked up my bass in one hand, amp in another and did my best to balance myself as I climbed up the stairs to the stage. Dropping the heavy amp down on its wheels, I rolled it over to Margo.

"Who's that?" she whispered.

"Ben, the singer for Lava Dance."

"That's Ben? He went to my high school. He was kind a dork back then. Oh, shit. Here come my parents. Act busy."

We gave them quick waves and smiles as they walked toward the stage with tall pink drinks in their hands.

"Break a leg, honey," Vinnie said, then pulled her husband over to a small crowd of regulars.

Margo and I plugged in and tuned. I noticed that Linda had transformed her pile of black bags into an operational drum kit. She seemed miles away, encased in drums. Gary soon joined us onstage to set up microphones for vocals and instruments. My heart was racing, but I tried to act cool, feeling Ben's eyes on me. Gary left the stage and returned to his small sound booth. He asked us, one by one, to create small performances as he checked the sound. When it was my turn, I stupidly thumped on the same note.

"Play a riff," Gary ordered.

This was not my specialty, but I faked my way through the most complicated melody I knew, which basically consisted of five repeating notes.

"Okay, now vocals," he said.

I pressed my lips to the microphone and spoke the anthem of musicians I had heard over the years, "Check. Check. Check."

"Okay, now guitar."

Margo slipped awkwardly back and forth between two bar chords.

"Now guitar vocals."

"Testes, one two three, testes."

"Cute." I smiled at her.

After an eternity of checking drums, guitars, and vocals, Gary told us to run through a song. Margo turned to us.

"Let's do 'Priscilla.'"

Linda clicked four times and we launched into the song. It was a simple E-G-C progression; I threw in a short run I just worked out. It sounded pretty good until Margo bent her head up into the microphone and mouthed the words. Nothing came out. Her brow wrinkled and she shook her head emphatically toward the illuminated sound booth, Gary glowing from its center like a wick. He pointed his thumb upward in approval. Now Margo and I both shook our heads. I alternately pointed to my ears, then to Margo, then back to my ears between strums. He leaned over the board like a surgeon, but Margo's voice remained lost in a cacophony of guitars. When it was time for my background vocals, I leaned into the mic and attempted harmonies. I felt the air forced over my tongue, but could hear only the wall of guitar behind me. I shook my head and twisted my face disapprovingly. Three minutes passed and we reached the end of the song. Margo and I stared at each other, exasperated. Gary walked toward the stage.

"Sounds good."

"I can't hear my vocals at all," Margo said.

"Me neither," I said.

"You sound fine out here," Gary said. "Our stage monitors aren't very powerful so you may not be able to hear yourself that well on stage. But, trust me, you sound fine. You should start in about ten minutes."

After Gary walked away, Margo said, "That sounded like shit."

"I know, but I guess we have to trust him. He seems to know what he's doing."

"That was great, honey!" Orlando said, walking back up to the stage. "You might want to tune your guitar, though."

"Thanks for the advice, Dad."

"I'm sorry, honey, just a suggestion. Can I buy you gals a drink?"

"A beer would be great," Margo said. "Kit, you want anything?"

"Yeah, a beer sounds good."

"Hey, Linda," Margo turned toward the back of the stage. "Want anything from the bar?"

"Ice water," she said, working her tuning key around the heads carefully.

Margo rolled her eyes and turned back to Orlando.

"Got that?"

"Got it. I'll be right back."

Margo walked back to her amp, turned it on standby, then yanked out her cord and shoved it into her tuner. Within a few minutes, Orlando was back juggling two bottled beers and a bottle of water in one hand, and two bonus shots of clear amber in the other.

"To take the edge off," he laughed, then joined Vinnie, who was surrounded by the crowd of men.

Margo distributed the beverages, then lifted her shot glass toward me.

"To being rock stars."

We clinked our glasses, and poured the burning liquid down our throats. I quickly countered with a sip of cool beer, and before long a warm rush raced through my veins. This was rock. We clicked on our amps and Margo walked toward the microphone.

"Good evening everybody. We're Broad Street, and we're here to rock your world."

The small crowd around Orlando and Vinnie burst into cheers and applause. Johnny moved in front of the stage, standing cross-armed in front of a gathering crowd of alcohol-soaked men. They were emaciated versions of our new bodyguard, clad mainly in flannel with the same slicked hair, cigarettes sizzling between bony fingers I doubted they were here for the alternative music.

Our first song was "Slander You," a punk fairytale we wrote about a woman in control. When our guitars kicked in, they were huge. Even the drums were heavily miked, so the toms filled the air with a thick primal rhythm. Margo looked at me worriedly, then stepped toward the mic. Suddenly, the guitars were accented by a piercing squeal that caused the small audience to clasp their hands to their ears in agony. Margo jumped back from the mic and looked at glowing Gary, once again hunched over the board in great concentration. Hesitantly, she leaned in again and was able to sing feedback-free. I could just make out her words beneath the swell of noise; Margo shook her head throughout the song. I stepped to the mic and started my background vocals without reference. I could only find the notes by how I remembered them feeling in my throat, but I doubted this method was accurate. I was convinced that on their fabulous sound system—that everyone in the room but us could hear—our vocals were comically flat.

The crowd didn't seem to mind. They flocked to the stage as we played, cheering us enthusiastically. Not the cheers of a crowd enjoying the music, but the catcalls of men encouraging us to strip to our pasties. When Margo's pick flew out of her hand, ten grown men lunged at it like hungry piranha. She looked down, stunned, then grabbed another pick from the top of her amp. We mouthed the words:

You go cruising down the Jersey shore,

Getting lucky with the local whores,

I don't care if what they say is true

I just feel the need to slander you.

We launched into a limited instrumental. Margo's guitar squealed as she slid bar chords high on the fret. I attacked my strings with the pick, slamming only on the downbeat to increase intensity. The volume felt good now, powerful. I glanced out toward the crowd to see Vinnie and Orlando dancing along. The men in the crowd bobbed their heads in time with the rhythm. I locked eyes with one of them, who responded by grabbing his crotch and sliding his slimy gray tongue out until it came to a point. He then snaked it back and forth obscenely, his eyes as cold as a killer. I quickly moved my eyes back to my fret, aware that I was now hitting the wrong notes. I struggled to focus, listen to the guitar, and find my way back to the right notes. We were back at the last chorus. I thought I could find my way to the end from here. But we still had ten more songs.

At the end of "Slander You," we kicked right into the next song, "Take That." It was my turn to attempt leads. I shrieked my vocals, and it felt good. The volume and insane drunken crowd had started my adrenaline pumping.

We plowed through the next few songs with equal vigor. The energy of our potential accosters was contagious. We fed them with suggestively churning hips and smiles; Margo flirted with them between songs. As we neared the end of our set, we were both high with the acceptance of our new adoring fans. Our last song was a cover of the Monkees' "She." Our version was stripped down and raw, with all three of us singing the chorus of a person desperate to win the affections of a young temptress. I pounded chunky root notes in time with Linda's slamming toms. As Margo began the first verse, I noticed a figure out of the corner of my eye emerging onstage. When it moved into the light, I saw it was the man with the snaking tongue. He started dancing behind Margo, moving his hips in time to the beat, but not getting too close. She ignored him. I looked for Johnny in the crowd below, but saw only more flannel-clad drunks. Even the pink and teal splash of Margo's parents seemed to be missing.

The man swayed and wiggled his way over to me. I decided to play it cool, go with it. I smiled as he danced around me, first behind me so I could only sense his presence by odor. Then, he was in front of me, spreading his legs and thrusting his pelvis toward me. Stay calm, we're almost done, I told myself. Then he moved closer, the microphone stand my only bodyguard against his drunken hormones. His gray tongue slithered out between thin chapped lips. Brown teeth emerged in a reptilian smile. He moved the tip of his tongue slowly up and down in air cunnilingus. I kept smiling and tried to stay focused on the notes, but I realized we were nearing the chorus and I would have to step toward the microphone to sing background vocals. And then we were at the chorus and not knowing what else to do, I stepped forward and opened my mouth to sing. Suddenly, the man's arms locked behind me and pulled me into him; his gray tongue plunged into my mouth. I twisted my head to separate from this hideous slug, trying to pull back, but he was too strong. He thrust himself against me over and over, the bass throbbing dissonant tones with each new push. The song never seemed to end. I felt suffocated and helpless; the pungent smell of alcohol and sweat choked me, but I tried to stay focused.

Then, suddenly, the man was pulled from me, arms flailing, eyes wide like a cartoon. He was airborne, falling from the stage in slow motion until his hideous body thudded onto the dark floor below. Around him, the crowd burst into laughter, pulled him from the floor, and patted him on the back, high-fiving him. I realized that the song was over, the guitar was ringing the final chord and I was staring down in disbelief at the men that writhed before me. When I broke the gaze, I looked up I saw Ben standing in front of me, smiling. My knight in Doc Martens.

"A big thanks to Kit's special dance partner!" Margo smiled at the crowd, who responded with high-pitched whistles and howls. "We're Broad Street! Thanks for coming out! Stick around for the very groovy Lava Dance!"

I was stunned. While the taste of violation still coated my tongue, Margo cheerfully swallowed the ugly cheers of these misogynists.

"Are you all right?" Ben asked.

"Yeah, thanks." I attempted a smile. "That was a first for me."

"What, you're not used to getting mauled in public?" He smiled. "I consider that the ultimate compliment."

"I'll take simple applause, thanks."

He stared at me for what felt like a long time, then Gary interrupted.

"Kit, I need you to start breaking down. We have to get Lava Dance up here right away."

"She's moving," Ben replied for me. He turned back to me. "You gonna stick around for our show?"

"Definitely."

"Great." He smiled and walked away.

As I packed up my equipment, Margo came over to me.

"That was awesome."

I looked at her in disbelief. "Did you not see what happened to me?"

"Oh, that guy was harmless."

"That was revolting."

"Come on. He was just having fun."

Disgusted, I turned my back away from her and started to pack up my bass and amp.

"Whatever," she snorted and walked away.

She packed up her equipment, pushed it to the back of the stage, then walked down the stage steps. Her parents rushed over to her and pulled her back to their trashy entourage.

"Kit, I really need you to hurry up," Gary said.

I moved my equipment to the back of the stage, then walked out to the floor. I saw my attacker in the front bar, hunched over a large, flannel-clad woman.

"That was great, Karen!" Vinnie exclaimed as I walked past them. "And you had your very own fan! I remember those days. Orlando used to kick about ten guys a night right off the stage."

"Twenty!" Orlando said.

My plastic smile hardened. "Anyone want anything from the bar?" I asked.

"No, thanks, Honey," Vinnie answered for the crowd. Margo looked over at me coldly.

As I walked away, I wondered if maybe I was exaggerating. I was dressed like a hooker. I had just thrust my hips at a sea of beer goggles. I had made my choices, and these were the consequences. Sex, drugs, and rock and roll, right? I ordered a beer and sat in a quiet corner of the bar. I watched as Linda joined the bevy of Bevilacquas, looking uncomfortable as Orlando put his arm around her and shook her.

Lava Dance was onstage now. The band was a montage of trends. The drummer wore a baggy T-shirt, oversized shorts, and a thick ponytail at the base of his skull. The stocky keyboardist looked slightly like a serial killer, the lanky bass player had Deadhead long stringy hair, and the guitarist wore clean preppy jeans and shirt. Ben was definitely the hottest one on stage. He turned to the band behind him, and asked:

"Ready?"

Oh yeah.

The drummer nodded. Ben leaned into the mic.

"Thanks to Broad Street for a great show."

Margo's crowd erupted in catcalls.

"We're Lava Dance." A shriek of high-pitched voices emanated from the front bar, and a group of women swarmed into the room. Where did they come from?

Lava Dance launched into their first song, a Velvet Underground-tinged swirl of psychedelic guitars, punctuated with Ben's low growling vocals. He strummed the guitar confidently as he leaned into the mic, legs spread like a boxer ready to pounce. Ben leaned back between words to slide his fingers up the fretboard, then pumped a wah-wah pedal to further distort the frequencies. The sound washed over me, hypnotizing. It was sloppy and sexy and angry. Any melody was buried under deafening volume, but to me it was all about the delivery. Ben kissed the mic again and again, his deep voice distorted with reverb and echo. At the end of the song, his vocals hung in the air, echoing with creepy intimacy; the guitars pulsed in time with soft blue lights, growing quieter until the air became still.

The crowd of curvy silhouettes screamed, applauding over their heads. Ben smiled humbly and nodded his head in appreciation. My heart sank.

Four more clicks, and they began again. Each song was a variation of the first, changing mainly by tempo and key. The girls swirled their hips to the drone, swooning dreamily at Ben's sexually charged lyrics.

Lava Dance's last song was another long dirge. This time the feedback rang as one by one, each musician abandoned his instrument and walked down a set of stairs behind the stage—first the drummer, then the guitarist, then the keyboard player, then the bassist, then finally, dramatically, Ben took his guitar off, leaned it against the amp and walked away, feedback growing louder and louder until everything suddenly snapped to black.

The hum of the guitar and the curtain of blackness disoriented me. It became the warm buzz of a whiskey shot, the gray invading tongue, Ben's rough hand on my elbow. And then the feeling was gone. The light burst back to life and Ben was working his way through the crowd, greeting the fans as he walked. Margo's crowd had moved to the front bar; I could hear their laughter. Linda was onstage grabbing her drums. I ordered another beer.

After a few minutes, Ben walked over and sat next to me.

"Great show," I smiled.

"Thanks, we had fun."

"You have a few fans out there," I said, an unwanted hint of jealousy in my voice.

"I'd say you gals did pretty well yourself."

"Thanks. It was interesting."

"So, when do you have to head back to Philly?"

"I don't know. Margo seems to be having a good time here."

"I can give you a ride home if you want."

I didn't want to ride home with Margo. I didn't want to be alone. And of all the girls in this room who screamed as Ben performed, he had chosen me.

"Sure," I said.

"Good. Let's go grab our stuff and get out of here."

We walked to the stage. Ben walked over to the keyboard player and started talking. Linda was leaning over a large black bag and pulling Velcro straps tight around it.

"Hey, Linda," I said. She looked up and raised her eyebrows. "I'm getting a ride home with Ben. Are you okay with this stuff?"

"Sure."

"Great show tonight."

"Thanks. You, too. I'll see you next week."

I picked up my amp and guitar and carried them down the steps and toward the front bar. I nervously paused before the Margo crowd.

"Kit!" she yelled, running over and throwing her arms around me. "Come on, honey, don't be mad at me. I love you!"

"How could she possibly be mad at my little angel?" Vinnie slurred, bringing her palm down hard on the bar.

"I'm not mad at you, Margo," I said, stepping out of her embrace. "I was just a little freaked out, that's all."

"Well, honey," Orlando said, leaning awkwardly off his barstool. "If that jerk freaked you out with just a little attention, you're in for a rude awakening. You're a sweet girl, but you're gonna have to be tougher than that to survive this industry."

"You're probably right," I said quietly.

"Oh, sweetie," Margo said, pulling me next to her. "Come have a drink with us."

"Thanks, but I'm going to grab a ride with Ben."

"Oh, really!" she said, raising an eyebrow. "Hey, ma, Kit's getting a ride with Ben."

The three Bevilacquas burst into laughter at this hysterical concept.

"Well, goodnight," I said. "It was nice meeting you both."

"You're not getting off that easy!" Orlando said. "Come here and give us a big hug."

I put my amp and guitar on the floor and walked into their circle. Their arms laced around me like a drunken Vishnu.

"See you next week, Honey," Margo said, kissing me on the cheek. "I'll let you know how much we make. Good luck tonight!"

Group laughter again.

"Okay, see ya."

I picked up my equipment and left. Outside, the black parking lot sparkled with the glow of quiet street lamps. A cluster of cars in front of the club contrasted the large empty parking lot behind them. Behind me, the door opened with a small rush of white noise, then closed to dampen it. It was Ben.

"Hey," he said, carrying his own amp and guitar case. "My car's over there."

He pointed to a powder blue Chevy Vega. We walked over to it, loaded our stuff in the back seat and climbed in. It smelled of old mothballs and cigarettes. Ben pulled out a pack of Marlboro Lights and offered one to me. I didn't want one, but took it anyway. I placed it in my lips and leaned over to let him light it.

"Thanks." I smiled, exhaling a plume of blue toxins.

"Where to?"

"Just take 76 down to the Broad Street exit."

"All roads lead to Broad Street," he said, starting up the engine and smiling.

As we pulled out of the parking lot and drove toward the highway, I began to vaguely regret my decision. Margo was back at Caper's having a blast and I was in a car with a virtual stranger. There was a song in there somewhere.

"You look really good tonight," Ben said softly, causing me to pull down my short skirt. "You used to go out with Dale, right?"

I was not expecting this. The breeze blowing through the car window suddenly felt cold; I wrapped my arms around myself. "Yeah."

"He seems like a pretty cool guy."

"Most people think so."

"I guess you know now that guy has quite a reputation."

A slight wave of panic washed through me. Why was he telling me this?

"Really?"

"I'm sure you've heard some things."

"Sort of."

"Well," he hesitated. "The first time I met you, you were with Dale. It was at a show, about a year ago. We played with his band. I thought you were cute."

I thought back to the blur of Dale's shows.

"I remember meeting you," I said. "But I'm not sure at which show."

"I think you may have been fighting with Dale that night. You looked pretty pissed." He took a drag of his cigarette. "This girl, Sara, was there that night. She's kind of a regular of ours. She and Dale were always pretty friendly."

And then I remembered. I had told Dale I would meet him at the club that night. When I walked into the bar, he was draped over a girl with stringy brown hair and a snake tattoo that crawled up her naked calf. His eyes had glided away from hers to spot me across the room, his face flashing a millisecond of hand-in-the-cookie-jar panic, then quickly to a slick smile that said: "Hi, honey. I'm just being my usual friendly self. If you think anything different, you're overreacting." This look always crushed me.

"I just remember thinking that you deserve better," Ben said. He pushed his cigarette through the window, creating a brief fan of red sparks.

These gentle words caused my eyes to moisten; I looked out the window. Ben popped in a Lava Dance tape, then moved his calloused hand across the seat to rest it on mine.

When we got to my house, I examined it through fresh eyes. The living room was dark and cavernous, occupied only by the same two folding chairs. The walls and floors were bare of color; there were no quirky lamps or furniture to identify it as mine.

We carried our equipment into the room. I clicked the switch by the front door, which ignited the one ceiling light in the middle of the room. The room was flooded with harsh green fluorescence.

"Want a drink?" My voice rang in the empty room.

"No, thanks."

Ben walked over to the switch and turned the light off. The room was illuminated only by the soft glow of the street lamps, which painted checkered windows on the hardwood floors. I stood stupidly by the switch. He wrapped me in his arms and pressed his mouth to mine, his breath sweetened by mint gum. I tilted my head to press my lips closer and parted them to feel his tongue against mine.

"Let's go to your room," he whispered.

I took his hand and guided him up the stairs, down the dark hall, and into my bedroom. We peeled off our clothes and slipped under the cool sheets. My body melted gratefully into his; echoes of our music rang through me like a serenade.

CHAPTER

I spent Monday morning in my tiny office trying not to think about Ben—his warm skin against mine, his sex-crumpled hair rolling away from me, his deep breaths that caressed me to sleep. Not thinking about Ben made proofreading extremely difficult.

Since the Dr. De Medio debacle, work had become an exercise in restraint. Jean tiptoed around me as if I were a sleeping child, speaking only in patronizing tones. I greeted her over-enthusiastically and asked inane questions about the medical newspeak I had to read every day. One of us was bound to snap.

"Do you think you can have the Demedio job done by three?" Jean cooed in my doorway this morning. I half expected her to pinch my cheek.

"Sure," I turned and smiled, my lips quivering with the effort. "I should be done by lunchtime."

"Great!" she exclaimed, then softly closed the door behind her. I was becoming convinced that these were the scenes that preceded workplace shootings. Bosses and employees, all swallowing their hatred for one another behind strained smiles.

But this Monday had been touched by the delicious memory of Ben's kiss as he left my house Sunday morning.

"I'll call you," he said.

I'd watched his jeans shift as he walked away, clinging to the threshold as if I were in a bad TV movie.

When I got home from work, I went straight to the phone and picked it up. No messages.

An hour went by. The phone didn't ring. I made instant macaroni and cheese and watched a *Simpsons* rerun.

Another hour went by. No call. I ate Ben & Jerry's out of the carton and watched a biography of Tanya Tucker.

Another hour.

Should I call him? No. Too pushy.

I lit a cigarette and opened a beer. Time for *Law and Order*.

10:00. I opened a third beer. I touched my cheek softly, remembering. Why shouldn't I call him?

Because he said he would call me.

I looked at the clock again. 10:30. Not too late. I pulled the crumpled piece of paper with his number out of my guitar case and dialed. After four rings, the machine picked up. Lava Dance played in my ear.

"Sorry we missed your call," Ben's voice spoke breathily. "Leave a message for Ben or Lava Dance and we'll get back to you."

Beep. Shit. What should I say?

"Uh," I stammered. Should I hang up? Shit. "Uh, hi Ben. It's Kit. Just, uh, calling to say hi." I hung up, then stared at the phone in disbelief. What did I just do? I had just vocalized the antithesis of rock hipness. I had sunk to groupie. I was a loser.

I lit another cigarette, picked up the phone and dialed again.

"Hello, dahling," Margo's machine purred. "I'm so glad you called. You know what to do."

I hung up.

This became my routine for the next three days. I left a message for Margo on Tuesday. My anger about the slimy tongue had dissipated with solitude. I was willing to concede to save one of the last relationships I had left. But I hadn't heard back from her, so I obsessed over that, too. No band. No boyfriend. I just stared at the phone, willing it to ring, and consumed more calories. By Thursday, I was fairly sure I had gained ten pounds.

Finally, I came home to three messages. The first was Margo, sounding congested.

"Hey it's me," she began, sniffling. "Sorry I haven't called. I've been kind of sick. I'm canceling practice tonight, sorry. I'll call you later on. I'm going back to bed now."

Great. I was one for one. The second call was Nikki. I saved it without listening to her whiny voice. The third call made my day.

"Hey Kit, it's Ben. Sorry I missed your call the other day. I've been out of town. Give me a call. There's a party this weekend. I thought you might like to go."

Relief—or was it desire?—washed through me. I was not an asshole after all. Unless I counted the waiting by the phone bit, but I had no witnesses to that. I called Ben and made plans for Saturday night. I tried to stay calm, but could hear my voice shaking as I agreed to be picked up at nine. When I hung up the phone, I sat in silence, trying to keep my hands from trembling.

Saturday night, I tried on six outfits, torn between rock and girlie, before deciding on a compromise of black jeans and a silky lavender blouse. Ben arrived late, looking good in beaten jeans, a Bauhaus T-shirt and a leather jacket.

"Hi," I smiled, but pulled back from him nervously.

"Hi." He stepped through the door and kissed me on the lips. "You ready?"

"Sure."

We walked out to his car and climbed in. He pulled a cigarette from his pack and handed me one.

"Thanks," I said. He leaned over with a lighter and snapped it to life. I took a deep inhale. He lit one for himself.

My heart was racing. I hadn't been on a date in almost two years and was having trouble remembering protocol. Do I say how much I thought of him this past week? Probably too needy. I needed to make small talk. I hated small talk.

"So who's having this party?" I asked.

"A friend of mine, Charlie. He plays in My Pet Rhino."

"Never heard of them."

Oh shit. I probably should have heard of them.

"I'm not surprised," he said. "They've been around forever, but no one ever goes to see them. Anyway, he lives with some guys in an old warehouse."

"Sounds like fun."

I watched the night unfold as we made our way up Broad Street. The prostitutes were in position on the Lombard Street intersection. A few blocks up, the graying audience was milling outside the Academy of Music. Around City Hall, a homeless man curled over a steam vent, despite the warm night.

"Seems like a lot of people out tonight," I said.

"Yeah, I guess so."

I drummed my fingers on my thighs.

"I really liked your show last week," I said. "You guys are good."

"Thanks. We had a great time. We're actually heading into the studio next week to cut our second record. Want to hear some of the new songs?"

"Sure."

I tried not to remember Dale saying those exact words a dozen times.

Ben put in a tape and we listened to a muddled practice recording. Each song started with male voices, but I couldn't make out the words. Then I heard four drum clicks and the noise turned to mush as a tiny microphone attempted to compress too many elements. It sounded horrible.

"What do you think?" Ben shouted over the loud volume.

"It sounds great!"

Ben drove toward Old City, a cramped historic area that showcased Philadelphia's beautiful people. He turned north, and drove up Third Street. The streets grew darker as we left the business district and entered an ominous collection of warehouse buildings. Ben parked on the dark street.

"It's right over there," he said, pointing to a building on the right.

We crunched our way through broken glass until we got to a freight elevator entrance. Ben pushed the button, and we waited silently in darkness as the clank of the elevator descended to meet us. We stepped inside. I stared at the closed door for what felt like a long time and Ben reached up to rest his calloused hand on the back of my neck. The doors finally opened and we climbed out.

I was immediately intimidated. The large open space was occupied by a variety of rock species: a sampling of curvy silhouettes from the other night, Bohemian naturalists, punk rock throwbacks. In one corner, a group of guys were sitting on worn green couches. One was taking a long toke from a large red bong. In another corner, Lava Dance's bass player was talking to two attractive girls I remembered from the Caper's show. The rest of the room held clusters of semi-familiar faces, ones I had seen in the shadows at Dale's shows.

"I'll introduce you to some people," Ben said, taking my hand and pulling me over to one of the attractive girls. She was a thin blonde wearing a black dress and funky black heels that accented her long legs. Her deep red lips burst into a perfect smile.

"Hey, Ben!" she said, leaping forward to embrace him.

"Hey, Christie," he replied after what seemed like a very enthusiastic hug. "This is Kit from Broad Street. They opened for us the other night, remember?"

I shook Christie's limp hand.

"I got there late, sorry," she chirped. "It's nice to meet you. Come on in and get a beer!"

We followed our hostess to a trashcan filled with ice and a potpourri of microbrews. Ben fished out two Yuenglings and handed one to me.

"Is this okay?" he asked.

"Sure."

"Where do you live, Kit?" Christie asked.

"South Philly. How about you? Is this your place?"

"Yeah, I live here with four other guys. They're floating around here somewhere."

"Yeah, poor Christie has to live all alone with four men," Ben said, smiling at her flirtatiously. "Tough life."

"You have no idea, Ben," she flirted back.

These two had definitely slept together.

"It's a lot of space," I interrupted.

"Yeah, it's a lot, but we're artists, so it makes great studio space."

Artist. Gorgeous. Cool. I hated her.

The elevator door opened behind us to reveal more guests. Christie excused herself.

"Come on, I have some other friends I want you to meet." Ben pulled me toward the corner of the room occupied by the bong-passers. They looked up sluggishly as we approached.

"Hey, Ben," they said.

"Hi, guys. This is Kit"

"Hi," I said stupidly. They stared at me with glassy eyes.

"Kit, this is Charlie. He lives here." Charlie was attractive in a rugged sort of way. He had thick sandy hair and a growth of stubble. His blue flannel shirt covered a faded Tiffany T-shirt. I assumed that was a gag.

"And this is Dave," Ben continued, pointing. "He plays guitar in Charlie's band."

Dave had tired brown eyes and looked like he'd slept in his dirty Stooges T-shirt for days.

"And Brian is in a band with those two over there," Ben said, pointing to two guys who looked like Brian—thick and short with dyed black hair, combat boots, and tattoos.

"Kit plays in that new girl band, Broad Street," Ben said.

"Really?" Charlie said. "Do you sing?"

"Sometimes. I mostly play bass."

Charlie looked almost impressed.

"So," Dave said. "Is she in?"

"I'm sure she is," Ben answered. "You party, right?" he asked, turning toward me.

"Yeah," I answered, not sure to which intoxicant he was referring. I drank. I'd smoked pot. Did that qualify me as a partier?

Ben pulled over two beat-up avocado green chairs and smiled slyly at Dave.

"Dave here has generously offered to allow us to sample some very special mushrooms."

"Cool," I said, trying to act it. I had never taken mushrooms before and wasn't sure I wanted to. I wondered why Ben hadn't mentioned this before, but maybe this was part of the whole rock package.

Dave reached into the back pocket of his jeans, pulled out a ziplock bag filled with what looked like dried shriveled turds, and handed it to Ben. He opened it, pinched a small handful and popped it in his mouth. His face contorted in disgust as he chewed, then he washed the mushrooms down with a long swallow of beer. He handed the bag to me.

I took a pinch, put the mushrooms in my mouth and chomped down on them. A liquidy burst of shit exploded in my mouth, making me gag. I quickly took a swallow of beer, but the taste stuck to my tongue, my teeth, the roof of my mouth. I swallowed again and again trying to wash down the hideous flavor. Ben and his posse laughed at my very uncool reaction.

"Yum," I managed to say, at which they all burst out again. I handed Dave the bag.

"Let the games begin," he said.

I finished what was left of my beer and Charlie handed me another one from a cooler at his feet. I sat quietly as the guys swapped passions for music they'd heard recently, obscure musical instruments, flea market finds that proved they were savvy consumers. As I sat and watched, smiling and nodding at what I hoped were the appropriate times, a slow tingling sensation began climbing the back of my neck. I looked at the faces around me and wondered if they were also experiencing this. But they just kept chatting about bargains and equipment and reminding me of the inane ramblings of Dale and his pals and I started to feel uncomfortable. I swallowed my beer, hoping this would kick start a more familiar intoxication, but somehow it was empty already and I was incredibly thirsty, but I was afraid to move my mouth.

The room was beginning to change. The music swirled around my ears three-dimensionally. The lights and people walking around me started to smear slightly into brilliant colors that were both beautiful and frightening. Everyone's talking began to drone like a record on the wrong speed. This was not what I expected. I was out of control.

No. I was okay. I could just sit back and take this all in and enjoy it and it would all be over soon.

"How are you feeling?" Ben's twisted face interrupted the scene before me. His eyes had become giant black Satanic pupils.

"Fine." I managed to smile, but my face felt disconnected. I didn't like this.

"You coming on?"

I didn't want to be discovered like this. I tried to fill my lungs with oxygen, but felt only angry smoke sucked through my nostrils.

"I guess so," I said.

"Me too," he grinned, his teeth yellow and pointy.

He fell back into his chair and laughed loudly. Dave had found a guitar and was strumming along and shrieking and then they were all talking again about the same shit over and over—flea markets, instruments, recording…was this all these losers ever talked about?

I was okay. This would all be over soon.

I looked around the room, and in the corner, I thought I saw Dale. But he couldn't be here. It was just someone who looked like Dale. Flirting with someone who looked like my sister. No, impossible. I was just seeing things. But I couldn't stop the thought of him screwing my sister, and my father dying before I ever achieved anything of worth, and my only friend Margo would just let it all happen like that guy onstage because no one could protect me.

As the circle around me kept talking and talking, I realized that I couldn't get home. I was in the middle of nowhere encased in a moat of broken glass and I would never get home and this might never end. I rubbed the back of my hand to soothe myself, but everyone was too close and too loud. I had to get out of here. I pressed my hands on the arms of the chair and tried to pull myself up.

"Where are you going?" Ben asked and I felt all of the eyes in the room look at me, their faces melting into skeletons.

"I don't feel well," I said.

"It's okay," he said, and stood up with me. "Come on."

I had no choice but to trust him. I clung to his arm as he pulled me through the crowd.

"What's wrong with her?" Christie asked.

"She's all right," Ben answered. "She just needs to lie down."

"Take her to my room," she dared me, her lips wet with blood.

We walked through the noise and the lights and down a dim hallway until we were in a quiet dark room. He led me to a mattress and guided my tingling body down to receive it.

"You're safe here," he whispered.

I embraced the blanket of lightlessness, the music and people safely muffled through the closed door.

"Feel better?" Ben asked.

"Hmm."

My blouse was unbuttoned and I tried not to think of the yellow teeth and dark eyes. I was paralyzed. A sandpapery palm scraped against my breast. My jeans were unzipped and pulled off. Rubbery flesh scraped against mine, inside me, but I was dis-associated from it. My mind was flying through colors and senses and there was something inside me and it felt good but wrong somehow but I was helpless to stop it but it was okay because I was safe. I closed my eyes and let the darkness swallow me.

I woke with a piercing headache. I slowly remembered where I was, and whose room I had been occupying. Shit. How would I get out of here? I lay there for a long time, hoping somehow to disappear. Finally, the door cracked open. It was Christie.

"Hi Kit," she said softly. "How are you feeling?"

"Better, thanks." I'd never felt so humiliated.

"Do you want some coffee?"

I managed to sit up and shake my fingers through my matted hair.

"What time is it?" I asked, pulling my fingertips under my eyes to scrape off any leftover mascara.

"It's about five."

"I'm sorry I stole your room."

"Oh, that's okay. I was up anyway."

"Where's Ben?"

She hesitated. "Um, he had to give someone a ride home. He asked me tell you he's sorry he missed you and hopes you feel better."

"What?"

"Yeah, I know. He can be kind of an asshole sometimes. Charlie said he could give you a ride home if you want."

This was the last person I wanted to share a car with. I remembered twenty dollars in my purse, assuming it was still in the next room.

"Can I get a cab around here?"

"Don't take a cab. Charlie's harmless."

I didn't have the energy to argue.

"Okay. That's nice of him to offer."

"He's out in the living room. I actually think I'm going to try to get some sleep."

"I'm sorry."

"Don't worry about it, really. I usually roll in around this time anyway."

"Thanks."

Christie smiled. Her face was more real this morning, her complexion imperfect, her lipstick gone to reveal small pale lips. I found her reality comforting.

"It was nice meeting you," she said.

I walked out to the living room. The large windows glowed with the pale orange of early morning. The room I had feared last night looked so normal now. My face burned as I remember running out of this room just hours before, terrified.

Charlie was lying on the battered couch. Early morning cartoons danced on an old color television set on the floor. The volume was low, so I could only hear a faint hint of high-pitched giggles and music. Charlie shifted his eyes to me.

"Morning."

"Hi."

"How are you feeling?"

My face burned again. "Better, thanks."

Charlie sat up and patted the remaining space on the couch next to him. I hesitated, then sat down.

"I'm sorry you had a bad time. If you're not in the right mindset, mushrooms can go pretty wrong."

He smelled of beer and cigarettes, his eyes glazed and bloodshot. His thick hair was mashed under a ski hat, and his feet were bare. I hated feet. But his weren't bad, cleaner than I expected. This hint of nudity made me feel an odd intimacy with him.

"I'd never done mushrooms before," I confessed.

Charlie wrinkled his brow. "Didn't Ben tell you we were going to do that? We've had it planned for a while."

"No."

"Hmm."

We watched Beavis and Butt-head rock out to music I couldn't hear.

"Do you want to get some breakfast?" Charlie asked.

"Actually, I'd like to go home."

"No problem, I'll take you. Just let me just get a quick shower so I don't smell like a brewery."

I pretended to stare at the cartoon, but watched Charlie walk away out of the corner of my eye. When he shut the bathroom door, the loft became still, except for the muffled sound of running water and the TV. I swallowed the desire to cry. Ben had screwed me when I was in no position to argue. And what possible reason could he have had to abandon me? I could think of only one. I remembered the silhouettes at the show and was hit with the sickening realization that I had stumbled onto another Dale.

A few minutes later, Charlie walked out of the bathroom with only a towel wrapped around his middle. His wet hair hung over his freshly scrubbed face. He had muscular arms that contradicted a loose stomach.

"I'll be right back," he said as he quickly walked to one of several closed doors. He emerged again shortly covered with jeans and a black T-shirt splashed with a band name I didn't recognize.

"Ready?" he smiled.

We drove quietly back to my house down Delaware Avenue, a street that skirted the river. The sun sparkled on the river as a cruel contrast to my ugly life. When we got back to my house, Charlie double-parked in front and I popped open the door.

"I'm sorry about Ben," he said. "Maybe I'll see you around sometime. Here." He handed me a small paper that advertised a show. "My band's playing next weekend. If you have any interest, you can use this as a pass."

I pulled the piece of paper from his hand.

"Thanks for the ride," I said and shut the door, maybe a little too hard.

CHAPTER

T he next day, I reached new depths of self-loathing. I lay on the couch, my head still buzzing from residual chemicals, and watched a nature program. A male lion hung lazily from a thick tree branch, its tail twitching as flies attempted to land on his tawny hide. The camera cut to a pride of lionesses chasing a gazelle, leaping to its neck, and sinking their long teeth deep into its flesh. After a nauseating display of power, the group dragged the heavy carcass back to the den. The male looked up sleepily at his six concubines, then climbed down slowly to dine. I thought of my mother's weakness with my father, of the girls shrieking as Ben spread his feathers at Caper's, of Dale stepping down from the stage looking for his dinner. I had been cursed with the philosophical desire for female independence without a clue how to achieve it. I pulled my bass from the floor and plucked on the strings until I had created the semblance of melody. I tried to wrap words around it.

The evening started like every one else,

Another night to express ourselves

Under the moonlit summer night,

We faced the end of a losing fight.

After a marathon of tired plucking, as lame nature specials continued to amplify my gender theory, the phone rang. Being an obedient behaviorist, I dashed over, hoping it was Ben.

"Hi, it's me." Margo sounded as if she'd been crying.

"Hey. How are you?"

"Not good. Listen, I'm sorry about the other night." Margo choked on her tears.

I was not expecting this. I was willing to write off Margo's reaction to the guys at the show as my over-reaction, but now she was admitting that something happened. This vindication filled me with affection for her. I wasn't alone in this mess I'd made. We could stand up to that jerk in the tree.

"Thanks," I said, "I really appreciate that. It really did freak me out, I mean his tongue was in my mouth, and…"

There was quiet sobbing on the other end of the phone.

"Margo, it's not the end of the world, really. This is what bands are supposed to do, right? Disagreements are just part of getting better."

She managed a small laugh, but her breath still sputtered.

"Pete and I broke up," she said.

This caught me off-guard. This call was not about me, or the band, or our friendship. She wanted solidarity. I felt guilty about the slow burn of anger that formed at the back of my throat.

"What happened?" I asked, trying not to sound annoyed.

"I don't know," she said, her voice pausing through intermittent tears. "Things haven't been going very well and we've been talking a lot and tonight, I don't know, it just sort of ended."

I tried to focus on the conversation, but I had been betrayed. When I needed Margo, she walked away. But this was different, I rationalized. I had been in these painful shoes not long ago, left to wander the jungle alone.

"Can you meet me at Fergie's Pub?" Margo asked.

"Sure."

I took the subway to Center City, and walked the two blocks to the small corner bar. I stepped into the dark room. It was packed with the usual eclectic mix of scenesters and old drunks. I spotted Margo sitting at one of the booths, and she waved me over.

Her face was puffy and void of makeup, something I'd never seen before. Her lips were pale, her round blue eyes glazed with fatigue.

"I'm sorry about Pete," I said.

Margo looked down at her hands and twisted a ring on her finger.

"It was bound to happen sooner or later. Things have been bad for a while."

"Why didn't you tell me?"

"I don't know. I thought I could handle it."

Two beers arrived and we each took long sips. Margo pulled out a cigarette and handed one to me. She pulled another out for herself and lit both.

"You know, you deserve better than Pete. He just let go of the best thing that ever happened to him."

"Thanks."

"I mean it."

"We both deserve better," she said. We took another drink from our icy mugs and let the bad jukebox music hang in the air.

"He's moving out next week," she said. "At least I get to keep the apartment."

"Well, that's good," I said. "That's a great place."

"The guitar's going with him, though."

"Shit. I forgot about that." I thought back to the kid who sold me his bass amp. I'd found him in a local paper littered with ads for cheap stuff. "Don't worry about that. I know where we can look for a replacement."

She dragged on her cigarette, lifted her head to blow out the smoke, then looked back at me.

"I hope you know how much your friendship means to me," she said.

You have an interesting way of showing it, I thought.

"Me, too," I said tentatively.

"I mean it. It was hard being an only child. I always wanted a sister."

"You've helped me a lot, too. It hasn't been easy since Dale and I broke up."

"Well, you're not alone any more. We're two hot babes on the prowl. Any man would be lucky to get us." She sipped her beer. "Speaking of which, what ever happened with Ben?"

I took a deep breath.

"It's not really working out."

"What do you mean it's not working out?" she asked. "You guys looked pretty chummy at the show. I just assumed he took you home and gave you a little lovin'."

"Well, there was that, and we actually went out again last night."

"What? Why didn't you tell me?"

"I don't know. You were sick, and I guess the way we left things at the show, I don't know…"

Margo reached out to touch my hand.

"I know you were freaked out by that guy. I'm sorry I gave you shit about it."

I was more grateful than I expected for her words, and swallowed back tears.

"So what happened last night?" Margo asked. She moved her hand back to pull the burning cigarette from the ashtray teeth, then put her elbows on the table to lean closer.

I told her about the party and the mushrooms and Ben leaving me in a stranger's house. Sharing this with Margo depleted the humiliation somehow. It started to sound like an interesting story. I decided to leave out the details about Ben in the room with me.

"What an asshole," Margo said. "I can't believe he just left you there. What is wrong with these guys?"

We both shook our heads at the shocking temerity of men, finished our beers and ordered two more, adding a request for two shots of Jamison's.

"That's why we have to totally kick ass with Broad Street," Margo said, tossing back the small glass of warm liquor. She grimaced and wiped her mouth. "Pete's band meant more to him than anything else, and he is truly delusional if he thinks his lame-ass cock rock will ever sell. What we're doing is a million times better. It would completely kill him if our 'cute little project,' as he calls us, started getting some notoriety."

I threw back my shot and cleaned my lips with the back of my hand.

"Yeah," I said. "Ben just played me some stuff for his new record and it was really horrible."

Margo pulled another cigarette out of her pack and lit it off the one still burning, stamping the smaller butt out in the ashtray.

"You know," she began, "I've been thinking. We really should do a demo tape so we can start sending it out to more clubs. One good thing about Pete was he passed along a lot of contacts in Philly and New York, a few places in DC. I say let's record soon. I have this guy Dan who records local bands at his house. He's supposed to be pretty cheap."

"Sounds great."

"We could start sending it out to small labels, maybe some zines and some college stations. It would be awesome."

As we continued to talk, the buzz of the liquor dissipated the loathing that woke me this morning. I felt incredibly lucky to have Margo and the band in my life. By 1:00, we were making plans for our rockumentary.

CHAPTER

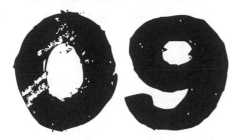

Margo set up the recording date with Dan, who had a 16-track studio in Center City. I tried to stop waiting for Ben to call and apologize, but my skin froze in anticipation every time the phone rang. I wanted to understand why someone who told me I deserved better would treat me so badly. I wanted to understand why I couldn't see this as a lie. But Ben never called.

We decided on two songs—"Banana Dreams" a fun, surfy number and, "Not My Fault," a recently penned song we wrote about a woman scorned. At least Ben was good for material. Both songs featured simple rhythms, shrill background vocals, big rock endings... the perfect ingredients for a demo tape.

We met Linda at Dan's studio on a warm day. Parking our cars illegally on the sidewalk, the three of us began the long, sweaty process of lugging our equipment up three flights of narrow stairs. Dan's studio was in a warehouse space in which he lived with many species of musicians and animals. As soon as we walked in, I was hit by a blast of cold air.

"Hey man," Dan greeted us each quietly, speaking in a deep, soothing baritone drawl. "Go ahead and take your stuff into the back room. Sorry about the cold in here. The air conditioner's broken, and we can't turn it off."

Dan stood about five-feet tall. He had the face of an old man and the wardrobe of an unemployed teenager. His semi-stoned grin was painted beneath a large round nose and sleepy brown eyes. Curly neon orange hair peeked out from under a navy ski cap.

We snaked our equipment through kitty litter boxes, empty liquor bottles, motorcycle parts, amps, clothes. The back room was a large space littered with more musical equipment than I had ever seen in one place. A wall of beat-up amps sat piled high against a wall. Drum pieces lay scattered around the room, except for a complete kit assembled in a corner. A microphone hung from a beam that dangled over the drum kit. Additional microphones were clipped to most of the pieces in the kit. A large bass amp hid behind a gray free-standing wall that I assumed was a sound barrier. Another smaller amp was placed in an open closet. Headphones rested in what seemed to be our designated areas.

"Go ahead and get set up," Dan instructed us. "You can tune while I get ready to run a few sound checks. Kit, you're over there." He pointed to the large amp. "And Margo, you'll be plugging into that. I need to separate the guitar sounds. They really bounce around this room."

I walked over to the big amp and started tuning. Margo walked to her designated area. Linda tuned the heads. Once I finished, I stood there stupidly waiting further instructions. The door finally opened and Dan popped his head in.

"Okay," he said. "Margo and Kit, you guys come up front with me while I check the drums. Linda, you can put that headset on so you can hear me."

Margo and I followed the little man back through the debris and into a small front room. A large soundboard took up most of the space, and Dan's small body looked childlike as he stretched his arms across a sea of sliders and buttons. We huddled in our coats, watching our breath as Dan twisted the knobs, raised and lowered sliders. He pressed a small button and spoke into it.

"Okay, Linda. Start with the bass drum."

Through the monitors that sat on top of Dan's board, we heard Linda, once removed.

Boom boom boom boom boom boom boom. Spike spike spike on the monitor.

"Okay, now toms," Dan commanded.

Pop pop pop pop pop pop pop pop.

"Okay, play the bass drum again."

Boom boom boom boom boom boom boom.

"Good. Now the high hat."

Pssst tap psst tap psst tap psst tap psst tap psst tap.

And so we waited, and smoked, and drank from the six-pack we brought, and wondered if our frozen fingers would be able to play the songs.

Finally, Dan set us free. "Okay, you two head back there and get set up."

Obediently, Margo and I wound our way to the back room.

"It's freezing in here," Linda said, shivering behind the kit.

She was right. We rubbed our hands together as we pulled our guitars over our necks and turned on our amps. Dan had miked our instruments and the drums, so when I slipped the headphones over my ears I could hear my bass, Margo's amp, and Linda's drums. And, of course, Dan, the voice in our heads.

"Okay gals, start playing something."

Margo mouthed "Not My Fault." Linda clicked four times and the song exploded in my ears. Guitars, drums, vocals—with headphones on, these elements become strangely detached from the reality in the room. My fingers were going through their routine, but I felt like an isolated bystander. My breath began to tighten. The harder I concentrated, the more wrong notes I hit. We finally reached the end.

"Okay that was pretty good," our head voice reassured us. "Now give me a few minutes, and we'll try a take."

A take. A chill ran through me. Suddenly, knowing that what I was about to play would be recorded forever, that the two people in this room were depending on me to play every note perfectly, I was struck with a suffocating claustrophobia. My headphones squeezed down on my skull; the cable tied me to the wall like a rabid dog on a leash.

"I have to go to the bathroom." I pulled off the headphones and bass.

"Now?" Margo asked.

"I'll be right back."

I found the bathroom off of the large center room and closed the door behind me. The toilet bowl was disturbingly dark brown. Crumpled dirty towels of dingy grays and pinks lay on the floor. The sink was also discolored, with a variety of questionable hairs stuck to the porcelain and faucet. I turned on the hot water; it ran ice cold. I stuck my finger under it for what felt like a very long time. Still, it ran cold. Fuck it. I cupped my hands under the water and splashed it on my face, as piercing as a slap. I looked up into the mirror as beads of liquid pulled off mascara, lipstick.

"You can do this," I told my reflection. "You can do this."

Just one more test. I pulled my sweater up and dried my face on the coarse wool. When I looked up, my brown eyes seem darker against my bare face, stronger. I was tired of that gnawing voice that continued to doubt me. My father's voice. I had to ignore it.

I took a deep breath, then opened the door and returned to the back room where Margo and Linda sat shivering.

"Sorry," I said.

Margo's expression changed from annoyed to concerned.

"Are you all right?" she asked.

"Yeah, thanks."

"I don't know about you guys, but I'm pretty nervous," she said.

"Let's just do it," Linda said. "My hands are getting numb."

Margo shot her a look, then slightly shook her head. After a few minutes, the headphone voice was ready.

"We're rolling."

We plowed through the song again. My numb fingers mostly fell on familiar strings at the right times, but I hit a few duds along the way. Margo played a wrong chord and winced. Linda sped up the song until we were at a lightning pace by the end.

"Okay," Dan said. "let's try that again. I'm going to blow over that one."

"Hold on a second," Margo said loudly into the room. "Dan, can you hear me?"

"Yeah, what's up?"

"How was that speed? It sounded kind of inconsistent."

Linda snapped her head up from the drums and glared at Margo.

"It could have been tighter," Dan said. "But, you guys are just warming up."

"Okay, I just thought it was a little fast," Margo said.

"That's the speed we always play that song," Linda said.

"Kit, what do you think?" Margo turned to me.

"You know," I started, wary of the need to get this recording done without killing each other. "I really didn't notice. I was too busy trying to hit the right notes."

"Why don't you just try it again?" Dan suggested curtly.

"Whatever." Margo sniffed.

Linda clicked off again and the song came together a little more smoothly, but there were still many performance flaws. When we reached the end, Margo looked over at me, but her comment was to Linda.

"That was definitely too fast. There's no way I can keep up with that speed when I sing."

Linda exhaled loudly.

"Margo, I've recorded two records with The Pussy Willows. I've been playing for five years. I think I know when I'm playing the same tempo."

My stomach tightened. Margo smiled coldly toward Linda.

"I know I don't have your vast experience," she said. "But I know when something is too fast. And that's too fast."

"You guys want to take a break and figure this out?" Dan said.

"No!" Linda snapped. "I want to get this done."

"Okay," he said. "Let's try another one."

This time Linda clicked slower, much slower than we had ever played it, and we followed along. Margo smiled and nodded, so I just went with it. The slower pace actually helped me keep up with the bass runs, and the take sounded pretty good.

"Okay, better," Dan said. "Let's do it again."

And again. And again. Each new version had its own idiosyncrasies. When Linda's performance was almost consistent, I hit a few wrong notes. When Margo played through flawlessly, Linda's time was off. After the ninth attempt, Dan said he thought we had it.

"Come on back and take a listen."

We returned to the front room. I nestled into one of the many trash-picked chairs, lit a cigarette, and listened to our efforts. Margo sat in a chair next to me. Linda sat on a couch across the room. The song boomed out of the speakers, loud and angry. The tempo wavered slightly. But, overall, it almost sounded like a real rock band.

"We can punch in some of those flubs," Dan commented on my few wrong notes.

"What do you mean?" I asked.

"You'll play along with the recording, then I'll punch in the new right notes for the wrong old notes. The most important thing is the tempo, and it's pretty consistent."

Punching in parts that weren't quite right. Erasing mistakes as if they never happened. I found this idea very intriguing. Maybe I could apply this philosophy to my love life.

After doctoring our imperfections with "Not My Fault," we began the whole process all over again for "Banana Dreams." And again.

"I'm quitting."

Linda twirled her sticks as she delivered the news at our next practice. Margo and I stared at her in disbelief.

"We just finished the demo tape," Margo said.

"I know. Sorry," Linda continued, not sounding that sorry. "But The Pussy Willows asked me back. They're going on tour."

"You hate The Pussy Willows," I reminded her.

"I know. But it's a West Coast tour. They have gigs lined up in LA, Frisco, Seattle. I really can't pass this up."

We sat in silence. I thought the timing between the awkward recording session and the invitation to rejoin The Pussy Willows was a little too convenient. Margo's big mouth was going to cost me the only thing keeping me sane. I couldn't let it end. The empty nights between band events were just too big.

"Maybe we can wait for you," I attempted lamely. Margo shot me a look I tried to ignore.

"Thanks, Kit," Linda said. "But this is just too good an opportunity."

"Shit." Margo dropped down on her amp and lit a cigarette, knowing Linda wouldn't dare complain now. "Everything was going so well."

We sat in silence, Linda still in her jacket, still clinging to her sticks. Should she play or should she go?

"I do know of another drummer," Linda offered. "He saw us play at your house, Kit. He thought we were really good and he's looking for a band to play in."

Margo and I looked up cautiously. Linda continued.

"His name's Gino. He's the boyfriend of a friend of mine. He's a great drummer."

"I don't know. I like the all girl thing," Margo said. "Shit."

"Can't hurt to try him out," I said.

"I don't know," Margo shook her head and stared at the floor, her shoulders hunched like a beaten dog. "Everything was going so well."

The band lay flailing on the ground, gasping for air. I knew it was up to me to resuscitate it.

"Why don't you give me his number?" I said to Linda. "I'll call him and see what he says."

"I really think we should look for another girl," Margo said.

"It can't hurt to call him," I said.

"I don't know," Margo sighed. "This sucks."

I ignored her. I was going to make this work. I booked a two-hour rehearsal for the next night. As soon as I got home, I called Gino.

"Yeah?" a sleepy voice answered. It was only 8:30 at night.

"Hi, is this Gino?" I asked.

"Yeah?"

"Hi, my name's Kit. I play in a band called Broad Street. I got your name from Linda."

"Yeah?"

"You probably know that Linda's leaving the band to go back with The Pussy Willows. She mentioned you might be interested in playing with us."

A pause. I felt like I was going a little too fast for this guy.

"Yeah."

I waited for more, then realized I wasn't going to get it.

"Can you make rehearsal tomorrow night at 7:00? We practice at Fishtown Studios."

"Sure."

"Okay. Great. I guess we'll see you then."

"Yep."

The next night, Gino arrived twenty minutes late. I vaguely remembered him from the party at my house. He was short and thin, with dark, rockabilly hair, beady brown eyes and a big Italian nose.

"Hi Gino," Margo bellowed, all faux confidence. She seemed nervous. "I'm Margo."

"Hey," he replied sheepishly, staring at the floor and peering up through tousled hair.

He slithered across the room to the drum riser, hunched over a cymbal bag in one hand, a snare case in the other. We glanced nervously at each other as he quietly set up the drums. It was just a tryout, I consoled myself. If it didn't work out, no big deal.

I attempted another intro. "Linda said you saw us at Kit's house."

"Yeah."

I was just about to launch into another lame comment when he continued.

"You guys were pretty good."

This cheered us up.

"Thanks," Margo beamed. "The sound system sucked, but we had a blast. Want a beer?"

Test number one.

"Sure."

She grabbed a lukewarm bottle of Yuengling out of a paper bag and walked it over to him.

"Thanks."

He unscrewed the cap, tipped it toward his mouth and poured over half the bottle into it, his large Adam's apple pumping to keep up. He wiped his mouth.

"Mind if I smoke?" he asked, passing test number two.

"Not at all," Margo smiled.

He pulled a pack of Camels out of his leather jacket, popped one into his mouth and lit it, cupping his hand around the end as if there were a breeze in the still room. He left the smoking cigarette in his mouth, squinting one eye, as he continued to assemble his cymbals and tune the heads. The end of the cigarette glowed intermittently as his lungs brought it to life, the ash growing into a long pupa skin. I caught Margo's eyes and we raised our eyebrows, not sure what to make of this guy. Gino finished setting up, dropped his cigarette onto the stained green carpet and ground it into the floor with a combat boot. He picked up the beer and polished off the remaining half.

"Want to try one?"

"Sure," Margo said. "'Take That' is pretty straight-forward. Let's try it." She counted us off.

As soon as Gino attacked the drums, we knew we were crawling our way up the food chain of percussive quality. Gino meshed perfectly with our simple garage style—no complicated rhythms, just straightforward 4/4 time, thick with the rumbling tones of bass drum and toms. It was louder, punchier, more ballsy than ever before. After we finished the song, Margo and I exploded.

"That was awesome!" we said in girlie unison.

"Thanks," he said. "That's a pretty cool song. Mind if I have another beer?"

"No," I said, happy to fuel this monster. I handed him another one, which he sucked down furiously.

"Let's try 'Falling'," Margo suggested.

We plowed through the three-minute song the same way—loud, furious, punk rock. We turned our guitars up to meet the slamming drums and became a whole new animal. My head spun with the rush of volume and adrenaline. My slight infatuation grew into full-blown lust for rock and roll. Maybe we could jump the hurdle of delicate egos and get somewhere with this band.

Gino finished with a big ending and his face revealed the slightest hint of a grin. He picked up his beer and took another long gulp. Margo and I took quick swigs of ours, trying to keep up

"You're great," Margo said, lighting a cigarette. "Have you been in bands before?"

"Not really," he answered. "I played with some guys when I lived in New York, but mostly I just bang around at home. I've been playing since I was six. I love it."

"How about your girlfriend. Is she in a band?" I asked.

Gino stopped smiling. "Yes."

Leave it to me to kill a good time. I tried another angle.

"What kind of music do you listen to?"

"A lot of glam, mostly. T. Rex, New York Dolls, The Sweet, that kind of stuff."

"Do you like anything new?" Margo asked.

"New music sucks."

"I know," Margo continued. "Most crap out there is all production and fake boobs."

He leaned unsteadily toward Margo. "Well if that's the criteria for a record label, it looks like we'll just need a good producer."

"Hey, these are one hundred percent natural, baby."

The two laughed. Was I in this room?

"Want to try another one?" I asked.

The two looked over at me, as if startled to see me still there.

"Sorry, babe," Margo smiled. "You're right. We only have about 45 minutes left. Let's try that new one we were working on the other week, the one that you start."

I started the introductory bass line. Margo interrupted.

"Sorry, that's a little fast. Gino, maybe you can count it off on the high hat."

I tried to stay calm, but felt the anger rising. Why was I always so easy to step over? Gino clicked off four and I played along at what felt like the same speed I just played.

"Perfect," Margo said into the mic.

CHAPTER

The lunchroom was empty on a dreary Wednesday. Rain spattered against the large window that framed downtown Philadelphia. I walked toward it and stared down at the city. Ten floors below our office, multicolored umbrellas twisted and weaved on the sidewalk. Cars clogged the street, blocked by the dam of a parked bus. The bus driver was out in the rain. His navy uniform darkened to black as he worked to fit a wheel-chair-bound rider onto a pneumatic metal contraption that emerged from the back door. The rider was a large black woman with a bright orange hat and matching suit. She sat calmly with her hands folded in her lap as the driver struggled to fit the weighted chair onto the device. Muffled horns scolded him; the small crowd protected by the clear bus stop watched him struggle. Someone should help. Finally, she was attached to the gadget. He pressed something by the door that made her lift slowly into the air. Then, the bus swallowed her. The doors folded closed. The driver pulled a white handker-chief from his pocket, wiped his damp face, then returned to the bus. Just as he started to inch toward the light, it turned from yellow to red.

The horns scolded once again. I could definitely relate.

I turned away from the scene and sat down at the empty table. It was a perfect day for my mood. It had been over a week since Ben abandoned me at a stranger's house without apology. I was nervous about the new drummer. I had yet to talk to my sister. My new life seemed always slightly out of reach.

I pulled my salad out of the white plastic bag, popped open the clear top and stabbed my plastic fork into a piece of broccoli. I crunched down on it, thinking that what I really wanted was a cheesesteak. The lunchroom door opened. It was Rachel.

"Hey," she said, plopping down an identical salad bag.

"Hi," I responded, my mouth full.

Rachel pulled out her salad. It looked more appetizing than mine, dressed in tuna, black olives and spiral pasta. She pulled out a diet Snapple, twisted off the lid and took a sip.

"I don't know about you, but Jean is driving me nuts," she said. "She's taken micromanagement to a new low. She actually tidied the paperclips and pencils in my drawer last night."

"How do you know?"

"Because I worked late last night, and she was still here. I saw her leaving Post-its all over Cheryl's desk. She was making her way through the office."

I thought of the contents of my desk, trying to recall any incriminating evidence. I couldn't remember anything too damaging.

"So how did that new guy work out last night?" Rachel asked.

I swallowed a chunk of broccoli.

"Margo seems to like him."

"Well that's good." She pulled her plastic knife and fork from their plastic wrapper and began slicing through her salad. "What do you think?"

I wanted to tell her how I felt left out of my own band, how I thought Margo seemed always quick to sell me out. But a bigger part of me wanted to protect my fragile dream of having a successful band. Realist Rachel would interpret my feelings for what they were—legitimate concerns.

"He's a good drummer, but kind of a jerk. He didn't say a word until he plowed through three beers, and then all he said was new music sucks and Margo had nice tits."

"Hmm." Rachel scooped up a forkful of tuna and pasta. I followed suit, jamming a dressing-coated tomato onto my fork and stuffing it into my mouth, the cool jellied interior exploded between my teeth. After a few seconds of chomping, Rachel asked, "Did he like your music?"

"Yeah. He actually was pretty complimentary in his own oblique way."

"Well that's good. You're not looking for a friend, right? Just a good drummer to play with."

"You're right. He was a lot better than Linda."

"Better is good." Rachel responded, looking quizzically into her salad, deciding which treat to choose next. She chose a hardboiled egg-tuna combo and stuffed it in her mouth. "And if Margo likes him, things will probably cool down at practice."

Rachel's simple rationale made sense. Certainly a little flirting was better than the stomach-wrenching tension of practices with Linda. Maybe I do overreact. Maybe this band could turn into something decent.

We were interrupted by the lunchroom door opening. The sight of Jean Zimmerman's bird nose peering around the corner made us halt mid-chew.

"Oh, Kit," she said, sweet enough to make my teeth ache. "I am so sorry to interrupt your lunch, but we have a little situation. I was hoping you might be able to help out."

There were no little situations with Jean.

"What's up?" I asked.

"Well, Dr. De Medio is here and he had some questions on an article you proofread recently."

"Questions?"

"It will just take a minute."

I glanced at Rachel who raised a concerned eyebrow.

"Okay," I said. I closed the lid on my salad and pushed my chair back from the table.

I followed Jean down the hall away from the lunchroom and around the corner. Through the glass façade that shielded her office, I saw the back of Dr. De Medio's bald pate, accented by a Friar-Tuck-like fringe of hair. When he saw me, he leaned down and pulled something from his tattered brown attaché. He sat back up, crossed his legs, and tapped the papers on his knee to tidy the pile. As we got to the door of her office, he turned and smiled. He was a ferret of a man—small beady eyes made beadier by thick glasses, a potato-shaped nose, and thin lips that revealed small yellow teeth. He nodded to Jean as she rounded her desk to assume position. I was sure they were going to destroy me.

"Hello, Kit," Dr. De Medio said in a high nasal voice. We had met several times before, most notably at a recent medical convention cocktail party where he drank too much wine and told me I had nice eyes.

"Have a seat," Jean said, pointing to the empty chair next to Dr. De Medio.

As I sat down, he began nervously tapping the papers against his knee. Jean turned to Dr. De Medio and smiled impatiently. I thought maybe she was so afraid that I would have another emotional reaction that she had to bring in this wimp to do the dirty work for her. Finally, he spoke.

"Now Kit," he began, laying the neat stack of papers in his lap. "You know that we have been very happy with your work. And, overall, you have been quite good at ensuring that articles are accurate. I don't have to tell you how important that is."

"Thanks," I said cautiously.

"Now," he cleared his throat, "of course you know about the adenocarcenoma table that we had some problems with. Jean told me that you and she had a little talk about that and she told me that you were going through some personal things and that's okay. It happens to the best of us sometimes."

This was completely embarrassing. I wanted to melt into the carpet.

He cleared his throat again.

"But it has come to my attention recently that another serious error has slipped by the proofreading department." He pulled the latest issue off the top of his neat lap pile and handed it to me. "Please turn to page 672."

I took the slippery journal from him and fanned through the folios with my thumb until I reached the correct page. I opened to an article on asthma treatment.

"Please note the Estrogen in the Prevention of Atherosclerosis article. The outcome results for the 'HIV-1–Infected Patients' was supposed be the outcome results of the 'Placebo-Controlled Trial.' The last proofreader to see this was you."

Jean cast her cool gaze in my direction.

"Am I fired?"

Dr. De Medio started tapping his paper stack again. Jean exhaled loudly.

"No, Kit," she said, tossing an angry glare toward Dr. De Medio. "You are not fired. Our company has a very forgiving policy toward inadequacy. You must acquire three warnings before you are dismissed. The first mistake seemed to be a temporary lapse in your ability. Unfortunately, this lapse does not appear to be as temporary as I had hoped. Consider this your second warning. You will also receive demerits that will be considered when we hold your annual review."

"Okay," I whispered. "I understand."

"We also cannot allow any more mistakes to go out of this office," Jean continued, "so all of your work must now be cleared by a senior proofreader and myself before being released to the journal. I need a daily task sheet each morning that itemizes what jobs you have and when they are due. We will meet at the end of each day to discuss any deviations from this task list."

I had just entered hell.

"Fine," I answered.

"Thank you for your time," she said.

I stood up and looked over at Dr. De Medio. He pulled his eyes up to meet mine and smiled faintly.

"I'm sorry it has to be this way," he whimpered like a beaten dog. "You've really done great work up to now. I'm sure things will turn around for you."

Poor schmuck.

"Thank you," I said.

I walked out the door and back to my office, thinking that I was on my way to completely ruining my life. What else could go wrong?

The answer was on my desk, in the form of a handwritten message next to my phone. Your mother called. Please call her. Urgent.

The cell phone rang four times before my mother answered.

"Hello?" Her voice broke with the static of a weak battery.

"Mom, it's me. What's wrong?"

"Hi Honey," her voice crackled, "it's your father. He came in for tests today and we..." Her voice disappeared into a murky hiss of static.

"Mom!" I yelled, too loudly for my small office. "I can't hear you! Where are you?"

I heard her voice, but couldn't make out the words.

"Where?" I asked loudly.

"...ferson...Ward."

"Jefferson?" And then she disappeared into silence. Thomas Jefferson Hospital. That was only six blocks from my office. I grabbed my purse and coat and walked quickly back to Jean's office. Dr. De Medio had slithered away; she was on the phone laughing loudly. I walked in, rather than waiting by the doorway until she was finished as was protocol. She glared at me and asked her charming phone colleague to hold for a moment.

"Jean, I'm sorry," I said. "I just got a call from the hospital. It's my dad, some kind of emergency. I have to go. I'm sorry."

She stared at me, attempting to decipher the truth of my rude interruption. Even I, she appeared to think, the bumbling proofreading dolt, would not be so bold as to choose this moment for a little R&R.

"Okay," she said hesitantly. "Make sure you give your jobs to Rachel so they get done today."

"I will. Thanks."

I turned and walked away before she thought of other last-minute crises that in her world superseded the mortality of my family. I went back to my office, grabbed my pink folders and left them with Rachel.

It wasn't until I stepped out of the building that I remembered my umbrella was still in my office. Heavy rain quickly soaked my hair and clothes as I stood on the corner futilely hailing a cab. Cars whisked past me, each one creating a new tidal wave of muddy water from the street that landed on my leather pumps. I gave up and started to walk quickly toward the hospital, across Broad Street, then 13th, then 12th, each step feeling heavier. What could have happened? Did Mom tell me she was taking him in? Am I so self-absorbed that I forgot this information? I was a terrible daughter. I was a terrible person.

Finally, I reached the automatic doors of Thomas Jefferson Emergency Room. I walked to the desk where a young black woman stared down at a clipboard. Her hair was cropped short, accentuating large silver earrings that looked like snakes wrapped around a tree. Her cleavage peeked out between aqua green scrubs. She looked up.

"May I … Wow, is it that bad outside?"

My wet clothes pulled down on my shoulders and spine. A small puddle formed around my feet. I pushed my wet hair out of my face and wiped the rain from my eyes.

"Yes. I'm here to see my father, Pierce Greene. I believe he came in for some cardiovascular testing."

She reached under her desk, pulled out a roll of paper towels and handed them to me. They were decorated with dancing teddy bears.

"I think you could use these," she said.

"Thank you."

As I tore small bears from the roll and smeared them onto myself, she pulled out another clipboard.

"Now, let me see. Greene." She ran her finger down a list. "Yes, here we go. He was admitted about a half an hour ago. You want to go to C302. Just go through those doors there." I turned to follow her pointing finger and saw two large swinging doors. "There's an elevator on your right. Take that to the third floor and follow the signs to C302."

"Thank you." I tore off a handful of paper towels and handed her back the roll. I wiped my face and neck as I walked through the doors, wrinkling my nose at the scent of decay and sterility. I took the elevator to the third floor and followed the arrow that directed me to C302. I tried not to look in the rooms occupied by the healing and dying, but instead noticed the eerie silence of the living. Only the mixed noise of television shows softly occupied these rooms. I shifted my eyes slightly to see a withered old woman covered to her sagging breasts by a white sheet. Her eyes were closed, her lips parted slightly, the remote control clutched in a shriveled brown hand that rested on her belly. I snapped my head away and walked to the next room.

My father was sitting up in bed. A pale pink curtain separated him from the occupied bed by the window, where all I could see was the hint of sheet-covered feet. Tubes snaked from my father's arm into bags of different colored liquids. My mother was sitting down with her back to the door.

"You're drenched," Dad greeted me, his voice soft and gravelly.

My mother stood up, turned around and walked toward me, giving me a gentle hug to avoid getting soaked.

"I'm sorry to scare you, Honey," she said "I forgot to charge my cell phone."

"What happened?"

"It's just precautionary," my mother said quietly. "Your father was in for tests today and the doctor was concerned about what seemed like a blockage in one of his arteries."

"They're going to open me up," my father added with dramatic flair.

"What do you mean?" I asked.

"Angioplasty," he grumbled. "They're going to stick a tube in me and vacuum me out. This body of mine is falling apart."

"Dad," I responded. "You're hardly falling apart. Maybe this is just a sign that you should start taking better care of yourself. Maybe cut out some of that scrapple you eat for breakfast. Maybe get out of your reading chair and take a walk once in a while."

"Honey," my mom interrupted, lightly touching my wet arm.

"Mom, you know it's true."

"Hey," my father said, "I need to survive surgery first, then I'll worry about other things."

"Pierce," my mother turned to him. "This is minor surgery. It's performed all the time and this is one of the best hospitals in the city. Dr. Goyal says the risks are very minimal."

"I don't have time for this," my father said, shaking his head.

My mother and I let the ironic statement hang in the air.

"When is the surgery?" I asked.

"Six o'clock tomorrow morning," he answered. "I have to stay in here tonight for no reason I can figure out, other than to rack up my hospital bill."

He turned toward my mother, and despite his words, he looked scared. Fear was not something I was used to seeing in my father. I looked down at my muddy feet. The clock on my life kept speeding up. What have I done? I screwed around in college and barely escaped with moderate grades. I couldn't keep a relationship going. I'd been demoted from an already lowly proofreading position. My band seemed to be moving in futile circles. I had to slow this down. I needed my father to witness some modicum of success in my life.

"What happened?" Nikki's voice interrupted behind me. She walked quickly over to the bed, dropping her smiley-face umbrella along the way, and hugged my father and mother. I stood by as they reviewed the events with Nikki. She sat on the bed with the two of them, dry and comforting. I felt my clothes stick to my skin and wished I, too, could make my parents proud.

By the time I left, it was almost 4:00, too late to return to the office. My mother wanted to stay until visiting hours were over at 8:00, but told us it was okay to leave. Nikki walked out with me and we stood beneath the building overhang. The rain continued to beat against the sidewalk; the water pulled pieces of garbage into a clogged drain on the street.

"So why haven't you called me back?" she asked.

"I think you know."

"You seriously think that I would fool around with Dale?"

I didn't answer.

"Kit, what have I done to you to make you think I'm that kind of person? You're my sister."

"Well, there was the time you went out with George in high school when you knew I had a crush on him."

She laughed.

"You've got to be kidding. I went to a Phillies game with him and about ten other people and it wasn't my fault he called later to ask me out. I didn't go out with him, did I?"

"Whatever." I was determined to make my point, however irrational.

"Come, on. I think we could both use a drink."

She popped open her bright yellow umbrella and stepped out from the dry safety of the overhang.

"You coming?" she asked.

I followed her out into the rain and wrapped my arms around myself. As much as I didn't want to spend time with Nikki, the thought of walking to the subway in the rain and returning to my empty house was too depressing. We walked three blocks to a small bar called Oscars, Nikki holding her umbrella high above our heads to try and protect us. Instead, we both got wet.

Oscars was another dive, but unlike Fergie's eclectic crowd, this dump was primarily occupied by college students. We briefly splashed the occupants with a wave of light before the door slammed closed behind us. I blinked a few times, adjusting to the dim room, until I saw the peninsula bar in front of me. It protruded like an inefficient border around the bartender, giving her most of the floor while patrons crammed barstools into what little space was left in the room. The bartender had long twisted dreads that she had sloppily banded together in back with a red string. A silver nose ring and thick Buddy Holly-style glasses accented her childish face.

On one side of the bar, two young buttoned-down guys looked in our direction, then leaned into each other to whisper. They each smiled and turned back toward us, then gripped their frosty mugs of beer and took long swallows. On the other side of the bar, a young Indian woman straddled the leg of a lanky white guy. She had hiked her colorful dress up to fit his leg between hers, baring brown skin and chunky black mules. She leaned in to him, her long black hair shining red against the glow of the neon beer sign that hung behind the bar.

Nikki and I walked to an unoccupied corner and ordered two beers. The bartender took two mugs from under the bar, filled them from a tap and handed them to us.

"Three bucks," she said, watching the door expectantly.

I tossed a five on the bar and she grabbed it indifferently.

"I can't believe this about Dad," Nikki said, taking a sip of her beer.

"Maybe this will be the kick in the ass he needs."

"I hope so."

We both sat quietly for a minute.

"How's the band?" Nikki asked.

"Pretty good. Linda left, so we're trying out a new drummer."

"Is she any good?"

"Actually, it's a guy."

"Really? I thought the chick thing was so cool."

"I know, but this guy seems decent. We'll see." I really wanted to change the focus of the conversation away from my pathetic life. We were only a few short steps away from the Ben debacle.

"So," I began, "How's work?"

Suddenly, Nikki started crying. She pulled her soggy napkin from under her beer and pressed it to her eyes. She's fucking Dale. I noticed the patrons glancing over at us. I pulled some dry napkins from a plastic cocktail napkin holder in front of me.

"What is it?" I asked, my voice shaking.

"It's my boss," she said quietly.

"What do you mean?"

"Kit, it's horrible," she pressed the napkin tightly into her eyes and then blew her nose. I felt all the eyes in the room on us.

"Come on, let's go to the bathroom."

I grabbed our purses and led Nikki back to the bathroom, weaving our way through a few small empty tables. We pushed the dark wooden door open and stepped into a small, dimly lit room. One small chipped sink hung from the wall; the back of the room housed a stall; its door hung by one rusty hinge. I shut the door, encasing us in musty dampness.

"What happened?' I asked, running cold water onto some paper towels and handing them to her.

"I haven't told anyone," she sobbed.

"You can tell me."

She blew her nose into the wet paper towel.

"We went out for drinks a few times after work. It always started pretty innocently, but each time we got a little drunker and a little flirtier, and last time…" She paused to pull a dry paper towel from its metal holder and pressed it to her eyes. "Last Friday night we went out with a bunch of people from work. We were having a great time, but one by one everyone left until it was just Ted and me. I was pretty drunk by this time, so I moved in sort of close to talk and he started rubbing his leg against mine and I didn't exactly resist. He is a very cute guy and I know he's married and I know it was wrong, but I just thought we were having fun. So we're carrying on like this for a while and then the bartender announces last call, so Ted asks if he could walk me home." She paused and turned her damp blue eyes up at me.

"You slept with him."

She quickly shifted her eyes back to the floor.

"It was stupid," she said quietly. "Totally fucking stupid." A tear splashed on the drab pink tile floor.

"Does anyone know?" I asked.

"Well," she hesitated.

"Well?"

"One of the people sitting at the bar when we left is a friend of Ted's business partner."

"Shit."

"I know. This is a mess. I could lose my job. He could lose his job. He could lose his wife. Although from what I hear that's no big loss."

"What does that mean? You're not still seeing him, are you?"

"Not really"

"Nikki, don't be stupid. You fucked up once and maybe you'll get away with it, but starting an affair with this guy is a really bad idea."

"I know."

"But you are."

"No. I just, I don't know. He's so sweet and really sexy and I just feel so comfortable with him."

"How old is he?"

"Thirty-eight."

"Does he have kids?"

"One. A four-year-old."

"And does starting an affair with an older, married dad seem like a good idea to you?"

"No."

I was surprised at how comfortably I'd slipped into this new role with my sister. Wisdom came so much easier when it was somebody else's mistakes.

"Seriously, think about this. This could ruin a great career opportunity, not to mention some innocent lives. Think about that poor kid."

"I know."

My anger at my sister's selfishness was coupled with an unusual satisfaction at her colossal screw up. What would dad and mom think of their perfect little girl now?

The alarm rudely awoke me the next morning at 5:00. I fought the crusty sleeplessness as my eyes split open to greet the dimly lit room. My night had been plagued with ugly visions of knives and graves and helplessness. I let my body walk through its routine—coffee, shower, getting dressed. I waited for the subway in the empty underground terminal, the distant lull of the train my only companion. I took the train three stops, then walked up to the sidewalk. A homeless man huddled in the doorway of a closed bank. As I walked by him, the sour odor of urine filled me with sadness.

When I got to Jefferson, my mother was already in the waiting room, which was small, with uncomfortable yellow chairs lining two walls. Also waiting were a small old man hunched over a cane and a pregnant woman with a young boy. The boy was asleep against his mother's chest. My mother smiled sadly when she saw me. I sat next to her and put my arm around her.

"He's going to be fine," I said. She nodded.

Nikki came in a few minutes later looking as tired as I felt.

"Hey," she whispered to us.

Our group sat silently, sipping bad vending-machine coffee, and waited. At 6:00, a nurse came in and asked for Shauntia Evans. The woman and her son got up and followed the nurse. Forty minutes later, a man with salt and pepper hair walked in with a taller, younger version of himself, and sat in two vacant chairs across from us. At 7:00, a white-jacketed man with large thick glasses walked in.

"Dana Greene?" he asked, looking at our cluster.

"Yes?" my mother answered. He smiled and walked over to us, pulling a chair from the wall until it faced us. This gesture worried me. It was never good news when the doctors on medical dramas pulled over sympathetic chairs.

The doctor leaned in on his elbows to share this horrible secret. "I'm Dr. Strook." He reached out and shook my mother's hand. "Are these your daughters?"

"Yes, this is Kit and Nikki," she answered.

Get to it already.

"The surgery went well. Pierce is very strong. We cleared the blockage in two of his arteries with the angioplasty. He's resting now, but I he should be able to go home tomorrow."

Tension melted from my mother's face.

"Thank God," she sighed.

"Mrs. Greene, your husband has a lot of life in him," Dr. Strook continued. "But he does need to start taking better care of himself. His cholesterol is dangerously high, and he's got to quit smoking. The damage to his lungs has caused a heart arrhythmia. I don't want to scare you, but with this history, he is a good candidate for a heart attack."

"He keeps trying to quit," she said, looking at her lap.

"He has to stop trying. He should also start an exercise routine. It doesn't have to be much, maybe just a 30-minute walk a day."

My father, exercise? I couldn't quite picture it.

"Thank you, Dr. Strook. I appreciate everything you've done. When can we see him?"

He looked at his watch.

"He should be waking up from anesthesia soon, but I'd give him another half hour or so. He's back in his room." He turned and walked toward the door. "It was nice meeting you all," he said, and walked out of the room.

"Thanks for coming, girls," my mother said, reaching out to squeeze our hands.

"I'm so glad everything went okay," Nikki said.

But I wasn't so sure that it would stay okay. My father had merely been handed a stay of execution. I knew how stubborn he could be, and this stubbornness could lead to a false, possibly fatal sense of invincibility.

Nikki and I both put our arms around our mother.

"Your dad should be rested up in a few days," my mother said. "Maybe you girls could come for a visit next Sunday."

CHAPTER

I spent the day at work avoiding Jean. I had filled Rachel in on what had happened, and she offered to take some of the pink pile in my office.

When I got home that night, I got a call from Margo. She had sent our demo tape out to all of the area newspapers and zines, and got a call from Laura Cook, a reporter from the City Paper. She wanted to feature Broad Street in an upcoming article on girl bands. Margo had arranged for Laura and a photographer to meet at my house the next night at 7:00. Maybe things were looking up after all.

I once again struggled with selecting the ideal wardrobe. First, jeans and a tank top, laid-back rock cool. The jeans made my thighs look big. Next, a black dress that looked fine as long as I didn't breathe. I probably needed to breathe. Then a retro mustard mini-skirt with a black body suit and black boots. Trying too hard. Finally, as I was pulling a black tank dress over my head, the doorbell rang. This would have to be my look.

When I answered the door, it was Margo. She wore a tight black skirt and handkerchief of a black top. I was instantly disappointed in my choice.

"Hi!" she said, sliding past me and tossing her purse on the coffee table.

My living room had evolved over the past few weeks. I had acquired a cherry red sectional couch from a friend of Margo's who was moving to San Francisco. It came with a matching coffee table that looked like a giant red pillow had swallowed a thick white slab of plastic. An overstuffed pine green chair enhanced the holiday look, courtesy of someone three blocks down from my house that had deemed it unworthy. I soon realized why the chair had been on the street, but one good flea bombing took care of that.

"This is great," Margo said, plopping herself into the green chair and lighting a cigarette. "I can't believe they're doing a story on us. Pete is going to be so fucking jealous. His band's had maybe one review in two years. Never a whole article."

"Yeah, I guess Dale never had an article either. That is pretty cool."

Gino arrived a few minutes later in typical rock costume—black T-shirt and black jeans. He barely filled an indent on a section of the couch with his bony butt. I got us each a beer as Margo and I talked nervously.

The photographer was a short, masculine woman with close-cropped brown hair and a plain, friendly face. A large gray camera bag hung from one arm, a tripod in the other.

"Hi, I'm Tracy," she said, dropping the bag to the floor and extending her hand.

"I'm Kit." I shook her hand and then stepped back so she could walk into the room. "This is Margo and Gino." Her warm smile vanished.

"I thought this was an all-girl band."

The three of us looked at each other, panicked.

"Well," I began, "it was until a few weeks ago. Our drummer quit."

"Linda?" Tracy asked. "She's great. She used to kick ass with the Pussy Willows."

"Um," I hesitated. "I think she may have gone back with them."

"Oh," Tracy answered. "This should be interesting. They're one of our other stories in this issue."

"Great!" Margo hopped from the chair. "They'll be in good company. Now, where do you want us?"

Tracy clipped a flood light onto my stair banister and shone it toward the opposite wall.

"Let's start with some shots in here," Tracy said. "Stand in front of this wall."

We assumed positions. Tracy bent and shot, climbed a chair and shot, her camera came at us from all directions.

"Now, girls standing, Vito kneeling."

"Gino," he mumbled.

"Yeah, Gino, sorry. Gino, you kneel in front of the girls. Girls, you lean in provocatively toward him." We followed orders. How do you lean provocatively? I attempted a sexy smirk.

"Kit, that's a little too serious. How about a sexy smile?" I softly brought up the corners of my mouth, leaned my head slightly down, then looked up.

"Good. Margo, you look great."

Tracy continued to click, the flash pulsing before my eyes until the room was broken by blue dots.

"Okay, let's shoot some outside."

We followed her out to my small back patio, where she arranged us in front of the ivy that crawled up the back of my house. We bent and stretched and embraced and pouted.

"Smile!" Tracy commanded. "No, not that much. Better. You're rock stars — act like it!"

I felt glamorous and stupid.

Laura arrived with a timid knock on the door. She was a plain mouse of a girl with short brunette hair that she nervously tucked behind her ear. Her head bobbed and turned as we introduced ourselves. She smiled and tucked, cowering as if she thought we would strike her.

"Aren't you an all-girl band?" she asked.

"That's what I said!" Tracy laughed from the back of the room where she was packing up her gear. "And get this—their drummer is back with The Pussy Willows. That's too perfect."

Laura pinched her tiny face.

"Hmm. This sort of changes things for the story, but maybe we can work with it. Let me think."

She pulled a small notepad from her battered brown backpack and flipped through some pages, pausing to read through notes. Margo and I looked at each other and raised our eyebrows. Laura continued to flip.

"Can I get you a beer?" I offered. It was my only recourse.

"Oh no, no," she smiled, peering cautiously up through her bangs. "Thanks."

Smile, tuck, flip. Laura slowly moved over to the green chair; the rest of us assumed positions on the couch. She pulled a pen from her backpack. Feeling a roomful of eyes on her, she looked up from her notes.

"Oh, I'm sorry," she giggled nervously. "Okay, I guess we'll start from the beginning. So, like, how did you guys get started?"

A pretty tepid question. Still, she was the gatekeeper between us and trumping our exes. Margo jumped in.

"We love the old girl bands," she said, lighting a cigarette. "You know, Old Runaways, Pandoras, Wanda Jackson. Ginger from Gilligan's island was a huge influence on my life." She beamed her million-dollar smile. Laura giggled and looked back at her notes.

"How did you get your name?" she asked.

"Isn't it perfect?" Margo said. "Kit and I were just practicing here one day and I was telling her this story about someone in South Philly who lived off of Broad Street, and it just sort of hit me."

Laura looked at me. I smiled and nodded stupidly. Gino picked at some dead skin on his fingertip.

"Anyway," Margo continued, shooting me a nasty look. "That's how it started."

"All right folks," Tracy interrupted. She was strapped up again with her camera equipment and headed toward the front door. "It was nice meeting y'all. See you in the funny papers." The door closed behind her and we were left back in the quiet room.

"Cool, cool," Laura said softly at no one in particular, looking back at her notepad. "Um… so when did Linda leave the band?"

Margo and I glanced at each other. Who knew Linda had such a following?

"Well," I began, "Linda was a great drummer. We all got along really well." Better plant some nice quotes; we may need to play with The Pussy Willows at some point. "But, The Pussy Willows offered her a great gig. They have a whole West Coast tour lined up. She couldn't pass that up. We understood."

"Really?" Laura asked. "I just interviewed them for another article and they never mentioned a tour. They said they're trying to set something up, but…" She stopped, then looked toward Gino and screwed up her tiny face. "Don't you go out with the bass player for The Pussy Willows?"

What? Margo and I spun our heads toward him.

"Yeah," he grunted without looking up from his finger experiment. This would have been a helpful piece of information prior to this moment. Margo and I caught eyes in a non-verbal agreement to act nonchalant. Laura scribbled more notes. We had just discovered a spy in our midst. I envisioned Gino blindfolded along my back wall, our guns poised to take him to his well-deserved fate.

"Interesting," Laura said. "What does she think about you being in Broad Street?"

"She doesn't give a shit."

Good, at least she couldn't print that. But she scribbled anyway, a small grin forming.

"Um, anyway, how long have you been together?"

As Margo filled Laura in on the logistics of our short-lived project, trying to sell us as the coolest new babes on the block, questions clouded my concentration. What would Linda and Gino's girlfriend say about us when Laura interviewed The Pussy Willows for this article? Would Linda complain about us? Would she tell the world that we dressed like sluts and acted the part by leaving with lead singers we barely knew? Would the new penis in our band lead to our demise?

"Do you have any gigs lined up?" Laura asked.

"Not really," Margo started to say, but I interrupted.

"We're finalizing a few things," I lied, feeling Margo's eyes burning through me. "I can call you later with the details. When's your deadline?"

"I have to turn this in by Thursday morning."

"Okay," I said, my underarm sweat glands pumping. "I'll call you by tomorrow night."

"Sounds good," Laura smiled. "Thanks for the interview guys." She loaded up her backpack and left. As soon as the door closed, Margo turned toward Gino.

"Why didn't you tell us you were dating a Pussy Willow?" she asked angrily.

He furrowed his brow at her.

"Because it's none of your business. Who cares?"

If Margo had been a cartoon, steam would definitely be pouring out of her ears.

"It would have been good to know," she said coldly. "And, you," she redirected her rage in my direction. "What show were you talking about? Is there something you haven't told us?"

"I just thought we couldn't let this article come out with The Pussy Willows bragging about their alleged West Coast tour and we don't even have a local show."

"An interesting point," Margo said. "But we don't have a show."

"I know. I'll think of something."

And then it hit me. Charlie. I didn't know why his name popped into my head, but he was the only music connection who had been kind to me recently.

Later that night, I dug through the basket of crap on my refrigerator that I used to hide my life scraps—a variety of key chains, a half-eaten energy bar, subway tokens, crumbled bits of paper with unclaimed phone numbers. I found the tattered piece of paper Charlie had given me the morning after the mushrooms. As I unfolded the small square, a black, distorted replication of a guy playing guitar was revealed. He was creased into tiny squares, the ink cracked at the folds. I stared at it for a minute. The figure could be any white male—Dale, Pete, Ben. Did they realize they were so ordinary?

My hand trembled as I dialed the number at the bottom of the paper.

"Hello?" a female voice answered loudly. In the background, I could hear the squeal of guitar and slap of drums.

"Hi, is this Christie?"

"Yeah?" she shouted back.

"Christie, I don't know if you remember me, but…"

"Hold on, I can't hear you." The room volume was muffled by a palm, through which I heard Christie's dampened voice. "Can you guys shut the fuck up for five seconds? I'm trying to talk on the phone!"

The muffled music continued.

"Ben! I am trying to talk on the phone!"

Oh shit. What was he doing there? The screech and pounding stopped, and the connection cleared.

"Sorry about that," she said.

"Yeah, Christie, hi."

I wasn't sure what to say now. Ben's presence had thrown me. What was I doing?

"Um, this is Kit. I don't know if you remember me. We met at a party at your place a few weeks ago."

"Sure, I remember. What's up?"

"I was actually wondering if Charlie might be around."

"Charlie? Well, yeah, sure. Let me get him for you."

The phone clunked down on the table and footsteps clopped away, diminishing in volume with each new step. Different, heavier footsteps returned and the phone was lifted.

"Hello?"

"Charlie, hi. This is Kit. We met at a party a few weeks ago?"

There was a pause.

"Yeah, I remember. Um, how are you?"

"I'm good, thanks. I know you probably think it's weird for me to call you, but I have sort of an odd question for you."

"Okay," he said cautiously.

"Well, I'm trying to get some gigs for my band, and we're kind of new to the scene. This is probably a stupid idea, but I just wondered if your band might need an opening act sometime."

Acts—was that the right word? It made us sound like a puppet show.

"Hmm. What are you guys like?"

"Punk rock. Chicks. You know, that kind of thing."

"Sure," he chuckled. "I've seen the type. What's the name again?"

"Broad Street."

"Broad Street, right. That's cool. Well, let me think about it and get back to you.

What's your number?"

He was blowing me off. Of course this was a stupid idea. Did I really think I could just waltz into the rock scene when Dale had struggled for months to get gigs? I sheepishly gave Charlie my number, my cheeks hot.

But a few hours later, the phone rang.

"Hey, Kit, it's Charlie." His voice was soft; muffled guitar and drums lurked in the background. "Good news. There's an outdoor festival at Clark Park in West Philly in a few weeks. I got you guys on the bill."

"Are you serious?" I was dizzy with excitement. "That was so quick."

"Apparently they hadn't met their chick quota."

I laughed. "That is so awesome, Charlie. Thanks."

"Don't worry about it. It'll be fun."

Charlie told me that the show would be the following weekend. We would play third on an all-day Saturday bill at this outdoor festival and share equipment with Charlie's band, My Pet Rhino. I hung up he phone and called Laura, letting her know about the show. Then Margo, then Gino. They were both impressed and I was flooded with gratitude for Charlie.

The *City Paper* came out the next Thursday. Through the cloudy glass of the corner newspaper box, two pictures stared out at me. One showed my pouting face coupled with Margo's sexy sneer. The other showed Linda and a group of girls straddling motorcycles in sexy leather outfits. The headline read: "Girl Power: Broad Street Takes on The Pussy Willows." Gino was nowhere to be found. Still, we had made the cover. My heart raced as I grabbed a stack of papers and ran home to call Margo.

The article was a two-page feature that painted Broad Street as the next chick band to take on the possibly-being-courted-by-a-label band, The Pussy Willows. Margo was painted as a sexy frontwoman influenced by vixens like Ginger of Gilligan's Island and Paula Pierce, late singer of the Pandoras. I was the Mary Ann of the group, the reserved rhythm section. The catfight between Broad Street and The Pussy Willows was said to be imminent, with the recent departure of fab gal drummer "Lodi," Linda's stage name, I presumed, leaving to rejoin The Pussy Willows under the vague pretense of a West Coast Tour. The article versions of Margo and me were still determined to plow forward with an interim male drummer, who was never named.

It wasn't quite the Nobel Peace Prize, but it was a start. I cut out the article and put it in an envelope addressed to my parents.

CHAPTER

That night, I got a call from Ben.

"Hey Kit," he whispered in my ear.

My stomach instantly twisted.

"Hi," I attempted indifference.

"I wanted to call and apologize for leaving the party early. I was pretty toasted and just sort of had to get out of there. You seemed to be all right when I left." I flushed with the memory of my exposed breasts in a stranger's room, of the violation I felt when Ben took advantage of me. Was I violated? That night was so surreal. Maybe I'd misinterpreted things. I wanted to believe that Ben thought I deserved better.

"You could have told me you were leaving."

"I know, I should have. I obviously wasn't thinking clearly. Christie said she'd make sure you were okay." He paused. "Are you okay?" His voice was warm and soft, a down pillow ready to smother me. I took a deep breath.

"I'm fine."

"I really want to make it up to you. I hear we're both playing Clark Park next weekend. Maybe we can go out for a drink after the show."

"We'll see."

"Okay. I'll accept that. If you guys need equipment or anything let me know."

"Thanks, but we're sharing with My Pet Rhino."

"Good old Charlie. I'm glad you two are getting along. He's a good guy."

I wasn't sure how to interpret this.

"Yeah, he is."

"So I guess I'll see you at the show?"

"Sounds good."

I hung up the phone, torn between loneliness and logic.

Saturday morning, Gino and Margo met at my house to pack up for the Clark Park show. The warm sun took a bite out of the cool fall day. We needed only our guitars and Gino's drum stands and cymbals; My Pet Rhino would let us use their amps and drums. We squeezed ourselves and equipment into Gino's behemoth green Malibu. Along the way, we stopped for a case of beer and packed it into a cooler filled with ice.

As we drove toward Clark Park in West Philadelphia, we passed beautiful, decaying homes that stood as reminders of the area's former prestige. These old houses had been taken over by college students from the University of Pennsylvania and Drexel, who had turned them into sloppy dens of drunken iniquity.

We found the park in an ugly corner of the neighborhood. I was surprised to find a littered oasis of green amid the decay, already crawling with young people tossing Frisbees and playing with their dogs and sipping bottles from brown paper bags. Along the edge of the park was a macadam path lined with vendors—food, incense, cheap jewelry, plenty of tie-dye. The path snaked along a slight hill that rolled down into a large, flat pit that housed a small stage. There was already a band on stage, blasting distorted punk to an apathetic audience.

We parked the car at the top of the hill opposite the blankets. My stomach was in knots as I scanned the park, adding up the hill's geometry: an average of 10 blankets deep times 40 blankets wide, each blanket home to at least two Bohemian-wannabes. In addition to the blanket critics, the path was filled with students sampling wares. The pit twisted with musicians I respected and feared.

We negotiated our equipment down the hill and found a void in the landfill of guitars, amps and drums. The sun beat down on the battered grass, patches of brown crushed beneath years of outdoor entertainment. As we neared the back of the stage, I saw a tough-looking biker chick with long tangled brown hair walking over to greet us. She was wearing a leather vest and bikini top that showcased her hairy armpits and stocky, tattooed arms.

"Hey!" she yelled over the band and held out her hand, first to me. "I'm Brenda!"

"Hi!" I shouted back. Her fingers wrapped like boa constrictors around my hand. "I'm Kit," I whimpered. "This is Margo and Gino." She mashed each hand in order.

"Cool!" she smiled. "You guys will go on after Renaissance Bitch! They should have about four songs left." I gathered this was the onstage noise preventing us from communicating.

"Thanks," I replied, wiggling my fingers to re-circulate the blood. "We're sharing equipment with My Pet Rhino. Do you know if they showed up yet?"

"You're sharing with those guys? Shit. They're not on 'til five. You'll be lucky if they…"

"What?" I craned my neck closer, wrapping my palm around my ear to hear better.

"You'll be lucky if they show up by five! Those guys are never on time. I need you guys to be ready in about 20 minutes!"

"But we didn't bring our stuff! Can we switch with someone?"

"No switching. Can you go get your equipment? Where do you live?"

Margo and Gino leaned in with worried looks and I knew that I had fucked up. Dale would have never been this stupid. He would have called and confirmed. No, he would just know that My Pet Rhino was always late. The pit was filled with his friends who would let him easily pluck the finest instrument from the pile. But my social connections left us with twenty minutes to climb back in the car, speed back to my house, load all of the equipment into the car—no, both cars because there was no way to fit Gino's drums and our amps into one car—of course my amp was on the second floor buried under a pile of boxes, then get back here, set up…

"Ben!" Margo called over my shoulder, waving her arm. I turned to follow the greeting.

And there he was. His white T-shirt had the simple words, "AlphaMale" in small black type across his right breast. The corner of his mouth turned up as he leered at me seductively. He walked over to us.

"Hey guys," his low voice cut through the noise. "What's up?"

"Ben," Margo said loudly. "We're in a little bit of a jam here. We were supposed to share equipment with My Pet Rhino, but they're not here yet. Is there any way we could use some of your stuff? We'd be glad to bribe you with beer."

Ben looked at me.

"Where's Charlie?" he asked.

"I haven't seen him," I answered, embarrassed.

"I told you the other night, you can use anything of ours you want."

I felt Margo shoot me a look, the gossip wheels spinning.

"Thanks, Ben," I answered. "I really appreciate it.

Ben guided us to Lava Dance's pile. Like Santa Claus, he fulfilled our wishes.

Gino got a beautiful silver glitter Pearl drum kit. Margo received a state-of-the-art Fender Vibrolux with built-in reverb. I was handed a Hartke head partnered with a 18-inch Peavey cabinet. We fished out cold beers and ogled our new toys.

I looked at the intimidating hill of cynics, and lit a cigarette. Ben had walked over to talk to his keyboard player. Gino was assembling the drums under the guidance of the Lava Dance drummer, who seemed a little nervous at the prospect of sharing these beauties. Margo was sitting on the amp and tuning and re-tuning her guitar. I pulled my bass out and did the same. My tuner was not giving me an accurate reading since it had to fight with the ambient volume, so I wasn't sure if I was helping or hurting my sound as I turned the tuning pegs. Before I had time to find out, Brenda came behind the stage.

"These guys are on their last song!" she shouted. "You guys are up next! Try to set up as fast as you can! We don't want too much of a lull!"

On stage, Renaissance Bitch was approaching their show's summit. The drummer smashed heavily around the kit while the guitar players forced screeching feedback from their amps. Over this chaos, the lead singer shouted.

"We're Renaissance Bitch! Come check us out at the Khyber next Friday night!" More pounding drums, more guitar feedback. "Thanks for coming out! Stick around for Broad Street!" Boom boom crash, boom boom crash, BOOM, and they were done. The silence that followed was only slightly interrupted by a smattering of applause. I found the crowd's indifference comforting; we would be mere background noise to a day in the park.

Renaissance Bitch started pulling off their equipment from the stage, and we began the job of replacing them.

"Great job, guys," I lied as the lead singer, a shirtless skeleton with bushy brown hair, walked past me.

"Thanks," he said. "Good luck with this crowd. They're brutal."

I lifted my equipment on stage—first the heavy speaker cabinet, next the head, next my bass and stand, finally my makeup case of miscellaneous cables, picks, and pedals. Brenda waved to me and pointed to a corner of the vast stage. I noticed an abandoned soundboard in front of the stage and realized she must do sound as well as coordinate. Gino had brought a six-pack of beer up with him, and had already emptied two bottles. He popped open a third. Margo was leaning over the amp, twisting knobs and looking perplexed. Shaking her head, she angrily put her guitar on her stand and walked to the back of the stage to motion the Lava Dance guitar player up for assistance. I turned my attention to my borrowed contraption, trying my best to figure out the complicated knobs on the front. Brenda walked over to me, grunted, then adjusted enough knobs and buttons to give me a decent sound. Next, she forced her expertise onto Margo, then the microphones. I could practically hear her mutter, "Girls!" I glanced back at Gino. Four empty bottles now stood by his feet.

"This kit sucks!" he shouted to no one in particular. He slammed down on the drums, made a face, then pulled his tuning key out to adjust the tones. I hoped the Lava Dance drummer was not watching.

I sighed as I waited for Brenda to return to her post at the soundboard. It seemed to take forever. I drank my warm beer, suddenly feeling dehydrated. I needed a cold glass of water. I licked my lips only to have them sucked dry again by a slight breeze. I squeezed them together for residual moisture, but they merely snapped back more chapped than before. The crowd before us milled and ignored. Brenda called up to Margo.

"You guys ready?" Margo looked at me, crinkling her brow. I shrugged.

"All right," Gino commanded from the back of the stage. He peeled off his T-shirt and threw it aside. "Let's go!"

A few Check Checks in the microphones, and Margo clicked on like a basement light.

"We're Broad Street!" she leaned flirtatiously into the microphone. "And we're here to rock your world!"

A few heads in the apathetic crowd turned toward the stage.

Despite the cool day, I burst into a sweat. It took all of my energy to ignore the eyes in front of me. My sweaty palms caused my fingers to slide helplessly around the fretboard. My sunglasses continually slid down my nose; I pushed them back up, they slid down again. I clung to my sweaty pick as it threatened to slip from my fingers. Still, I smiled, I moved to the music, I did the best I could to hide my misery.

The rest of the band seemed to fare better. Gino was solid and hit hard, twisting his face as he played. Margo was all confidence, belting out each song seductively. Still, the crowd ignored us. I grew annoyed as they tossed Frisbees and bought merchandise from vendors and ate hot dogs. Just one person ventured closer to the stage, moving his gaze between Margo and me, swaying slightly to the beat. He looked young, maybe late teens. His brown curly hair hung above wire-rimmed glasses, and a silver bike helmet dangled from his hand. He caught my eyes and smiled. I smiled back. Our first fan?

A half hour after climbing on stage, it was over.

"Thanks for coming out," Margo grinned. "We're Broad Street! Stick around for

The Young Mels up next!"

The guy dropped his bike helmet to clap enthusiastically, his face split by a big goofy grin. Ben, who was standing off to the side of the stage, noticed we were finished and clapped politely. The rest of the crowd pretty much ignored us. I tried not to care. I was happy that we had gotten to the end of the set.

As we pulled the equipment off and piled it again behind the stage, Ben walked over to me.

"Great job!" he said, giving me a peck on the cheek that took me off guard.

"Thanks," I blushed. "And thanks again for the equipment. You're a life saver."

"Let's just say you owe me one," he smiled.

"I'd say we're even." I instantly regretted bringing up the bad party, but Ben just laughed.

"Come on. We have a blanket and some beers up front."

I finished packing up my equipment and tucked it out of the sun. Gino was bending the ear of the Lava Dance drummer, who seemed anxious to escape. Gino clutched a full beer, by my estimates his seventh or eighth. Margo made a long, slow exit off stage, pausing to flirt with the other musicians. I waved her over and we followed Ben to a patchwork of stained blankets.

I said a slightly embarrassed hello to Christie, who was in one corner talking to the preppie Lava Dance guitar player. Aaron, the bass player, was sitting next to Ben with a bottle of Jim Beam jutting obscenely from between his crossed legs. He looked less grungy than he had the other night. His long hair was pulled into a ponytail that showed off big brown eyes. Ben made introductions.

"You guys sounded great," Aaron said, mostly to Margo. "Care to celebrate?" He held out his phallic liquor bottle; Margo grabbed it.

"Oh yeah," she said, twisting off the lid and tilting the bottle toward her mouth. Snapping it back down she grimaced and wiped her mouth with the back of her hand. She pulled the bottom of her black sweater up to clean the lip of the bottle, then handed it to me. I took the Jim Beam and poured it down my throat. The sun had baked it to the temperature of hot coffee. I fought the urge to gag. Ben handed me an ice-cold beer, which I swallowed gratefully.

"You guys were awesome!"

We looked up to see the fan from earlier. Upon closer inspection, he seemed older than I originally thought. There was still the hint of acne on his face, but his curly hair hid flecks of gray.

"Thanks!" Margo said. "What's your name?"

"Adam."

"Well, Adam," Margo said, patting a small corner of blanket by her feet. "Why don't you have a beer with us?"

He giggled and blushed, then sat down on his knees, taking the beer from Margo's grasp. He seemed delicate, not quite right for the rest of the crowd here.

"You guys are in Lava Dance, right?" he asked Ben.

Ben nodded.

"You guys are awesome. I saw you playing with The Original Sins at JC Dobbs a while back. You totally kicked ass. The Sins are great, too. Too bad that whole Pete Buck production didn't work out for them. I think garage is being killed by the whole grunge thing." His speech was choppy and quick. He reminded me of a little bird. "Not that I don't like grunge. The Flaming Lips are like one of the best bands of all time, even though they aren't totally all grunge. The Meat Puppets, Dinosaur Jr. All those guys are good. I have most of Dinosaur's early bootlegs. They're so much better live than in the studio. They were pretty good on the second album, but I just found a great European release at a garage sale last weekend."

He stopped. We all stared at him.

"So," Adam said, blushing. "Anyway, Broad Street totally kicked ass today. Do you guys have a mailing list?"

"Sure," Margo said, pulling a bank receipt out of her purse. "Write all your stats on this. We'll let you know when we're playing next."

Adam smiled as he jotted down his information.

On stage, the faint click of drumsticks launched the next band, Mothra, into life. The air filled with a dirge of guitar and guttural screams. Abandoning any attempt at conversation, we settled back and watched, sipping hot Jim Beam and cheap beer. After a few songs, Charlie emerged from behind the stage, spotted us and walked over. He looked panicked.

"I thought you were on at 4:00!" He said to me, cupping his hands around his mouth.

I shook my head no and held up two fingers. He shot Ben a look, then looked back at me.

"I'm really sorry," he shouted. "I thought you weren't on until 4:00. I was back there waiting for you."

"It's okay!" I shouted back, and at that moment it was. The beer and liquor had put me in a loving mood and I was willing to forgive anyone anything. Charlie shook his head, stood up and walked back toward the stage. I wanted to tell him I didn't care, that I still appreciated what he'd done for us, but he was already gone.

"Kit!" Margo's voice pulled me out of my lull. "Dale's here."

I sat up quickly and scanned the hill behind the safety of my sunglasses. Dale was coming down the hill, winding through the blankets, waving and smiling like the Queen Mother. Still, he had the forced expression of a party crasher. This should have been his party. He was the one who had worked so hard to get into this crowd. He approached our blanket, his eyes hidden by dark sunglasses, his teeth clenched in an angry smile. I smiled back, my heart racing with a surge of sadistic pleasure.

"Hey Dale!" I smiled. Margo flashed a glance at me, then turned to play along.

"Oh, hey Dale. How are you?"

"You remember Ben and Aaron from Lava Dance," I said.

Ben held out his hand. Dale shook it reluctantly. I introduced him to the rest of the group.

"Great," Dale said. "It's really just terrific to meet everyone." He turned toward me. "Kit, can I talk to you a minute?"

I inhaled deeply.

"Yeah, sure." My knees buckled slightly as I stood up. I quickly found my balance and followed Dale. The band grew muffled as we walked to the top of the hill, then toward a shady walnut tree away from the crowd. I followed Dale a few steps behind, watching his slumped posture. When we reached the tree, he turned to me.

"Kit, I need to talk to you. This isn't the place to do this, I know, but I knew you would be here and I just wanted to see you. You look good."

"Thanks."

"Drunk, but good."

I looked up at him like a child who had been caught stealing candy. He stepped toward me. The shade of the tree softened his dark eyes. I used to think those eyes held my entire universe. He gently put his arm around my waist and pulled me closer. He pressed his soft lips against mine. They responded. Instinct? Desire? Maybe a little of both. He broke the kiss to whisper into my ear.

"Please come home with me."

My head swam with booze, adrenaline, confusion. I wanted so badly to believe that Dale could be the savior I had painted him to be over the years. But an unfamiliar voice whispered into my other ear—"He is still an asshole."

I pulled myself from his embrace and stumbled backwards slightly.

"I can't."

Could he smell my fear? He paused, staring hard at me.

"You're drunk," he scolded.

"That's not your concern."

"What are you doing? You're hanging out with those dirtbags from Lava Dance. Don't you know what people are saying about you?"

What people? Who cared enough in this town to say anything about me? He had to be making it up.

"Margo already has a pretty fine reputation for being a slut," he continued. "Do you want to become like her?"

"No she doesn't. She was dating Pete for years."

"They had a pretty unconventional relationship."

I didn't want to hear any more. I would not let him cheat on me, then take away the life I was trying to build on my own.

"You know, it's amazing the lengths you'll go to to get laid." I turned to walk away, but he grabbed my arm and spun me back around.

"You don't believe me? Why don't you ask her where she and I were last New Year's Eve?"

He had achieved his goal. I was stung. New Year's Eve. Where was I? My mind spun backwards. I had gone with my sister to New York City to watch the ball drop. It was insane. We got there late only to be crushed by millions of tourists. We couldn't get anywhere close to the dropping ball, so we had meandered down to the Village, gotten drunk, then crashed on the floor of her friend's apartment. Dale told me he was going to spend the night at his parent's place in the burbs. The whole evening, suspicion gnawed at me, but that was nothing unusual. When I came home that morning, he greeted me with fresh coffee and bagels. But this couldn't be true. He had to be lying.

"I'm going back to my friends now," I said softly.

I turned away from him, expecting to be pulled back by words or touch. But he let me walk away, back down the hill, back to my new life. It looked different when I got there.

"What happened?" Margo asked.

"Oh, nothing," I tried to sound indifferent, but I couldn't look her in the eye. "He just wanted some money for an old gas bill."

I felt her studying me.

"Are you all right? Do you want to take a walk?"

I looked at her. I was not about to let Dale ruin our friendship. I was finally feeling like I could survive on my own.

"I'm all right, thanks. Really."

"Great." She leaned over to rescue two more beers from the cooler, opening them and handing one to me. "Let's have a good time."

I took the bottle and swigged. Adam was still ranting about music trivia – something about how Pavement were a complete rip-off of The Fall, not that he didn't like Pavement and in some recent interview the singer said his real influence was The Replacements, blah blah blah.

"So," I turned flirtatiously toward Ben. "What time do you go on?"

It was late afternoon when our blanket buddies climbed on stage to play a fierce rock set. Ben sang in his deep, sexy growl. Aaron sloped drunkenly against a stack of speakers while his fingers danced around the fretboard. As the horizon swallowed the sun, the air cooled, drawing the crowd into the pit to dance enthusiastically. Margo and I joined them—Gino watched the drummer in awe.

When they were done, just Aaron and Ben returned to the blanket. I could feel my words becoming reluctant from alcohol, my eyelids growing heavy. It was close to 6:00, and I had yet to consume any food. I let Ben wrap his legs and arms around me. Dale would not ruin this for me. Ben nuzzled my ear and I turned to give him a long kiss. Aaron and Margo had assumed similar positions, laughing and kissing and smoking.

I felt like we owned this day, these guys, our music. I barely noticed My Pet Rhino come on the stage. It was not until they began that I thought I saw Charlie staring down at us. Was that anger on his face? The light was fading to dusty pinks and oranges and it was too beautiful to worry about Charlie. I laid my head back on Ben's shoulder, turned and tickled his ear with my tongue.

Some time later, I opened my eyes to a dark room that smelled like dirty socks. My stomach roiled in response, but I fought the rising bile. My head felt like it would explode. A sheet twisted around my naked body; mattress grit rubbed against my skin. I blinked to decipher the naked body next to me. His back was wide and smooth, except for a small patch of black hair developing at the base of his spine. I looked around the room. It was small. A Mr. Bubble beach towel served as a curtain for the one window. The floor was covered in clothes and albums and magazines and a shrunken used condom. Crap.

A light peeked under the door. What was on the other side? The air was still.

Anxiety started quietly at my toes, then slowly ate its way toward my stomach.

The body next to me stirred, groaned, then turned toward me. It was Aaron.

I couldn't move. How the fuck did I get here? I tore through fractured images—sitting on the hill with Ben, kissing Ben, watching Charlie's band. Dancing. I remembered dancing to one band, then, oh my God, I think Margo and I got on stage with The Tweeters and sang bad harmonies. In front of hundreds of strangers. And Ben. Where was Ben? I remembered getting into a car, but I'm not sure who got in it with me.

Aaron sucked some air percussively through his big nose, then blew out stale whiskey and sleep. My stomach turned again and I turned my head away, gagging. I slowly inched my way off the bed and untangled myself from the sheets, careful not to disturb him. I then slipped to the floor in a crouching position. My eyes adjusted enough so I could find my own clothes from the filthy ones around them—dress, shoes, bra. Panties? I lifted various specimens to no avail, then looked at the tangled sheets. Fuck it. I clicked on my bra, then pulled my dress over my head and slipped on my shoes and coat. I tiptoed to the door, turned the knob slowly, then slid out into the light, squinting my eyes.

I was in a living room now. A television glowed with the blue screen of an extinguished VHS tape. In front of it was a couch with its back to me. I carefully walked over and peered over its edge. There was Ben, alone. Shit. Where was Margo?

I found my bass in a hallway that connected the living room to the doorway. I picked it up and walked out the apartment door and into a dim lobby, glancing at a clock along the way. 11:30. I had managed to fuck up my life just as Dale had predicted.

I walked to the street and glanced around. It looked like I was still in West Philly. I found Market Street and hailed a cab, aware that I probably looked like a crazed homeless person. The dark-skinned driver looked at me suspiciously as I climbed in, gave him gruff instructions, then nestled into the cracked vinyl of the back seat. I should have told him to just drop me off by the Schuylkill River so I could put an end to my misery. Or maybe I could just move to a new city and start all over. I would figure something out. Tomorrow.

When I got home, I dropped my equipment by the stairs and unplugged the phone. I twisted my Venetian blinds shut and pulled the blanket off the back of my couch. I crawled underneath and pulled the blanket high over my ears.

A knock at the door woke me. When I opened my eyes again, slits of light crept through the blinds. Go away. I closed my eyes again. It was probably a Jehovah's Witness. But the knock came again, this time louder.

"Kit!" Margo's voice called through the door.

I did not want to deal with her. Maybe she'd think I was away. She knocked again.

Shit.

I tossed the blanket aside and stood up, bracing myself on the back of the couch. My head was pounding. I looked into a small mirror by the door and was surprised that my reflection didn't look as bad as I felt. My hair was matted, but my makeup was still relatively intact, except for faded, smeared red lipstick. I turned and opened the door.

"Where have you been?" Margo plowed through the door angrily. "I've been calling all night."

"I unplugged the phone," I answered, falling onto the couch.

"What happened? I've been going crazy. I had to get Ben's number from Pete, and there was no answer there."

"I don't know what happened," I said, rubbing my temple. "I was hoping you could fill in some of the blanks for me."

She stared at me in disbelief.

"You don't remember?"

"No," I said, then dropped my face into my hands. My eyes teared up. I was completely disgusted with myself.

"Kit," Margo sat next to me. "What happened? When I left you at the park, you were having such a good time. You said you didn't want to leave. I should have insisted. You were so fucked up. But then again, so was I."

"When did you leave?" I asked, wiping my tears with the blanket.

Margo turned away and looked down.

"Pete showed up. It was stupid. I was drunk. We were dancing, then we sort of made out and then we went back to his place and, you know. I feel like shit about it."

We both sat in quiet self-pity for a moment.

"Anyway," she continued, "I left his place around midnight and I've been calling you ever since. I was so worried about you. I don't know, I get kind of a weird vibe from Ben. When I left, you were on the blanket with him and Aaron and they were both sort of teasing you. God! I never should have left you. If we had both just gotten in a cab and gone home, we could be celebrating a great show this morning over Bloody Marys instead of feeling like shit."

I tried to decipher the facts. They were both teasing me. Had I slept with both of them?

"So what happened?" Margo asked softly.

"I need that Bloody Mary."

I pulled my hair into a ponytail and washed the evening off my face. Margo drove us down to a restaurant on South Street that served Bloody Marys and Eggs Benedict on a deck that overlooked the out-of-season punks.

"So what happened?" Margo asked, stirring her drink with a celery stick.

And then I had an idea. Maybe I could punch in new parts to cover up the flubs. Who knew what the reality was? If I started my own version of the truth, maybe I could circumvent the rumor mill.

"I passed out in some apartment. I'm not sure if it was Ben's or Aaron's. I woke up on the couch and Ben was there. I think Aaron was in the next room. I have no idea what happened."

That part was true. This was starting to sound better. Almost convincing.

"So I snuck out before they woke up and took a cab home."

Margo looked at me, disappointed. Or was that suspicion? I wrapped my lips around the straw of my Bloody Mary.

"That's it?" Margo asked.

"What do you mean, that's it? Who knows what I did before I passed out?"

She mulled this over.

"Were you dressed when you woke up?"

"Yes," I lied. "But I did seem to misplace my underwear." I thought this tidbit was okay to include. I could live with the implied story that I fooled around with Ben. It was predictable, hardly worthy of gossip. Maybe we would be hailed as the new rock couple in the scene. That would be better than a bad solo reputation.

Margo started at me. I kept my eyes cast down toward my glass. She sighed.

"I'm just glad you're all right. I can't do this without you, you know."

I lifted my eyes.

"I hear bass players are a dime a dozen."

"You know what I mean."

With the evening behind us, we turned the conversation to the success of our show the previous day. We talked about our new fans and friends, and it wasn't until well into my second Bloody Mary that I remembered I was supposed to visit my father at home that day.

"Oh shit," I said.

"What?"

I looked at my watch. It was still early enough to get out there.

"I totally spaced. I'm supposed to visit my parents today. Did I tell you he was in the hospital?"

"Uh, no," Margo said. "But I wish you would have."

"Sorry, it's been so crazy." I downed my entire glass of ice water. "Damn, I'm hung over. You should come with me. Take the pressure off a bit."

Margo shook her head. "I don't know. I'm feeling pretty skanky today."

"Pleeeeeeease," I begged, hands pressed together.

She rolled her eyes.

"Okay. I just have to stop at home and wash the drunk off me."

We both cleaned up at Margo's apartment. I called my mother while Margo was in the shower and told her the plan. She sounded exhausted.

When Margo came out of her bedroom, she had on a pretty floral dress and her hair was tied in a neat ponytail.

"Is that your 'meet the parents' getup?" I asked.

"Fuck you."

"You might want to clean up the mouth a little."

"Very funny. Let's go. I'll drive."

As we walked to her car, I noticed Margo carrying a Tupperware container.

"What's that?" I asked.

"Oh, just thought I'd bring your parents a little something. I made some short-bread the other day."

"Made shortbread? Impressive."

"Get in the car."

We rolled the windows down slightly to feel the cool breeze against our faces. I was nervous about my parents meeting Margo. They had a tendency toward pretension, grilling friends with questions about politics and literature. It had prevented me from bringing home rock-guy Dale for a while, but it eventually became unavoidable. He charmed them, of course. How would Margo fare under the over-educated microscope of my professor father?

We took the Swarthmore exit off of the I-95 highway and into the serene setting of the suburb. The sun was interrupted by the tall old trees that lined the small road to my parent's house, breaking patterns of shadows through the windshield. A canopy of fiery leaves dripped into the quiet street. Charlie Parker played on the radio, serenaded me with a calming lullaby that echoed our environment perfectly. This tranquil place seemed so far from my life in Philadelphia.

My tranquility ended at the sight of Nikki's Cabriolet in the driveway. We pulled behind it.

"This is beautiful!" Margo said, shutting off the engine and leaning forward to get a better look.

The house and property did look beautiful. The giant oak tree in the front yard was a rich palette of oranges and reds and yellows. The porch was decorated with bright orange pumpkins and gourds of varying shades. Even though it was late fall, the yard was still flush with color.

My mother appeared on the porch, waving to our car. I took a deep breath, and stepped out. Margo climbed out, too, pausing to reach into the back seat to grab the shortbread. We walked toward the porch and my mother embraced me.

"Mom, this is Margo."

Margo shifted the shortbread container to the crook of her elbow to free her right hand, and shook my mother's hand.

"It's great to meet you Mrs. Greene," she said.

"Please, call me Dana. It's nice to meet you, too, Margo. Kit's told me a lot about you."

"Your yard is beautiful. I didn't think German primroses bloomed this time of year."

I turned toward her. When had Margo ever noticed a plant? My mother looked impressed, too.

"Actually, I manage to get it to bloom into late fall. Plus, it hasn't been that cold this season."

"And how old is your winterberry? I've never seen one so big. The root structure must really be established."

My mother smiled. "Actually, my husband and I planted that when we first got married. It's older than Kit. Do you have a garden?"

"Unfortunately, no. I live in an apartment now. Growing up, I never really had much of a yard and my parents weren't really the outdoor types. But I've always been interested. I've read a lot and try to get down to Longwood Gardens a few times a year."

Who the hell was this person?

"Do you want a tour?" my mother asked.

"I'd love it."

"Kit, why don't you take in Margo's purse and say hello to your father and sister?"

There went my buffer.

"I'd love to," I smirked. Margo followed my mother down the steps and into the garden. My mother pointed to various foliages, seeming to glow with the adoration of her audience. I took a deep breath, and opened the screen door. The door squeaked noisily as I pulled it open.

"Hello?"

As I entered the house, I heard Nikki and a man's voice laughing. I walked into the vestibule, and there they were. Sitting at the huge dining room table that was rarely used except for holidays and special occasions, Nikki was sitting shoulder to shoulder with an attractive older man. He had dark hair and blue eyes that brightened against dark skin. His muscular arms were folded in front of him. My father sat across from them with his back toward the door. I walked into the room, and all three turned toward me. Nikki looked nervous.

"Hi Dad," I said, walking over to him and putting my hand on his shoulder. "How are you feeling?"

"Falling apart, as usual," he grumbled.

"That's nice," I said.

"Hi Kit," Nikki interrupted, annoyed.

"Oh, hi," I said, pulling my lips into a fake grin. "This must be the guy I've heard so much about."

Nikki glared at me, but Ted stood up and extended his hand.

"I'm sure you have," he said with a dazzling white smile. "I've heard a lot about you, too. I'm Ted."

I looked at him skeptically as he stood and we shook hands. What did he mean he'd heard a lot about me, too? My father moved his eyes between Nikki and me. Behind me, I heard the porch door open and close.

"Kit," my mother said, "you didn't tell me Margo was such an expert on horticulture."

"I had no idea," I said, to which Margo smirked at me. "Margo, you remember my sister Nikki." I said.

"Sure, we met briefly at the party at Kit's house," Margo smiled coldly. "But you left pretty early that night so we didn't really get to talk."

Nikki blushed. Cool dig, I thought.

"Nice to see you again," Nikki said quickly.

"And this is my dad," I said. "Dad, this is my friend Margo from our band."

"Margo," he said, shaking her hand. "Isn't there a Margo in Walker Percy's Lancelot?"

I rolled my eyes, embarrassed that my father began the cultural interrogation so quickly.

"I think so. My mother was a huge All About Eve fan, but I've seen the name pop up elsewhere. Apparently Kevin Stewart wrote a novella recently called Margot. I'm sure you know it. Kit tells me you were an English professor."

Once again, I was in the presence of a stranger.

"I haven't read that one," he said. He turned to me. "I didn't know you had friends who actually read."

"She's amazing," I said, to which Margo shot me a look.

"Who wants Mimosas?" my mother asked.

"Mimosas!" Margo said. "You Greene's know how to throw a party."

We started to follow my mother into the kitchen, but my father walked away from the group and over to his reading chair in the living room. He seemed stiff and old. I noticed my mother watch him with a worried expression.

"I'll be right in," she said.

We went to the kitchen and pulled up stools to the counter island that floated in the middle of the room. We waited for a few awkward silent moments before my mother returned.

"Sorry. Where was I?"

"Is Dad okay?" I asked.

"Oh, he's fine. Just tired."

I wasn't sure if tired meant sick or just grumpy. My father had never been much for socializing, which I usually resented, but his recent health scare made me more sympathetic. My biggest concern was having him meet Margo, and she seemed to have passed his test. I hoped that gave me a little more credibility.

My mother pulled out a large crystal pitcher and placed it on the island. She popped the champagne cork and poured champagne into the pitcher, then added orange juice and poured us each a glass. I sipped at the sweet tanginess of the drink, grateful for the light buzz.

"How's the band doing?" Ted asked.

"It's great," Margo said. "Kit is an amazing bass player and has written some really good songs."

"I didn't know you wrote, Kit," my mother said. "That's great. When you were little you never wanted to practice your piano lessons."

"Consider the material, Mom," I answered, but I liked this new appreciation of my ability. I hoped my father could hear this from the other room.

"She's great, Dana. You and your husband should come see us play some time. You'd be very impressed with your daughter."

"I'm sure I would," she beamed at me, as if seeing me for the first time.

"But you do most of the singing," Nikki interrupted. "Right, Margo?"

"We split it up," she smiled back. "Kit has a great voice, too."

"Oh," Nikki said, annoyed.

"Why don't you kids sit outside on the porch while I get dinner ready?"

Did this exclude Ted, who looked to be in his late 30s? We followed orders and walked out to the porch. Ted and Nikki went first, Margo and I followed. Just as we got to the door, Margo stopped.

"I'm going to go help your mother," she said. "You should probably spend some quality time with your sister."

Ted and Nikki sat on the porch swing and I took a rocking chair next to it. We sat quietly sipping our drinks.

"So, how's work, Ted?" I asked.

"Fine, thanks, Kit," he said smugly. "How's band life? I hear bass players pull down big salaries these days."

"It works for me."

"That's great."

We all rocked in silence, arms folded across our chests.

"So, Nikki, how's the job going?" I asked.

"Maybe we should go, Ted," she said, standing up and sending Ted swinging.

"I guess that means not very well," I said,

Nikki stormed past me and slammed the screen door behind her.

I let out a heavy sigh and crossed my arms in front of me.

"Why are you giving your sister such a hard time?" Ted asked.

"Well, let's see. She's fooling around with a married father and she's ruining a good job opportunity."

"Don't judge what you don't understand, Kit."

"I understand perfectly."

"Really? What is it you think you know?"

"Just the facts I laid out for you. Those are enough."

"Okay, let's dissect these facts. First, I care about your sister very much, and I know that I've put her in an awkward situation. She's helped me through a difficult time, and she knows I appreciate that. My wife and children are really none of your business, but let's just say that things are not that great in that department. And last,

I'm doing everything I can to make sure nothing happens to Nikki at work."

"So you have it all worked out."

"I'm trying to. I know that's hard to understand."

I sipped my Mimosa and rocked, trying to determine if I believed him.

"I just worry about her, that's all," I said.

"I know you do. You're the big sister. Believe me, I have a little brother that I would do anything for. But Nikki is tougher than you think. You should give her some credit."

"Maybe."

"Who wants more Mimosas?" Margo said loudly through the screen door.

The door creaked open and banged shut. She had a full pitcher in her hands and used it to refill our drinks. Nikki followed behind her with her purse on her shoulder.

"Ready?" she asked Ted.

"Nikki, don't be a drama queen," I said. "Just stay. I'll be nice, I promise."

Nikki dropped into the porch swing.

"That would be a first," she said.

"Margo," I said. "Why don't you pull up a chair and join us 'kids.'"

Margo grabbed a chair and pulled it next to mine so we were all facing the garden. A soft breeze whispered through the trees and lifted the leaves into a slow dance.

"This is nice," Margo said.

The door opened behind us and my mother pulled up a chair next to Margo.

"Margo, did you notice the Christmas heathers?" my mother asked. "I think they're going to turn out really well this year."

"They're gorgeous."

The rest of us rocked stupidly and looked at the pretty colors.

Eventually, we went inside to the dining room to consume ham and potato casserole and fruit salad. Margo and my parents continued to talk as Ted, Nikki, and I sat quietly and watched. I felt a little removed, but I was proud of Margo. She had justified the band to my cynical parents as a creative, worthy endeavor. She proved that you could be eclectic and literate, as well as play guitar. She even made me proud of myself. At least for the moment.

On the ride home, Margo was serene. The sun was setting, turning the sky a brilliant orange. Charlie Parker was again scoring our environment with smooth saxophone.

"I love your parents," Margo sighed. "I wish my parents were more like them."

"What do you mean? Your parents are great."

"I could never discuss gardening with my mother. She could kill a plastic plant. I think she has."

"I could never discuss music with my parents, unless it was released before 1955."

"Well, I just wish sometimes my parents wouldn't be so…much. They would never support me pursuing something that wasn't in the spotlight, like being a landscape architect. I would love to do that."

"Really?" I couldn't picture Margo in gardening gloves with dirt crunched into her knees.

"Yeah," she said. "Ever since I was little I loved to plant things. I used to buy little seed packets and clay pots and plant them in my room. Marigolds, Snapdragons, Gerbera Daisies. Not once did my mother ever ask me about them."

"I had no idea."

"I know, it sounds stupid."

"No it doesn't. If that's what you want to do, you should do it."

"I don't know. I'd have to go back to school, but it would be too much. My job is fine. And, maybe we'll become rich and famous with the band."

"Maybe. If we can keep a drummer for more than two shows, we could be on our way."

As we drove further from the serenity of the suburbs and the skyline of Philadelphia began to loom on the horizon, tension crept up from my toes as I thought about how much I'd screwed up the previous night. I did not want Dale to be right about me.

When I got back home, I pulled my bass out of its smoky case and propped it on my lap. I plucked the strings until I found a dissonant arrangement of notes that captured my mood. I played them over and over, adding the beginning of a hook, then hummed a melody along with it. Words began to form:

You keep on asking questions; I can't help but tell you lies
Cause looking in the mirror, I can't see through this disguise
The stranger here beside me is my best friend tonight
I guess I'll kiss you baby cause I'm too tired to fight.

CHAPTER

T he next groggy Monday, Rachel knocked on my office door.

"Hey," she greeted me. "Did you hear about Dr. De Medio?"

"No. What about him?"

"Apparently he was fooling around with that little Catholic-school intern and now she's pregnant. The parents are filing charges."

"Dr. De Medio? I can't believe that."

I pictured him at our last meeting, shrinking away from conflict like a turtle. He would be the type to fall for the plaid-skirted bad girl.

"That's so awesome," I continued. "Jean must be having a fit."

"Of course—but the only way she has a fit, which is to scream at anyone in her path."

"Thanks for the warning."

"There's also been some talk that she and Dr. De Medio were actually having a little thing."

"Jean does not have sex. Impossible."

For some reason, I was suddenly feeling much better. Maybe I wasn't the only fuck-up.

"I'm just telling you what I heard." Rachel shrugged. "I guess we'll never really know. Anyway, how was your show on Saturday?"

"It was a blast." I lied. "How was your weekend?"

"It was my grandmother's birthday on Sunday so we had a little party. She turned 85 this year and she's still amazing. Racist, loud-mouthed, but always entertaining. It wasn't anything big, just the family."

Once again, Rachel's life tugged at me. It seemed so simple and easy. Rachel would never get drunk and sleep with two guys. She'd found her true love through a network of caring family and religious friends. Her boyfriend would always honor and cherish her. Being a single gentile sucked.

My phone rang.

"I'll talk to you later," Rachel said, closing the door behind her.

I picked up the phone, bracing for Jean.

"Kit Greene," I said.

"Kit, hey. It's Ben."

The blood scurried from my brain and I swallowed hard.

"Hi!" I said in my overly enthusiastic work voice. "How are you?"

"Are you okay? I've been trying to call you all weekend. You just disappeared Saturday night."

He was not making this easy. If I slept with his friend, why did he care if I left? I cursed my empty memory.

"I guess I never plugged my phone back in. Sorry."

"That's all right. I'm just glad you're okay. Things got a little wild the other night."

New York City was nice. I always wanted to live in New York.

"Did you have fun?" he asked.

"From what I remember. I was pretty drunk."

"Yeah, I guess we all were," he laughed. "After we put that movie in, I guess I passed out."

Movie? I remembered the blue screen on the television. Something told me we did not watch Citizen Kane. Spanking Citizen Jane was probably more likely.

"Me too," I said. "I woke up at around 11:30 and took a cab home. Sorry I didn't tell you."

"I guess we're even now."

I was dying to know what happened, but afraid to ask. Were we all watching the movie? Did I go to bed with Aaron after Ben passed out? Did I go to bed with both of them? It was too horrible to think about.

"Well," Ben continued. "I'm glad you're okay. I was calling to see if you might still like to go out for that drink I promised."

A drink? After all that, Ben wanted a date? Maybe nothing had happened. Maybe we could become the hot new rock couple.

"Sure."

"How about Friday night after work? Maybe I could meet you at Oscar's?"

"Sounds good."

I got off the phone, hoping this was the beginning of something good.

After a few hours of avoiding the wrath of Jean Zimmerman, my phone rang again. I once again said a small prayer for a voice other than the Wicked Witch, and was again rewarded. Sort of.

"Kit, it's Nikki," my sister said. She was sobbing.

"What is it? Is Dad okay?"

She laughed through garbled snot. "Dad's fine, I'm sorry. But I'm not so good. Can you meet me?"

What had she done now? I looked at the clock. Noon. I had to blow off Rachel for lunch, but it was an acceptable time to slip out of the building.

"Sure. How about the McGillan's?" It was the first dark place I could think of.

"Okay. I can be there in about ten minutes."

McGillan's, like most of my favorite haunts, was an old dark tavern. Actually the oldest if you believed their claims over several other pubs in the area. I arrived before Nikki and scoped out a table in the back. They had a cafeteria-style buffet set up for lunch, so I made a tray of comfort foods—macaroni and cheese, meatloaf, mashed potatoes, two Diet Cokes. I walked to the table and waited a few minutes before Nikki appeared, silhouetted by the backlight of the open door. I waved her over.

As she approached the table, I could see her face was red and puffy. She grabbed the soda and took a long swig. She sat in a chair across from me with her back to the room. I pushed the soda and tray toward her.

"So what happened?" I asked.

"It was awful. Ted's partner called me in this morning for my 'exit interview.'"

"What's that?"

"Basically a sugar-coated way to tell me I'm fired," she said, her eyes filling with tears again. "They even escorted me out of the building. I felt like a criminal."

"What happened? Did he find out about you and Ted?"

She blushed and looked down at the tray. She picked up a fork and started playing with the bright orange macaroni and cheese.

"Nikki, what happened? I thought you were going to stop seeing him."

"I know, I really meant to. But last Friday we went out for happy hour with a bunch of people again. I got pretty drunk because I hadn't eaten anything all day, and the next thing I knew he was back at my place."

My face flushed as I thought of the irony of our parallel dysfunction.

"We ended up passing out. He didn't wake up until almost 3:30. He ran out of the apartment, but his wife was up when he got home. Apparently they had made some plans and she was totally pissed. He called me from a pay phone the next day. He said he explained everything and thought she believed him. But, I guess not."

She poked at the noodles, then set the fork down and took another sip of her soda.

"What happened to Ted?"

"I don't know. He wasn't in today. I tried calling him at home, but got the machine and obviously couldn't leave a message."

"So you get fired and nothing happens to Ted?"

Her blue eyes look up at me from her drink.

"That's the way the world works, Kit."

"You've got to have some kind of rights here."

"I'd rather just drop it."

"So what will you tell your next employer? Spirit is one of the biggest names in Philly. And you know how small a town this is. If you get a reputation as a trouble-maker, you may have problems getting another job, especially in design."

"What do you think I should do?"

"I don't know. Maybe you should encourage Ted to help you find a new job."

"You mean blackmail him into finding me a new job?"

"Hey, it got Monica Lewinsky in the door at L'Oreal."

"Yeah, and look how that turned out."

"Okay, bad example," I said. "But Ted owes you something. I'd say he's getting off pretty easy, so to speak. Do you have any friends there who could get a message to him discreetly?"

Nikki paused.

"When did you get to be like this?"

"Like what?"

"I don't know. Vindictive."

"I'm not vindictive. I am so fucking sick of men who wave their dicks around and act like they have every goddamn right to fuck whoever they want and no one ever questions them, just the girls who fall for them. Our parents shoved this whole equality shit down our throats our whole lives, and it's a fucking lie."

Nikki looked stunned. "What are you talking about?"

"Wake up, Nikki. You know I'm right."

She shrugged and jabbed at the ice in her drink. "Yeah, you are. Which sucks."

"It doesn't have to. We just have to let people know they can't fuck with us. We have to be stronger than that."

Nikki nodded, but I wasn't sure she really believed me. Hell, I wasn't sure if I believed me. But, I liked this idea of power, that I could control an outcome in my life.

I just had to remember it the next time I saw Ben.

Friday came quickly. Jean had been out sick since Wednesday, and there was much speculation as to the nature of her absence. The resulting calm in the office was disorienting rather than comforting, and soon people began to run in circles like sheep in need of a shepherd. Being a link in this decaying chain, my workload dropped. Just two pink folders greeted me from my desk Friday morning, not nearly enough to distract me for the entire day.

I mulled about in the coffee room for a while with a handful of catty women, absorbing the day's latest about the great Jean/De Medio scandal. The official story was that Jean was at the corporate HR office dealing with the Catholic-girl slipup. But today, Cheryl, the receptionist whose wound still glistened on the back of her head, was sharing her unauthorized version. It seemed there were two possibilities. The first was that Jean had forgiven Dr. De Medio and the two had run off to Tijuana. The other was that Jean had hunted Dr. De Medio down, attacked him, and was now sitting in jail for assault. A third story claimed Jean was a transsexual. That made me laugh.

The rest of the day pushed sluggishly forward. I hadn't told anyone about my impending date with Ben and when the hour-hand finally hit five, I headed out toward the front lobby.

"Have a great weekend, Rachel," I said, walking quickly past her office.

"Hey, do you want to walk to the subway together?"

"Can't, sorry. I'm meeting someone."

I felt guilty as I ran out the office door and jumped on the open elevator just as the doors were shutting. I wasn't ready to tell Rachel about Ben—or about my bad behavior around him.

Oscar's was only two blocks from my office. The happy hour crowd was starting to grow, so I grabbed a small table in the back of the room and ordered a beer. My eyes scanned the room. The usual crowd was here—young professionals, grizzled barflys, trendy scenesters. Ben was late. Or blowing me off.

"Are you using this?"

"Yes!" I answered with increasing agitation as person after person walked to my table, touching the empty chair.

I was halfway through my second beer when Ben finally showed up.

"Hey," he smiled, pulling the empty chair closer to me and sitting down. He leaned over and kissed me on the cheek. "How you doing?"

"Nice of you to show up," I said.

He laughed and waved the chunky waitress over and ordered a beer and two shots of Jim Beam.

"How was work?" he asked.

"Great. There's a big scandal between one of the doctors on our advisory board and a Catholic-school intern. It would make a perfect TV movie. How about you?" I realized I had no idea what he did for a living.

"I was off today."

"Oh. You're at Tower Records, right?"

"No. I work over at Philly Record Exchange."

"That's right," I said, pretending to remember.

The waitress arrived with our drinks. Ben picked up a shot and handed it to me, then picked up his own.

"To new friends," he said.

"New friends," I agreed, then clinked his glass. I tossed back the liquor and quickly followed it with a large gulp of beer.

We continued making small talk, ordering two more beers and two more shots. My anxiety was dissipating into a warm buzz. He told me about Lava Dance's latest recording sessions, and how they were going to shop the demo to some indie labels. We talked about the Clark Park show and how much fun we had. I still had no idea what had happened and I no longer cared. Maybe I was wrong about Ben. Maybe he did just get too wasted the night of the party and went home. The more he spoke to me with his low, sexy voice, the more I wanted to believe that.

"So I had an idea for us tonight," Ben leaned over to me, his arm wrapped around the back of my chair.

I leaned in closer to him. His shirt smelled like baby powder. He nuzzled at my ear.

"There's kind of an interesting place near here that I thought you might be into."

I felt up to anything.

"Sure. What is it?"

"Why don't we settle up here and I'll take you there?"

"Okay," I said, kissing him on the cheek lightly.

Outside, the evening had cooled, and I wrapped my arms around myself. We walked quietly down the small street, then turned and walked a few more blocks.

"This is it," Ben said in front of a cement wall interrupted only by a single red door.

"What is it?"

"Open the door."

I reached out, grabbed the brass handle and swung it open. Red light poured into the street, creepily illuminating a large dark man seated on a barstool. Loud music pumped in the background.

"I.D." the man said, holding out a thick bear paw.

I turned to Ben, who smiled slyly. Where was I? I pulled out my wallet and my driver's license, then handed it to the bouncer. Ben did the same.

"Go on in," the man grunted.

We walked down a small dark hallway, then through a beaded curtain into a large bar. The room was half-full, depending on your point of view, of drunken men hooting at the scene on stage. My eyes were drawn to a naked blonde woman with enormous breasts who sat spread-eagle on a folding chair. Her hands were handcuffed behind the chair. She was gyrating her hips to the beat of house music as another equally well-endowed naked blonde danced around her, whip in hand. She snapped the whip in time with the music as the woman on the chair writhed in mock protest. The woman standing then wrapped the whip around the neck of the writhing woman, then pulled her forward into a deep French kiss. The men shrieked with excitement.

"What do you think?" Ben whispered into my ear.

"I don't know," I answered. I was pretty buzzed and as much as I didn't want to admit it, the music, the strippers, I was more than a little turned on.

"Let's get a drink."

I followed Ben through the room, drawing embarrassed stares by some men, curiosity by others. We walked through another curtain and into a small room that had a bar and a few tables. A large-breasted brunette in a thong bikini and cowboy hat waved to us from behind the bar.

"Hi Candy," Ben said as we pulled up stools at the bar. "This is Kit."

"Hi Kit," she said, blinding me with a synthetic smile. "What can I get for y'all tonight?"

"How about two shots of Beam and two drafts? You still having that special?" Ben asked, scratching his nose slightly.

"Anything for you, honey."

She poured us beers and shots, then nodded to a man sitting in a dark corner. He nodded back, then walked out of the room.

"So where you from, you pretty little thing?" Candy asked me.

"Originally from Swarthmore," I said. I couldn't help staring at her boobs. "But now I live in South Philly."

"They have some nice places down there. Cheap, too. Ben, you don't live too far from there, do you?"

Ben smiled. How did she know where he lived? I drank my beer and decided to ignore it.

"Kit plays in an all-girl band," he said.

"Do you really?" Candy said. "That is so adorable. You must be the singer."

"Bass player, actually. I do some singing, though."

"Listen, I have to hit the head," Ben said. "I'll be right back."

Watching him walk away, I felt awkward and conspicuous. Two men walked in and sat at the end of the bar.

"Excuse me a minute, sweetie," Candy said.

I watched her. She leaned forward until the men across from her could practically rest their drooling chins on her breasts. The two men tried to look unaffected, but Candy completely dominated them.

"What can I get for you boys?" she purred. "Do you want a cool drink, or maybe something a little hotter?"

She pulled a straw from its holder and put in her mouth, licking it lightly with her tongue before wrapping her bright red lips around it The men giggled like school-boys.

"I'll take a beer for now," the smaller of the two men answered.

"Yeah, make that two," the other one said.

As Candy turned away, the two men elbowed each other and whispered. She leaned down to pick up a stray napkin from the floor, her ass and vitals exposed by the thong bikini, then turned and smiled at the men before slowly standing up, running her long red nails along her thigh. They stared at her, jaws agape. She filled two beers, then slinked back to hand the drinks to them. I was mesmerized. My parents had always painted strippers as victims, but Candy ruled the room.

Ben returned from the bathroom.

"Miss me?" he asked, sitting close. He picked up his shot and held it up for an-other toast. "To new friends."

I laughed stupidly. "We did that one already."

"You've met a few friends since then," he answered, nodding toward Candy, who was still working the two guys.

"True," I said, lifting and clinking my glass with his. I tossed it back, then chased it with my beer. My head was swimming. It must have been close to 10:00, and I once again hadn't had any dinner.

Whoops.

"I bought a present for you," Ben whispered to me.

"Really," I smiled at him unsteadily. "What is it?"

"Let's go back there and I'll show you." He gestured the corner. "Behind that curtain."

Red curtains bordered the whole room. I looked back at him.

"What are you up to?"

"It's a surprise." He said, then got off his barstool and held my hand. "Come with me little girl."

I stepped off the barstool, catching my foot slightly on the rung and falling forward. Ben caught me and straightened me up. I clodded ungracefully behind him as he walked away from the bar and through a crease in the beaded wall. I felt like I was being swallowed into a Fellini movie. Surely circus freaks would be behind the curtain. But instead, it was only a small table and a few chairs. A matted red velvet loveseat was against the wall. He pulled me over to the couch. The sexual energy of the room was working its magic on me.

Feeling brave, I asked, "So handsome, what's a couch dance?"

"It's just another big tease, like everything else in this place. Come here."

He pulled me down next to him and took a small compact mirror from his back pocket. He clicked it open, then lifted a tiny clear bag from his shirt pocket. Coke. I had done some a few times in college and remembered liking it. I smiled.

"For me?" I asked.

"For us."

He poured a tiny white chunk onto the glass of the compact mirror, then got a small razor blade from his shirt pocket and crunched the chunk into powder. He expertly dragged the powder into two even lines, tapped the blade against the mirror, then licked the blade and stuffed it back into his pocket. He pulled out a small straw and handed it to me.

"Ladies first," he said.

I put the straw up my nose and leaned in. I closed one nostril with my finger, then sucked up the powder with the other one. There was a slight burning in my nostril that made my nose run, so I sniffed and wrinkled my nose. Ben devoured his line, then took another deep inhale.

"Thanks," I said.

In moments, I started to feel clearer. The cocaine dried the cloudiness of the alcohol buzz. Ben took another deep breath, then turned toward me.

"Wanna give me a couch dance?"

I smiled, then pulled my skirt up. I climbed on top of him so his crotch was between my thighs, and started to move my hips to the dull thud of the music from the main room, slowly rotating like the gyrating woman in the chair. I was in a dream, after all. An insane dream where people walk around naked and the world is hidden behind curtains and there are no rules. I felt Ben grow hard beneath me and it felt good. I reached down and worked his belt open and his zipper down, then worked him out of his underwear until the only thing between us was my panties. I slid back and forth on top of him.

"Did you bring protection?" I whispered in his ear.

"Hold on," he grunted. He managed to wriggle a condom on and I climbed back on top of him, grinding my hips against him. Ben threw his head back against the couch and groaned. I moved my panties aside and slipped him inside me. I was in charge here. I lifted myself up and down, up and down, matching the music like a pro. Ben moaned and grabbed my ass and started moving his hips faster and faster until he slammed himself against me and shuddered.

I fell on top of him, wrapping my arms around his neck. Maybe we would be the new rock couple. Daring, adventurous, alternative. We rested there for a minute, letting our heartbeats slow.

"We better get going," Ben said.

"What?"

"Yeah, the bouncer might come back any time."

"Oh."

I climbed off of him, embarrassed. I looked for a napkin, but didn't see anything so I awkwardly pulled my underwear back into place. I stood up and brushed myself off, still lightheaded. Ben tossed the condom on the floor, zipped himself up and stood up.

"Ready?"

"Yeah, I guess."

I followed him back through the curtain. The men at the bar had been joined by a handful of other guys. Candy commanded them all. Instead of stopping for another drink, Ben kept walking. I waved slightly to Candy as I left. She smiled and waved back.

I followed Ben into the larger front room, which had also grown more crowded. A group of young guys gathered in the back, laughing loudly and slapping each other on the back. A dancer was grinding on one of the guys, who looked too drunk to truly be enjoying himself. He would soon make some woman a blushing bride, I assumed. The rest of the smoky room was filled with older men who looked bored as they stared at the gyrating women on stage.

Then, we were back out in the street. Ben put his arm around me and kissed me on the cheek.

"That was fun," he said, and just as I was about to feel good, he looked at his watch. "Oh shit. I'm supposed to meet someone now. Do you mind if I get you a cab?"

I started at him disbelievingly.

"Are you serious?"

"What?"

I couldn't believe someone could be so blatantly stereotypical. I felt like I'd been kicked in the stomach.

"I'll get one myself," I said angrily, walking away. Tears began to blur my vision.

"Kit!" Ben called. He ran up behind me and turned me around to face him. He wiped a stray tear from my cheek and kissed me. "You're right. I'm sorry. I'm an asshole. I'll just blow off this other person. It's just a friend from out of town."

"Who?"

"My old college roommate. I haven't seen him for a while. He lives in Chicago. Um, I guess you could come a long if you wanted. It'll just be two guys reminiscing about the bad old days, but you're welcome to join us."

By his tone, I didn't feel welcome at all. I felt dirty and stupid. The last thing I wanted was to hang out with more of Ben's alternative friends. I wanted Ben to come home with me. I wanted him to be there when I woke up and have breakfast with me and spend some time with me sober. I wanted him to meet my parents and give me Valentine's Day gifts and cook dinner for me.

"Forget it," I said.

"Are you sure?" he asked, looking almost sincere.

"Whatever."

I walked away from him, feeling every angry footstep on the hard sidewalk as I headed toward Broad Street where a cab was waiting.

"I'll call you," he said from behind me.

I climbed into the cab and slammed the door closed, turning to see Ben through the grimy window. He smiled and waved as the cab pulled away, his grin as sly as a cat that had just swallowed the last bite of mouse.

Asshole.

CHAPTER

The next morning was all too familiar—headache, body ache, fatigue, confusion—all blanketed by a thick layer of shame. As the night crept back into my memory, I could only wince. What was I doing? Things had been so easy with Dale. Unpleasant, yes, but my current situation made this former life look pretty appealing.

I turned my head to face the digital clock radio by my bed. 1:30. Shit. It felt like 6:00 in the morning. I let my eyelids succumb to their heavy weight, when I suddenly snapped them open. Practice. I had band practice at 2:00.

I jumped out of bed and threw on the only pair of jeans that didn't completely smell of smoke, then a T-shirt. I pulled my hair back into a ponytail and splashed my face with cold water. It didn't help. My brain felt disconnected from the rest of my body merely watching the activity from a fuzzy distance. I dragged my bass and peripherals wearily out the door and to the car. The dashboard clock read 1:52. I would be fifteen minutes late. Not too bad.

When I got to the practice place, Frank stood in the door, watching traffic drive back and forth like a tennis match.

"Hi Frank," I greeted him as he moved his lanky frame out of the threshold to let me through.

"Heeey Kit," he said, as if he were introducing Johnny Carson. "Late night?"

"Hmm." I grunted.

"Well, you're still the first one here."

I dropped my cases in disgust.

"Are you serious?"

"Yep."

"Super."

I pulled my equipment up to the rehearsal space and began setting up my amp and microphones. By the time I was finished, it was 2:30. I sat on the floor and stared at the large clock face, the minute hand sweeping in slow circles.

At 2:45, I decided to lie on the floor. It was sticky and smelled of feet, but my need to be horizontal was strong enough to ignore it.

At 2:55, I heard footsteps clunking up the stairs. I pushed myself back into a seated position. Margo burst into the room.

"I am so sorry," she announced, dropping her guitar heavily on the floor. "I totally overslept. Long night with the co-workers." She looked around the empty room. "Where's Gino?"

"Beats me."

"That little shit. Where the hell is he?"

I shrugged. She pulled a cell phone out of her purse and dialed. After a pause, she rolled her eyes.

"Machine," she mouthed, then said flippantly, "Gino, it's Margo. We're at the practice place for rehearsal and wondered where you might be. I hope you're on your way."

She clicked her phone off.

"He's not on his way," she said. "Jerk." She sat down next to me and looked at me closely, cocking her head.

"So," she raised her eyebrows. "You look like shit. What did you do last night?"

"Thanks. I kind of had another date with Ben."

She slapped my leg.

"Why don't you tell me these things?"

"Well, I don't know. I don't know if it was even a date. It was weird. I can't figure him out."

"Well, he is cute, but there's something I just don't trust about that guy. I hope I'm wrong."

Me too.

We sat in silence as the clock inched to 3:15. We had only booked two hours. We would pay $30 to sit on a stinky floor.

"I guess he forgot," I offered.

"Yeah, I guess," she smirked. "But his behavior is getting a little old."

"What do you mean?"

"Nothing." Margo stood up and sat behind the drums, beating the bass drum softly with the foot pedal. "You know what we need? A girls' night. You're coming home with me and we're going to put on sweats and watch girlie movies and eat too much. What do you say?"

"Sold."

At 3:45, we decided Gino was a no-show and packed up our cars. I followed Margo to the apartment she had inherited after the breakup with Pete—the one I where I had met her a lifetime ago.

We brought our stuff to the living room. It looked smaller than I remembered, but maybe this was because of the clutter. There was stuff everywhere. Clothes piled high on the backs of the couch and chairs. The coffee table was littered with magazines that spilled onto the floor. A blanket and pillows were bunched at the seat of the couch. The small table that had served as a bar for the party was piled high with unopened mail, catalogs, and more magazines. The stereo had four large stacks of CD cases piled on it.

"Hmm," Margo grunted as she looked at the mess. "I guess I should have thought about this chaos before inviting you over. Oh well." She walked in and threw her guitar beside the couch. "Come on in and clear yourself a seat. I'll get you some comfy clothes."

She picked up the phone along the way.

"Gee, there's a shocker," she said. "Gino hasn't called." She replaced the phone in its cradle and disappeared into the bedroom.

"Make yourself a drink," she called. "While you're at it, make me one, too."

I silently hushed my wailing liver and walked into the kitchen. Dirty dishes were piled in the sink and on the counter. I opened a cabinet that had stacked coffee cups and plates. I tried another that had boxes of cereal and pasta. The last one had glasses. I selected two pint glasses, filled them with ice, then looked in her freezer for vodka. No problem there. She had three bottles of various flavors. I chose Citron and poured heavy shots for us both, topping them off with semi-flat seltzer I found in the fridge. Using my finger as a stirrer, I mixed both drinks, then licked the cold liquid off my finger. I went back to the living room.

Margo was still in the bedroom, so I pushed a butt-sized clearing on the couch and sat down, setting Margo's drink on the table. I took a long sip of mine, then grimaced at the strength. Oh well, hair of the dog as they say.

Margo emerged in a red cotton top and sweatpants. She tossed a similar pair to me, but mine was white with tiny blue daisies. Perfect. I wanted to feel innocent today. I exchanged my constricted jeans and shirt and instantly felt better. This was what I needed.

"I have the perfect movie," Margo said, rooting through a stack of videotapes. "*Same Time Next Year.*"

"Alan Alda?"

"Yeah. It's the perfect chick flick."

She plucked the disk from the middle of a stack, and the rest of the pile fell. Margo ignored it and walked over to the television, putting the disk in and turning on the TV. A few more clicks, and the movie bloomed to life onscreen. It was perfect. We drank our vodka and fell in love with these two people who were destined to be together but whose lives kept them apart.

"Ben would never bake me a cake," I said during a scene where Alan Alda made Ellen Burstyn a cake to reminisce over their song, "If I Knew You Were Coming, I'd a Baked a Cake." I was on my third drink.

Margo laughed.

"Pete would never sing me a song," she said. "Or cry over me. He would certainly never deliver a baby. He'd probably pass out, Mr. Tough Rock Star."

"Where are these men? I don't think they really exist."

"They do, but we think they're dorks."

"Maybe." I paused. "Dale did sing to me, though, the first time we met. I think that's when I fell in love with him."

I thought about the innuendo that Dale had made about Margo. I wanted to ignore it, but it kept lingering at the back of my mind. Part of me wanted to know, but only if it weren't true. I had just enough vodka in me to consider bringing it up.

"What did you think of Dale back then?" I ventured nervously.

"Oh, I don't know. It's hard to say now that I'm friends with you. I can only think of him as an asshole."

I took a long sip of my drink. Alan Alda was acting like a jerk to Ellen Burstyn.

"Did he ever hit on you?" I asked.

Margo turned and looked at me.

"Yes," she said flatly.

My heart began to race.

"Do you really want to know this?" she asked.

"No, but tell me anyway."

Margo flopped back into the couch and pulled her legs up to her chest.

"A few years ago, Pete and I were having some trouble, as usual. I had just had a huge screaming match with him at this club and was out in the parking lot, smoking. Dale walked out to see if I was okay. He turned on the charm as he does so well and we sort of made out a little. It was stupid and lasted like five minutes and that was it. One of Pete's friends walked out and we just sort of broke it up and that was the end of it. But every time I saw Dale after that it was just a little creepy. I got the feeling he felt entitled to me somehow."

Alan Alda sobbed onscreen in big, comical wails.

"It was so long ago, Kit. You know that I would never, ever do anything to hurt you or to jeopardize our friendship. You are one of the coolest people I've ever met."

I flipped between anger and betrayal and self-pity. Margo had been just one of many girls in my history, another faceless threat to my fragile life with Dale. Maybe things weren't so bad now.

"I know you wouldn't. I just had to ask. Dale said something at the Clark Park show, that's all."

"What did he say?"

"It was more implication than confession, as usual. It's history."

"What an asshole."

Now Alan was a hippie and it was Ellen's turn to be a conservative shrew. I knew they would work it out.

"Let's order a pizza," Margo suggested, pausing the movie.

"Great. I'll make us two more drinks."

I felt a weight lifted from me that I hadn't known was there. Part of me believed Dale's accusation, and I didn't want the truth to hurt my friendship. Even though it may have happened before I knew Margo, I didn't want her to be another Dale conquest. The phone rang.

"Could be Gino," Margo said, pushing herself up from the couch.

She walked to the phone and picked it up.

"Good evening," she answered. Pause. "Hi." Pause. "Yes." She looked at me, her face bursting into a grin. "That sounds great." Pause. "Okay." She pulled a piece of paper and pen from under a pile and wrote some notes. "Great. We'll call them and set that up. Thanks. Okay. See you then."

She hung up the phone and turned to me.

"Guess who's opening for The Venturas?" she asked.

The Venturas were only one of my favorite bands. I'd seen them once with Dale and was totally impressed. They were an all-girl three-piece that played pop songs with complete confidence.

"You're kidding," I said.

"Would I kid you about that?" she teased. "That was The Trocadero. We're playing with them in two weeks. I guess I should call that little shit drummer of ours."

She picked up the phone and again dialed.

"Great," she said. "Machine again." She paused. "Gino, it's Margo again. We just got a call from The Trocadero... Hello? Hey, where've you been?" Pause. "What?" Pause. "That's ridiculous." Pause. "I really think you're overreacting." Pause. "Whatever, Gino. We just got a call from The Trocadero to open up for The Venturas. If you want to miss out on that, that's your problem." Pause. "Okay. We're really sorry," she said, mock sweet. "All right. We'll see you at practice Thursday night."

She hung up the phone.

"What a lunatic," she said.

"What happened?"

"He said he got to the practice place at quarter of two and it was locked. He said he waited until quarter after two and gave up." She shook her head. "He was totally pissed and said we have no respect for his time, blah blah blah."

"What? When I got there at 2:15, Frank said I was the first one there. How could the place have been locked?"

"Who knows? I'm sure his watch is probably on some different time zone. Anyway, he changed his tune when I mentioned the show."

"Was he going to quit over that?"

"He's not now. He just mumbled something about trying to make a point. Whatever." She walked over to the pile of videocassettes on the floor. "How about Dr. Zhivago?"

"Sure."

As Margo was setting up the machine, I thought about Gino. As much as he annoyed me, he really hadn't been treated with much respect in this band. Was it just because he was a guy? Were we being sexist? I sighed. I didn't have the energy for any more guilt. I tucked my feet under myself and settled in as the famous opening music crept softly to life.

CHAPTER

Monday morning I got into work late, drained from the weekend. I left another message for Nikki, but only got her machine. I was worried about her, and felt bad for not having tried to reach her.

As I drank my morning coffee, I heard the tittering of female gossip out in the hallway. I popped my head out to see Cheryl's open wound bent in a huddle with two middle-aged women from bookkeeping.

"What's going on?" I asked.

Cheryl turned to me.

"It's Jean. She's disappeared."

The three women stood shaking their heads.

"What do you mean?" I asked.

Cheryl walked toward me to whisper the news.

"Apparently she was caught embezzling."

"Who told you that?"

"Lee-Ann, who works at corporate, called and told me this morning. That's why we haven't seen her. There's a warrant out for her arrest and no one can find her."

"So let me get this straight," I said. "Jean Zimmerman, a woman who has no history of showing any kind of imagination, has had an affair with our top medical consultant and is so upset she has run off with company funds."

"I know. Isn't that crazy?"

"Yes it is."

Cheryl looked at me cynically. "Anyway," she began, but then turned to rejoin a more appreciative audience.

I smiled and went back to my supply closet office. My desk was empty of pink folders. I'd cleaned up my files on Friday. I had no messages to return. Who was running this place? I picked up the phone to call Nikki. Again, got her machine. I didn't leave a message.

I drummed my fingers on the desk. I checked my email. Five messages. Three home-based business promotions. One proofreading style update. One medical listserv news. I looked at the clock. 10:18. This was going to be a long day. I picked up the phone again and called my parents. My mother answered on the third ring.

"Hello?" She sounded winded.

"Did you run to the phone?"

"Oh, hi Honey. I was just working outside."

"Where's Dad?"

"He's still sleeping."

"Sleeping? This late? He normally gets up at the crack of dawn."

"He's just been really tired lately."

"How's he doing?"

"Oh, pretty well."

"Is he walking?"

"Well, he gets out now and again."

"Is he eating better?"

She sighed. "You know your father. He's stubborn."

Translation—he's still smoking, eating scrapple, and not getting off the couch.

"You should come out for another visit soon," my mother said. "He'd like that."

"I will, I promise."

"Nikki was out again the other day. She and Ted surprised us with a visit."

She brought Ted with her? Unbelievable. So, not only had she not told my parents that she lost her job, she was flaunting the cause in front of them.

"He seems nice," my mother said. "How are you doing?"

I could have totally screwed my sister at this point. All those years I had to hear about the perfect one, the successful one, the flawless one. Here was my chance to show she was just as fucked up as I was.

But something stopped me, an image of my father lying on the hospital bed, tubes linking his arms to bags of liquid.

"Everything's great, mom," I said. "I'm really happy. The band is doing well and work has gotten a lot better."

"I'm so glad," she said. "I worry so much about both of you."

"We're fine. I better get back to work now. I just wanted to check in."

"Thanks. I love you, Honey."

"I love you, too."

I hung up the phone and stared at my screen saver. A swirling wash of color created a slow, pulsing rhythm. I started to tap my foot along with the movement as a melody slowly formed in my head.

I spent the rest of the day bullshitting with the gang, shopping, playing Free Cell. This Jean-less office was going to bore me to death. When I got home, there was one message.

"Hey Kit, it's Charlie. I was wondering if Broad Street might want to open up for us at The Khyber this Saturday. Our opening band backed out, not that we wouldn't want to play with you anyway, but I just thought it would be fun. Give me a call."

Good old Charlie. I hoped he hadn't gotten word on the loose new bass player in town. After clearing the date with Margo and Gino, I called him back.

"Hello?" A male voice answered. It wasn't enough syllables to decipher its owner and could possibly be Ben, but I decided to launch into a conversation anyway.

"Hi. May I speak to Charlie?"

"Speaking."

Relieved, I sat down at my kitchen table.

"Hey Charlie, it's Kit calling you back."

"Hey! What do you think about that show?"

"Yeah, we're in. Thanks. Sounds like fun."

"Great, great." I heard footsteps, then a door closing. "Listen, I wanted to apologize for the Clark Park thing."

"What Clark Park thing?" I asked.

"The whole equipment mix-up. Let's just say I was given incorrect information."

"What do you mean?"

"Well, Ben talked to Brenda about the schedule, and for some reason he told me you weren't on until 4:00."

"That's weird. I don't even remember discussing it with him."

"Well, anyway. I just wanted to apologize."

"Don't worry about it. You've been a huge help. I really appreciate what you've done for us."

"Hey, I'm glad to do it. I think you guys are great."

My face grew hot.

"Thanks. You, too."

This was a bit of an exaggeration since I didn't actually remember much of their performance. But Charlie seemed like a nice guy. Why not throw him a bone?

We discussed logistics—time, equipment sharing, money. I hung up feeling pretty good. We had two new gigs lined up, and Jean was out of the picture. If I could just mute that annoying voice in my head that kept whispering to me about Ben, I might even say I was content.

Thursday night at practice, Gino showed up late. He responded to our enthusiastic greetings with a low grunt, then clunked his equipment down noisily on the drum riser. Margo and I exchanged glances and shrugged. We continued our setup, tried to ignore him, and chatted excitedly about the show on Saturday.

"You can use their drum equipment if you don't feel like bringing yours," I said.

"I'll bring my own stuff," he said, not looking at me.

Margo distributed set lists.

"I thought we could play the same set we did at Clark Park," she said.

Gino pulled the set out of her hand and glared at it.

"'Take That' and 'Falling' should not be back to back," he said. "They're almost the same song."

"Hardly," Margo said.

"They have the exact same rhythm," Gino said. "And the same chords."

"Fine," she said. "We'll move 'Falling' toward the end."

She pulled her guitar over her head and checked the microphone.

"Ready? We'll start with…"

Before she could finish her sentence, Gino clicked four loudly and launched into the first song on the set list. Margo and I scrambled to catch up. Gino pounded angrily on the toms, then cracked ear-splitting snare hits. Margo struggled to sing over the volume. Gino invented busy drum rolls that stepped on the vocals and my bass line, and by the time three minutes were up, Margo and I were both lost.

"That's great, Gino," Margo said. "You're pissed. We get it."

"I find that hard to believe," he mumbled under his breath.

She put her hands on her hips.

"We said we were sorry about being late. We're sorry you weren't mentioned in the article. We have nothing but regret for the horrible way you've been treated."

"Let's play," he snapped.

I had an idea.

"Actually, I'm just going to run next door and grab a six pack. I'll be right back."

I pulled my bass off, switched my amp to the appropriate setting—stand-by—and ran over to the intimidating bar next door. Poetically named "Whiskey Dick's," the dark cave was occupied by mullet-headed men who gawked with ugly lust at any woman who entered.

I walked to the back of the room, trying to ignore the blatant staring at my ass, and pulled two sixes of the strongest beer I could find out of the illuminated cooler—Mickey's Big Mouth, the malt liquor that packed a punch.

When I returned to the room, Margo was sitting on her amp smoking a cigarette. Gino sat on his stool, a cigarette dangling from his mouth, as he loudly "tuned" his drums.

"I'm back!" I said, holding the beer out as a peace offering.

I handed a Mickey's to Gino, then pulled one out for myself. Gino twisted the barrel-bottle's cap off, then chugged half the beer's contents in several gulps. I cracked mine open, then sat it on the bass amp. Margo did the same. A few more gulps, and Gino polished off the rest of the beer. I quietly placed the six pack next to Gino's drums.

As we moved through the set, my plan seemed to work. The corners of Gino's mouth lifted slightly with each passing gulp. We tolerated the sloppy drumming since it came with an improved attitude. By the end of practice, Gino was drunk and happy. We made plans for Saturday night and Margo and I watched him stumble off to his car.

"This could be a problem," I said, watching him toss his hardware in the car, then turn back and give us a goofy wave.

"Do you think he's okay to drive?" Margo asked.

"I doubt this is the first time he's driven this way," I said through a grin as I waved back at him. I wondered how long it would be before our band would self-destruct.

I got to the club Saturday night at 8:30 as instructed. The Khyber was an alternative music institution just blocks from the Liberty Bell. Huge bands like Nirvana, Hole, and Smashing Pumpkins had cut their touring teeth here, so it had developed a regular crowd of local music fans looking to hear the next big thing.

I walked into the long bowling alley-like bar with my equipment dangling from my arms. The bar was draped with the tailend of happy hour drunks, most of whom were tattooed, dreadlocked and pierced. I scanned the crowd for Ben but didn't see him. I didn't see Charlie either. As I walked in to see if I could get a better view, a be-speckled guy hopped off his barstool and walked over to me, grinning widely.

"Hi Kit!" he greeted me. He looked familiar, but I couldn't remember where I'd met him.

"Adam," he helped me. "We met at Clark Park. I'm so excited to see you guys again tonight."

"Adam, right, I'm sorry." I put my equipment down and shook his hand. "You're the guy that knows everything about music."

He chuckled. "Here, let me get those." He leaned down and picked up my bass and makeup case.

"Thanks," I said, following him through a door that led into the music room. It was also long and narrow, with a stage taking up one end of the room, another bar on the other side. Charlie was on stage setting up his amp. He turned and smiled.

"Kit!" He hopped off the stage and thrust his hand out to shake mine. "It's great to see you."

He had cut his shaggy brown hair short, which made him look cleaner.

"Hi Charlie," I greeted him. "Thanks again for the gig."

"Oh, no problem," his eyes moved to Adam, who was standing awkwardly next to me.

"Oh, this is Adam. We met him at Clark Park."

"Yeah, I thought you looked familiar," Charlie said, shaking his hand. "The music man, right? You came up to us after the show, right?"

"Yeah, you guys were a lot of fun," he said. "Kind of reminded me of The Electric Love Muffin a little."

"I consider that a compliment, Adam. Thanks," Charlie said. "We just need to finish setting up, then you gals can go up there and get ready. We'll probably sound check first, then you guys. The third band hasn't shown up yet."

"Third band?" I asked.

"Yeah. Once I told the guy who books this place that you were playing with us, he added The Pussy Willows to the bill. I guess they're working the chick band thing. Not sure how we fit in exactly, but that's fine. You'll be on first, then us, then them."

Oh shit. I hadn't seen or talked to Linda since the article. This would be interesting.

"I thought the Pussy Willows were on tour in California," Adam said.

"We all did," I mumbled.

"Yeah, I read that article," Charlie said. "Do I smell a catfight?"

"Cute," I smirked. "Besides, we'd totally kick their asses."

Charlie smiled. "That I would like to see."

He climbed back on stage and continued setting up with the other two guys in his band—a white Rastafarian bass player and a black drummer with a shaved head and two gold earrings.

"So, do you get out to see shows much?" I asked Adam, not sure what else to say.

"I try to. I just saw an awesome jazz show last week at Bob & Barbara's. Nate Wiley's been playing there, like, a hundred years and he is still totally awesome. But, I still live with my mom, so I can't always get out when I want to. She can be pretty strict with the curfew."

"Curfew? I haven't heard that expression in a while."

Adam blushed. "Well, I'm trying to save up enough money to get my own place."

"What do you do?"

"I'm sort of looking for a job right now. I really want to do something in the music business. Maybe try to get a job at a label or radio station. I've been collecting records for a long time, I could really bring in some cool stuff that doesn't get any airplay. Maybe, like, on DRE or something."

Lives at home. Collects music. Unemployed. This would be the kind of fan we attracted.

"Great," I said.

Margo rescued me.

"Hey," she grunted, carrying her equipment over to us.

I reintroduced Adam to Margo before breaking the news about playing with The Pussy Willows.

"What? You never said that."

"I didn't know about it until thirty seconds ago. Apparently The Khyber added them to the bill once they found out we were playing."

Charlie called us up to the stage and Adam helped carry equipment. The Rastafarian showed me how to work his bass amp, while Charlie showed Margo how to set up his. Adam sat on a radiator by the stage and watched as we checked microphones and guitars. Finally, Gino walked in.

"Nice of you to show up," Margo said to him.

"Fuck you," he said, climbing to the stage.

"Excuse me?"

"Oh, lighten up," he slurred. "I'm just kidding." He put his hand on the side of the stage, then pushed himself up unsteadily. He turned and smiled at me, his eyes bloodshot, then walked back to the drums and plopped himself on the stool, almost missing it.

Margo walked back to him and leaned in.

"You're drunk," Margo said.

"Nah," he grinned.

"We have to play in an hour. You've got to sober up."

"Don't have a tittie attack. I'm fine."

"Drums," the sound guy's voice commanded through the stage monitor. "I need to check the drums. Start with the kick."

Margo and I stepped back nervously to watch the show. Gino tapped his foot on the bass drum pedal repeatedly.

"Okay. Now toms."

Gino slapped evenly on the toms. He seemed to be okay so far.

"Great, now snare."

He moved around the kit confidently. Maybe he would be all right, I hoped.

"Why don't you guys try a song?" the monitor voice asked. I peered back to the glowing booth, but could only see the back of the large mixing board.

"Okay," Margo said, turning toward both of us. "Let's run through 'Priscilla.' We both sing on that one so we can test the mics."

"'Priscilla,'" Gino laughed. "My favorite."

He clicked off four and we started the song. Gino's time was pretty close and Margo and I managed to keep up. We made it through the first verse, then the chorus, then back into the second verse again. But then came the bridge. Margo and I changed our tempo and chords to go into the instrumental break between the choruses, but Gino kept flailing away loudly as if we were still in the chorus. I noticed Adam out of the corner of my eye looking puzzled. I stood in front of Gino, trying to get his attention, but his eyes were closed and his mouth was in contortions. There was no bringing him back. Not knowing what else to do, I started playing the chorus again, which completely threw Margo off and she just stopped playing and singing. She waved her arms above her head to stop us, and eventually Gino did. I turned to notice the small crowd that had gathered in the room laughing and whispering. As my eyes adjusted to the dim light in their direction, I realized it was Linda with a group of girls. The Pussy Willows. Great. They were the last people I wanted to witness this.

"Okay," the sound guy said. "Let's get My Pet Rhino up here for a sound check."

I unplugged my bass and put it back in its case, aching to disappear with it. I leaned it against the back wall. Gino had hopped off stage and was walking over to The Pussy Willows.

"What are we going to do?" Margo asked.

"I can go get some coffee. There's a place right up the street."

We both turned to see one of the girls hand Gino a beer.

"I don't know if that's going to do it," Margo said.

"I wonder if we could get some coke," I whispered. Margo looked at me, surprised.

"What do you mean?" she asked.

"I don't know. Sometimes coke can sober you up." I neglected to tell her why this was fresh on my mind. "Let me see what I can do."

I looked at my watch. 9:00. We had an hour. I turned to see Adam standing next to us. He gave me a giant, goofy smile and I tried not to roll my eyes. What a dork.

The three of us watched My Pet Rhino run through a song. They sounded good—bluesy rock without being too pretentious. After they finished, I felt a tap on my shoulder. It was Linda.

"Hey guys!" she said to Margo and me. "Isn't this great that we're playing together?"

We both smiled through clenched teeth.

"Yeah," Margo said. "The Khyber's not LA, but it should still be fun."

Linda ignored the sarcasm.

"I know. The California thing is still on the back burner, but Tami's still working out the details. Come here, I want to introduce you guys."

We walked reluctantly over to the gaggle of rock chicks.

"Tami," Linda interrupted the laughing clique. "I want you to meet Margo and Kit."

A girl clad in black leather pants and a slim pea-green tank top turned toward us. Aging tattoos covered most of her arms, and I noticed long hair popping out from under her armpits. Her long brown hair was tied into a tight ponytail on top of her head, its choppy wisps dangling around her face. She had the leathery skin of a long-time smoker, and smiled wide with gappy yellow teeth.

"Hey," she greeted us hoarsely. "This is so fucking awesome that we're playing with you guys! We were just out with your little drummer boy here and he told us what a blast he's having with you!"

They had gotten Gino drunk. Cunts.

"Really?" Margo said, smiling angrily. "We wondered where he was tonight."

"Oh my god. We had such a fucking blast with this guy. We don't get to see him much since we keep his girlfriend on the road and in the studio."

I moved my eyes to Gino, who was standing next to a short freckled waif with long brown braids. Since Gino made no attempt to share his treasure with us, Linda made the introductions.

"This is Caroline, our bass player. Caroline, this is Kit and Margo."

We all smiled politely and shook her limp hand.

"Pussy Willows! Onstage for sound check!" the ghostly sound guy commanded. I craned my head to see around the mixing board, but saw only a jeans-clad leg and beat-up sneakers.

"Excuse us, gals." Tami said. "I think we're wanted."

Linda and Caroline followed Tami like obedient puppies. They climbed onstage and she pointed out their orders.

After a few minutes of setup, The Pussy Willows played their first song. The three-piece was solid. Linda seemed better than when she played with us; Caroline danced her fingers around the bass fretboard flawlessly; Tami strummed solid rhythm guitar. She leaned into the mic and belted a catchy powerhouse pop song. During the instrumental, she wailed through an impressive guitar lead. I hated them. As they were nearing a close, I heard a shrill voice behind us.

"Surprise!"

We turned to see Margo's parents. Vinnie was wearing tight Metamucil-orange pants, complete with matching heels and nails. Orlando wore a tan tunic over brown and white plaid pants. This was so uncool.

"Hi girls!" Orlando cheered, wrapping his arms around both of us. "Can you believe we're here?"

"No," Margo said, rolling her eyes.

"Oh, Honey," Vinnie squealed. "What kind of face is that to see your old parents? We read about your show in the paper, and decided we would surprise you! Now give Mummy a hug!"

Margo leaned in, barely lifting her arms to meet Vinnie's embrace.

"And how are you, sweetie?" she asked, giving me a squeeze.

"I'm good," I smiled, ready to crawl away and hide.

The tattooed hipsters at the bar were turning toward us with puzzled expressions.

The Pussy Willows had finished their song and were also looking our way. I felt naked in the music-less room and attempted to will the sound guy to put some music back on. Adam walked over and handed us beers.

"And who is this handsome fellow?" Vinnie asked.

"This is Adam," Margo said. "We met him at the last show."

"Ooh! A fan. How exciting."

Adam blushed.

"Since Margo is too rude to introduce us," Orlando glared jokingly toward Margo, "I'll take the liberty. I'm Orlando and this is Vinnie. We're Margo's parents."

"Nice to meet you," Adam replied.

"I'm sure she hasn't told you," Orlando continued, "but she didn't just find her musical talent. She received some good genes..."

"Dad, please." Margo interrupted.

"Oh, she doesn't like me to flatter her, but she has always been a musical child. She's obviously still learning, but she heard music all the time in our house. Vinnie and I had a little hit back in the late 70s called 'Can't Fake That Smile.'"

"That was you?" Adam lit up.

"You know it?" Vinnie asked.

"Sure. I have the original 45 in mint condition. I got a great deal on it at a flea market. The flipside is..." He looked up at the ceiling. "'800 Smiles?'"

"That's right!" Orlando said.

Margo and I looked at each other and rolled our eyes.

I saw The Pussy Willows descend from the stage and head toward the front bar. Various hipsters congregated to greet them, accentuating our nerdy entourage. I saw Gino walk over from the end of the bar to talk with them. He looked glassy. I craned my neck and saw Charlie sitting at the bar with the drummer. I decided to attempt my plan.

"Excuse me," I said to the reminiscing trio.

"Where are you going?" Margo pleaded.

"I have to go talk to Charlie." I raised my eyebrows and she nodded.

I walked to the front bar, weaving my way around a crowd to avoid The Pussy Willows. I left my beer on a table and squeezed into a void next to Charlie.

"Hey there," he smiled. "Can I buy you a drink?"

"Sure. I'd love a beer."

He ordered a beer from the bartender. I had no idea how to broach the subject of soliciting drugs. I took a long swig of my beer and decided to just jump in.

"So, this is kind of a weird question," I asked softly. The sound guy had put on loud music, and the white noise of the bar made for the perfect cover. Charlie leaned in.

"What?' he whispered back with mock seriousness.

"Would you by any chance know where I could get some coke?"

He snapped back and scrunched up his face.

"Now why would you ask me that?" he asked.

My face burned.

"I'm sorry. I'm just in a bit of a jam. I just don't know anyone that well in the 'scene.'"

"Are you calling me a scenester?"

"Well, no, but..." I stammered.

He smiled and put his hand on my shoulder.

"I'm just giving you a hard time," he said. "Maybe I can help you out. What's your jam?"

I turned and motioned my head toward Gino and the Pussies.

"He's totally bombed."

"Yeah, that was an interesting sound check," Charlie said.

"I don't know. I thought maybe that would help."

"It might. Temporarily. Let me see what I can do." He looked at his watch. "You guys are supposed to be on in a half an hour. We certainly wouldn't want to start late and fuck up the Pussy Willow schedule." He smiled and winked as he hopped off the bar stool. "Why don't you go back in there and I'll meet up with you in a minute."

"Thanks, Charlie."

"I don't know, Kit. The favors are starting to pile up."

"I know. I totally owe you."

He smiled and walked toward the front of the bar. I didn't want to witness anything, so I hopped off my stool and carried my beer into the darkened back of the stage room. Margo ran over to me.

"So?" she asked.

"I should be getting something soon."

"Shit," she said, looking at her watch. "We're on in like twenty minutes."

"They'll wait. Why don't you go out and buy a pack of cigarettes or something? They got rid of the machine here. I'll wait here. Then we'll have an excuse."

"You're good."

"Where are your parents and our little fan?"

"They're out at the bar reminiscing over the fabulous 70s and how it's an underrated musical era."

"I think I'll stay here."

"Probably a good idea."

She walked up to say something briefly to her parents, then left the club. I hid in the shadows, watching the group laugh and gesture flamboyantly. Adam had been joined by other young people who were watching Vinnie and Orlando like it was storytelling hour at the Wigwam Nursery.

I drank my beer and waited. The front bar was packed with smoke and loud conversation. I was on my second beer when I saw Charlie walk through the door into the room.

"One more favor," he said, handing me a pack of cigarettes.

I looked conspicuously around the room.

"What do I owe you?"

"I haven't decided yet."

I stared at him, wrinkling my brow.

"I'll let you know."

He walked back to the other room. Now, the challenge was going to be getting Gino to participate in my ruse. I knew there were two unisex bathrooms in the back stage room. We could use one of those. As I headed toward the entrance to the front room where Gino stood with The Pussy Willows, I saw the sound guy emerge from his booth. Shit. He was short and bearded and walked with a bow-legged swagger.

"I need you guys on in fifteen minutes," he grunted.

"Okay. Our lead singer just ran out to get some cigarettes."

"Fifteen minutes," he snapped, then walked back to his booth.

I walked to the threshold of the bar and called to Gino. He looked groggily up at me and waved. I motioned him over to me. He leaned over and gave Caroline a sloppy cheek kiss, then walked over to me.

"Hey, we have to go on in a few minutes. But listen, I got us a little treat."

His eyes tried to focus on my face.

"I got us some coke. Margo and I already had some and there's more in this cigarette pack. You can go in the bathroom right there."

Gino wrinkled his face.

"I don't do that shit. Not anymore."

I hadn't counted on this.

"What do you mean, 'anymore?'" I asked angrily.

"I mean I gave it up."

This opened up a whole new can of worms. Was he a reformed addict? He wasn't doing a very good job of it.

"Oh, come on." I said. "It's a special occasion."

"True," he said, thinking. He looked to the front room where he could see Caroline, then leaned toward me shakily. "You can't tell her," he motioned with his head.

"Of course not."

He smiled.

"Just for the special occasion." He took the cigarette pack from my hand and went into one of the bathrooms.

Margo appeared in the room, sneaked by her gabbing parents, and walked over to me.

"Well?"

"He's in the bathroom now."

"Good. Let's hope this works."

"I think I made a mistake."

"What do you mean?"

"He just sort of implied that he might be a recovering addict or something."

"Of course he's an addict! Please. He's a grown boy. He can take care of himself."

I wasn't so sure. The sound guy walked up to us.

"I need you guys up there."

"Okay, okay," I said impatiently. "We're going."

We walked toward the stage, but I kept an eye on the closed bathroom door. I pulled my bass out of its case and started setting it up. The door remained closed. I re-tuned to kill time. I pretended to search for picks. Then the CD snapped off. The crowd in the other room began to slowly spill into ours. The door remained closed.

Oh my god. He'd OD'd. Charlie had actually given me heroin and we would have to pump adrenaline directly into Gino's heart ala Pulp Fiction.

And then the door opened. Gino sauntered out coolly. He slinked past The Pussy Willows, and Tami handed him a full pint glass of beer and a shot and slapped him on the ass. Caroline seemed unfazed. He climbed on stage and winked at me, the remnants of white powder outlining one of his nostrils. It's for the show, I rationalized. But I couldn't shake the guilt.

"Ready gals?" Gino yelled confidently, then clicked off four and launched into the set.

He was a powerhouse of volume. He slammed loudly on the toms and snare, inventing new drum lines as he went along. His improvisation fueled by chemistry made it difficult to predict where he was going in the song, but Margo and I managed to keep up. Orlando and Vinnie gazed up adoringly at Margo as she belted the song. The crowd from the bar had filled most of the room, and more people kept being added to the mix. The Pussy Willows were not among them. Ben was not among them.

I tried not to think about him. I banged loudly on my strings, feeling the low thud against the soles of my feet with each strum. I couldn't believe the volume just three people could make. Gino seemed wired but in control. I was afraid to feel too confident.

When we reached the end of the song, Orlando, Vinnie, and Adam hooted loudly, accompanied by a slight interruption of crowd applause. Vinnie reached into her huge orange purse and pulled out a bouquet of plastic flowers. She split the bouquet in two and tossed one bunch toward me, the other toward Margo. My bunch bounced off the mic stand and ricocheted back into the crowd. Adam ran over and retrieved it, setting it carefully by my feet. Margo's flowers flew over her head and landed behind her amp. Vinnie clapped and hopped up and down excitedly.

"Thanks for coming out," Margo said into the mic. "We're Broad Street. The next song was written by my father, Mickey Dolenz."

She turned and nodded, Gino clicked off the intro, and we started "She." Once again, Gino was playing an entirely different part than he had at practice, but it was essentially the right groove, so we could fake our way through it. Ten more songs, I thought, then tried to keep that out of my mind. I needed to take this one song at a time.

I looked at the set list. Most of the songs we were playing were familiar, until the end. We had added a new song last practice, which I now realized was a horrible idea. I tried to get Margo's attention to tell her we should cut the song, but Gino kept plowing through the set.

"Hey," I leaned over Gino's drums. He stared back at me, his eyes manic. "Maybe we should skip this song."

Margo had turned to see what was happening. Gino stripped off his sweaty T-shirt to unveil a pale, hair-free chest.

"Fuck that," Gino said. "Ready babes?"

The song was supposed to be slow, driving, and angry. Gino chose instead a jumpy pace with all high-end percussion that transformed the song from turgid to poppy bubblegum. I tried to match my notes with his new creation, but it wasn't working. Margo struggled, too, and after a few minutes she stopped playing and waved her arms in the air. She leaned into her mic.

"Excuse us, folks, but our drummer has decided to write a new song for us. Unfortunately, he's neglected to share this little creation with us before now." She looked over her shoulder sideways. "Gino, sweetie, why don't you try playing the song the right way?"

From the corner of my eye, I saw Gino rise. I turned to see the pint glass of beer in his hand.

"Why don't you kiss my ass?" he screamed, then launched the contents of the glass toward Margo.

She jumped back, but not enough to avoid impact. Beer splashed in her face, soaked her hair, her dress, her guitar. She stood shocked, holding her arms in the air like she was being held up. Gino stood still, too. The whole room waited, holding its collective breath.

"Holy shit!" Tami said, laughing.

The crowd exploded with laughter. Even Orlando and Vinnie started to laugh. Adam laughed. It was infectious. Before I could stop it, a grin pushed its way onto my lips. The only one in the room not smiling was Margo. She glared at me and I tried to stop laughing but couldn't help myself. Her mascara was running down under her eyes. Her lipstick was smeared in the corners. She looked like a melting clown.

"Whoops," Gino said, which made the room roar even louder.

"You, my friend," Margo pointed a dripping finger, "are a dead man."

She turned to the mic.

"Thank you, thank you," she bowed.

The room flashed brightly for a second and I realized someone had taken a picture.

"I'm glad everyone enjoyed our little Three Stooges routine," Margo continued. "It's taken a while to perfect, but I think we're getting it down. The only problem is, like that Daffy Duck cartoon, we can only do the trick once," she said, pulling off her guitar and wiping her hands on her dress. "Thanks for coming out. We're Broad Street. If anyone knows of a good drummer, give us a call."

The audience laughed again.

Gino nonchalantly unscrewed his cymbals and started packing up his drums. I pulled my bass off and rested it against my amp, then walked over to Margo. She was placing her guitar in its soft case with her back to the audience.

"Are you all right?" I whispered.

She turned and glared at me.

"Oh, I'm great, thanks," she said. "And that little prick is done."

We both turned and looked at Gino, who ignored us.

"Did you hear me back there?" Margo said.

Gino kept packing his drums, stuffing his cymbals into a black soft case.

"You're done," Margo repeated.

Gino looked up slowly and smiled.

"That's the best news I've had all day," he said.

My fingers itched to smash Margo's guitar over his head. We were three weeks away from playing with The Venturas, and it appeared we were once again drummerless.

Gino packed up his stuff and headed over to the Pussy Willows, who greeted him with smiles and slaps on the back. Margo and I finished packing up, then climbed down from the stage. Vinnie and Orlando were waiting for us.

"Are you okay, Honey?" Vinnie asked.

"I'm going home."

The beer had started to dry. Her hair stuck to the side of her face, her dress was stiff.

"Oh, poor baby," Vinnie said. "Orlando, help her with her stuff."

"Need help?" Adam asked.

Margo smiled, "Sure, grab a handful."

They left me alone in the room, until Charlie walked up to me holding two beers.

"I thought you could use this," he said, handing one to me.

"Thanks. Know of any good drummers?"

"That bad, huh?"

"Yeah."

"You'll be okay." He touched me softly on the arm before walking to the stage.

But it wasn't okay. How would we find—and rehearse—a drummer in three weeks? Gino was insane and erratic, but at least he knew our songs. As My Pet Rhino was setting up to play, I noticed Laura, the reporter from the City Paper, and a photographer talking to The Pussy Willow group. Gino still had his arm around Caroline, but it looked more like support than intimacy. Tami was leaning close to Laura, who was jotting furiously in her small notebook. Then, Gino leaned in and said something that made Laura's eyebrows rise. She took more notes, then looked up and seemed to ask a question. I stood and watched helplessly. Where was Margo? I needed help with damage control. Shit. Before I could muster the courage to intervene, Laura walked away. Tami looked over at me, smiling triumphantly.

CHAPTER

Rachel popped her head into my office Monday morning.

"Jean's replacement is here," she said.

I quickly closed the solitaire game on my computer and spun my chair around.

"What's the call?" I asked.

"Too soon to tell. Could be okay. Not sure yet." She looked over her shoulder. "I have to get back. We'll assess at lunch. Good luck."

"Yeah, you too."

I had no work to fake. I hadn't had a proofreading job since last week, and that was only one small ad. My files were cleaned and organized. I had already checked my email. I scanned my tiny office for chores, but everything was tidy and in order. The stylebook. I could reread our thick stylebook that detailed in painful tedium how our company punctuates and attributes registration marks and colors its logo. I practically knew this manual inside and out, but I had to do something.

I pulled the heavy guide off the bookshelf that hung on the wall over my desk. It landed in front of me with a soft thud. I randomly opened to the annotations section and began to feign interest in abbreviations and accreditations. I heard an unfamiliar female voice down the hall chatting with Dawn, the executive editor. The unfamiliar voice moved closer, introducing herself to my neighbor, an associate editor. I debated my pose, wanting to make a good first impression. I propped the book on my lap and turned my chair so she could clearly see what I was reading. I heard soft footsteps approaching my door.

"Good morning," the woman said, smiling.

She was a youngish Asian woman with a business-smart haircut and simple pine green suit.

"I'm Nancy Lee," she said in a soft voice. "I'll be filling in for Jean Zimmerman."

"Hi. I'm Kit Greene. I'm a proofreader."

"Yes, I know. I've heard good things about you."

This surprised me, but I tried to keep my eyebrows from rising. She probably said this to everyone.

"If you wouldn't mind," she continued, "I'm trying to get together with everyone to review procedure. Would you be available at 3:00?"

"Sure."

"Great. I look forward to getting to know you."

She smiled and walked to the next office, repeating her routine. Her voice had a comforting maternal quality, but I'd been burned before. It was the passive-aggressive ones you had to watch out for.

At 12:30, I met Rachel in the lunchroom. Two other editors were there, Dawn and Sandy, as well as Joe, one of our graphic designers.

"What do you think?" Rachel asked me as I pulled my usual salad from its bag.

"She seems nice," I answered, "but I'm not sure yet."

"I know," Sandy said. Sandy was in her mid-forties, stocky, with dyed bright orange hair. She was in the process of finishing a chicken cheesesteak. "I had my meeting with her this morning and she was so sweet, asking me questions about my kids and husband. I don't think Jean even knew I had children."

Neither did I.

"I had my meeting this morning, too," Dawn said, her cheeks full of turkey sandwich. "I get a good vibe from her."

"Me too," Rachel said, unveiling her salad. "But we'll see."

I noticed Joe didn't even look up from his sandwich as he read the City Paper. He was cute in a little boy sort of way. I could only imagine what he thought of us catty women.

"Hey Kit," he said. "Isn't this you?"

He flipped around the newspaper to reveal a small black and white photo. I stood up and moved closer to examine it.

"Oh my god," I said.

In the photo, Margo stood dripping, her arms raised. Gino and I were gaping at her, mouths open, Gino with weapon in hand.

"May I see this?" I asked. Joe handed me the paper.

BROAD STREET TAKES A BATH

By Laura Cook

Could there be trouble in Broad Street paradise? Last Saturday night, the new gal band, opening for veteran grrrrl rockers The Pussy Willows, had a scuffle that resulted in the launching of a pint of beer onto the lead singer, Margo Bevilacqua.

"I was sick of hearing her sh*t," says drummer Gino Pistone. "She thinks she can push everyone around, but she's wrong."

Does this spell the demise of the young band?

"They can kiss my ass goodbye," Gino says. "Let them try and find another drummer who will put up with their sh*t."

Bayonne, lead singer and founder of The Pussy Willows, agrees.

"It's not easy to find good drummers in this town," she reports. "We tried a ton of people out and no one clicked. Luckily, Lodi was smart enough to come back where she belongs."

Ironically, Lodi was in Broad Street briefly before leaving to rejoin The Pussy Willows.

In related news, The Venturas will be heading our way next week. Broad Street and The Pussy Willows are scheduled to open for them. Will they kiss and make up? Stay tuned.

Meanwhile, DJ Scrappy Doo reports he'll be spinning Friday night at the new club on Columbus Boulevard...

I handed the paper back to Joe.

"What's that about?" Rachel asked.

"Oh nothing. Just the end of my band."

At 3:00, I went into Nancy's office. The room was lit with warm floor and table lamps, rather than the cold fluorescent tubes that striped the ceiling. The late afternoon sun spilled through the window behind Nancy. I knocked on the open door.

"Oh, Kit, hi," Nancy greeted me. "Come on in."

I walked over and sat in a chair across from her desk. The height had been adjusted so that I was at eye level with Nancy, rather than the child-height established by Jean.

"So, I know things have been a little strange around here," she began. "The company sent me down from New York to help us get this office back on track. I have a lot of learning to do, and I want you to know that I'm open to suggestions as we move along here."

Suggestions? That was a first.

"I'd like you to tell me about your normal procedure for proofreading, and then maybe we can discuss ideas for improving that procedure. But first, I'm just curious. Is it true you're in a band?"

This caught me off guard. How would she know this? Maybe she saw the article. Great. She thought I was an alcoholic musician slacker.

"I am, but it never interferes with my work schedule."

"Oh, I'm not worried about that," she said. "I was just curious. I used to play a little guitar myself in college." I could not picture this sophisticated professional jamming. "But, that was a million years ago. What do you play?"

"Bass. I do some singing, too."

"Really? That's great. I'd love to come see you some time."

If this was a snow job, the woman was good. She was the first grown-up to give me what felt like genuine praise.

We spent the rest of our meeting reviewing work logistics and for the first time I saw myself in a career, not just a paycheck, with an integral role in the company. When I got back to my desk, there was a message from Margo on my voicemail.

"Did you see it?" she asked when I called her at work.

"Yeah."

"He is so fucking out of this band."

"Crap. What are we going to do about this show coming up?"

"I don't know. Hold on, I'm getting another call."

She clicked me into Muzak purgatory. After a minute, I hung up, feeling guilty about spending too much time on a personal call. She would call me back.

There was a soft knock at my door, then Rachel popped her head in.

"So? What do you think?"

"I think she's great, which scares me."

"Yeah, me too. We'll keep our guard up. I also came to deliver these." She handed me a pile of pink folders. "Back to the grind," she said, then closed the door behind her.

As I flipped through the folders to organize them by deadline, my phone rang.

"That was Gino," Margo said. "He called to apologize. The guy was literally crying."

"You're kidding."

"Nope. He said he didn't remember a thing. He doesn't remember throwing the beer. He doesn't remember talking to the reporter. Nothing."

"That doesn't change the fact that he did those things. Everyone will think we're chumps if we take him back."

"Well, I was thinking. We need him for this show anyway. Let's let him play it, then we'll dump him afterwards. He'll definitely be on his best behavior this time."

"I don't know. That seems kind of cruel."

"Crueler than throwing a beer on me and humiliating us in print?"

"True."

"Believe me, this is for the best. It will buy us more time to find another drummer."

This did not feel right. I could see her point, but to string along an obviously troubled guy just didn't seem like the best answer. But we did need a drummer for the show. What choice did we have?

"How'd you leave it with Gino?"

"I said I'd talk to you and get back to him. What do you think?"

"I guess so. Maybe he'll redeem himself."

"Please," Margo snorted. "This is Gino we're talking about."

When I got home that night, I pushed open the door to familiar silence. Ben hadn't called since our sleazy tryst, and every time the phone rang my heart jumped in unrewarded anticipation. I tossed my bag on the couch, kicked off my shoes and went upstairs to strip off my workday clothes and climb into baggy gray sweats. Being single could be so liberating, I told myself. I nuked a Lean Cuisine and sat down on the couch to watch *American Justice*. The phone rang.

"Hello?"

"Hi, is this Broad Street?" a young female voice asked.

"One of the Broads, yes."

"My name's Keri. I'm a drummer. I got your number from your friend Noelle. I saw your article in the paper today and I just wondered if you guys really needed a drummer. I saw you at Clark Park and thought you totally rocked."

"Um, well, we're kind of undecided right now, but it's a possibility."

"I couldn't believe that jerk threw a beer on you."

"Actually, I'm the bass player. The one looking stupid and helpless."

She laughed. "Hey, what could you do? Throw yourself in front of her? Anyway, the guy sounds like a jerk. But, whatever you want to do is fine. I've been playing since second grade. I love drums and I think your band is great. If you're interested, I can give you my number."

I promised I would let her know if we were interested. I hung up the phone, then picked it up again and dialed in my code.

"You have four messages," the computer told me in broken digital English.

I'd never had this many messages. Panicked, I started playing them.

"Hey, this is Joanne. I'm a local drummer and I saw the article in today's paper. I got your number from the City Paper. I'd like to try out if you're looking for someone . . ."

"Hi. This is Tom. I saw the write-up in the paper today and wondered if you really were looking for a drummer..."

"Kit, hey it's me," Margo said. "Call me. This whole article is nuts."

The last call was Ben.

"Hey, Kit," he said. "I saw the article today. That's some crazy shit. Sorry I missed it. Give me a call if you feel like it."

I called Margo first.

"You'll never guess what happened today," Margo started.

"You got a bunch of calls from drummers."

"How'd you know?"

"I got a ton of calls, too. Friend of friends kinda thing. It's crazy!"

"I know," I said, "but what the hell. I say let's return some calls and set up some tryouts."

"Works for me."

After hanging up the phone, I thought about the many phone calls I would have to make. A call to Ben would be exhausting. Interviewing strangers would be exhausting. Debating the qualification of these drummers later with Margo would be exhausting. I was too young to be this tired at 6:30 at night. I picked up the phone and called Charlie. He answered on the second ring.

"Nice article today," he said.

"I know, that was pretty weird. I guess any press is good press, right?"

"So they say. What's up?"

"I just wanted your opinion on something. Would you kick out a disturbed drummer if he threw a glass of beer on you?"

"It depends on the drummer. It's never happened to me, but it's happened plenty of times in bands. The Ramones don't event speak to each other."

"You didn't answer my question."

"Personally, I probably would. I spend too much time with my band to be treated like that. I'm lucky, though. My band is just a bunch of pretty normal guys."

"Would you play a gig with that drummer, then kick him out later?"

"This doesn't sound hypothetical."

"Is that Kit?" I heard a male voice in the background. A hand went over the phone and I couldn't make out the voices. The muffled conversation went back and forth a few times before Charlie came back to the phone.

"Ben's here," he said. "He'd like to say hi."

I'd anticipated this conversation since our last horrible encounter, but once he was on the line, I didn't know what to say.

"Hey, Kit."

Ben's voice was a husky whisper. My breath caught in my throat. I was pathetic.

"Looks like I missed quite a show the other night."

"Yeah. Looks that way."

"I'm really sorry. I was up at a show in New York that night."

"Hmm."

"I'd love to make it up to you. Have any time for a drink this week?"

I wanted to see Ben again, to have his calloused hands against my skin, his smoky tongue in my mouth. What the hell was wrong with me?

"Sorry, I can't."

What? Did I say that out loud?

"Oh," Ben said, sounding surprised. "Okay. Maybe some other time."

"Maybe."

"Great, well," he said. "I'll see you later then."

"Yeah, see you."

I hung up the phone, stunned. I knew I had done the right thing because it felt horrible. I sat down, lit a cigarette, and started calling potential drummers.

After two hours of listening to various stories of percussive potential, histories and histrionics, drumming and dysfunction, of dreams snuffed out and waiting to be rekindled, my gut kept moving back to Keri. She seemed down-to-earth, and I that sounded really good to me about now.

I called Margo and we discussed our options. She had come away from her calls with the same concerns I had. We decided to audition Keri and another girl, Tia, the next night.

Margo volunteered to tell Gino practice was canceled.

Margo and I arrived first at the studio at 7:00. Tia would try out at 7:30. We set up our equipment and waited nervously, chain smoking and chatting about unrelated issues. I didn't mention Ben. I didn't ask about Gino. Anxiety and excitement nibbled at me. I took long, deep breaths as I watched the clock tick closer to 7:30. Finally, there was a knock on the door.

"Come on in!" Margo called. The door opened.

Tia was thick and manly. She wore torn jeans with chunky combat boots and an old black T-shirt. Her arms were covered with tattoos and her black hair was buzzed short. Drumsticks protruded from her back pocket. She certainly looked the part.

We introduced ourselves.

"Hey," Tia grunted in a low voice. "Good to meet you guys."

She plunged her hands into her jeans pockets, rocked on her heels, and surveyed the room.

"I used to practice here with my old band. I see Frank's finally updated a few equipment dinosaurs in here."

Tia walked up to the drum riser and inspected the equipment, pulling a cigarette from her breast pocket and lighting it. Margo and I glanced at each other and raised our eyebrows, not sure what to make of her. Tia plunked herself onto the stool and pulled the drumsticks out of her back pocket. She tapped around the kit, scrunching up her face as she hit each drum. She stood up and lowered the stool, then sat back down and tapped again.

"Yep," she said. "Still sounds like crap."

"Who was your last band?" I asked.

"Ass Fault. We were kind of a thrash metal chick band. It was fun, but our guitar player had a bit of a drug problem. When she came back from rehab, Ass Fault was not one of her 12 steps."

"Oh," I said. "That's too bad."

"Yeah, well. What are you gonna do?"

"So you said you saw us at The Khyber, right?" Margo asked.

"Yeah, that was hysterical. It's too bad that drummer was pschyo. He really played his balls off."

Sure, with chemical assistance.

"But, I guess it's good for me," she continued. "What do you guys want to play?"

"We were thinking 'Priscilla' would be a good one to start with. It's pretty straight-forward," Margo suggested.

"Why don't you start and I'll jump in?" Tia said.

Margo counted off four in the mic and we kicked in. After a few notes, Tia started playing. She ticked off on the high-hat at first, then suddenly exploded into a roaring fill on toms. It was completely inappropriate. Margo stopped playing.

"That's good," she began. "But, it's not quite as metal. It's more garage-y. Toms are good, just maybe not as loud."

Tia looked a little pissed, but shrugged.

"Fine. Let's try it again," she said.

Margo counted again and we began. When Tia came in, she played exactly the same thing. I caught Margo's eyes and saw her lips twitch, fighting off a laugh. I quickly looked to the floor to avoid the same. Tia crashed on the cymbals and beat the drums as if they were trying to break into her house.

When we got to the end of the song, I still couldn't look at Margo for fear of breaking into a laugh.

"That was pretty good," she said. "Maybe we could try one that's a little mellower. Kit, what about 'Falling'?"

"Sure."

Margo again counted off four, and we kicked in. The song used the classic Nirvana formula—start off slow and quiet, then crescendo into a loud chorus, then back into a quiet verse. Tia's version was one big crescendo. I tried to sing along, but all I could do was shriek. The melody was completely lost under the volume.

"Okay," Margo said at the end of the song. "Maybe we should try rocking out a little. Let's try 'Take That.' That's nice and loud."

"Sure," Tia said, wriggling in her seat excitedly.

She seemed to possess no awareness of her one-note act. Margo shrugged her shoulders, smiled, and counted off four. Tia's drumming almost worked in this song, but even though her style was better, her time was terrible.

When we finally reached the end, Margo looked at the clock. It was almost 8:00, time for Keri's tryout.

"Cool, very cool," Margo said. "We have a few more people to try out, but we'll give you a call when we make a decision."

Tia looked flushed and excited.

"Excellent," she said, pushing her drumsticks back in her pocket. "That was a lot of fun. I'd definitely love to play with you guys."

"Great," Margo said. "We'll let you know."

As Tia pulled the door shut behind her, we waited to hear her footsteps pad down the steps before exploding into laughter.

"What the hell was that?" Margo asked between breaths.

"Oh my god," I sputtered. "I love what you said before 'Take That.' She had no idea."

"Guess which Ass won't be playing with Broad Street?"

There was a light tap on the door.

"Come on in!" I said.

I watched the door creak open to unveil an attractive wisp of girl. She was rail thin and short, the exact opposite of the behemoth who had preceded her. She wore a pink oxford shirt tucked into khaki chinos. Her dirty blond hair was short and professional; black penny loafers topped off the outfit.

"Hi!" she said, bursting into a grin. "I'm Keri. Am I too early?"

"No," I said. "Come on in. I'm Kit, we spoke on the phone."

"Yeah, sure, hi," she said, walking over and shaking my hand. "And you must be Margo."

She walked over and shook Margo's hand.

"I'm so glad you guys let me try out. I told Kit on the phone that I saw you at Clark Park and thought you totally rocked. When I read that article, I couldn't believe that guy was such a jerk to you."

Margo smiled.

"Well," she said. "That's why you're here. Our little drummer Gino has a few issues to deal with. That incident was just the proverbial icing on the cake."

"That's too bad," Keri said,

"Enough about that asshole," Margo said. "You can get set up if you want."

Keri walked up to the drums and sat down. The stool was so low for her tiny body. She looked like a small child engulfed in metal and calf skin.

"Geez," she said, standing up and spinning the stool top to make it taller. "What ape was in here last?"

Margo and I looked at each other and smiled. When Keri sat back down, she was now visible, but still looked diminished by the drums. How could this tiny girl handle this big instrument?

"What do you want to try first?" she asked.

"How about 'Priscilla'?" Margo said again. "It's pretty straightforward."

Keri unzipped a neat pack of sticks.

"What kind of sound are you looking for on this one?" she asked.

Margo and I glanced at each other, impressed.

"It has kind of a garage-y feel to it," Margo said. "Not too fast, king of dirgy."

"Okay," Keri said, selecting a set of sticks from the pack. "Let's try these."

Keri tapped on the toms and nodded to Margo. Margo counted off four and we started the song again. But, this time, the drummer got it. Really got it. From the first chord, Keri fit like a warm glove. She accompanied instrumental breaks with rolling toms that propelled the song forward. When the verse started, she pulled back with lighter cymbal splashes that lifted the vocals weightlessly above the guitars. Chills ran up my arms when we kicked into the chorus. When we went back into the verse, she consistently returned to light cymbal splashes. Where Gino hit hard throughout, Keri approached the song more stylistically, tastefully. It was the best I'd ever heard this song, and it was the first time she was playing it.

"That's great!" Margo said.

"Really? I feel like I'm a little rusty. I haven't played for a while."

"Well, you're the best drummer I've heard," Margo said. "That was great. Kit, what do you think about trying 'Falling'?"

"Sounds good."

We spent the rest of the hour running through songs on the set, from hard rockers like "Take That," to softer songs like Wanda Jackson's "Right or Wrong," where Margo and I harmonized throughout. Keri wrapped drum choices perfectly around every note. Her short hair bobbed enthusiastically as she played—her mouth puckered in concentration. For the first time, I didn't have to fight to lead the way like I did with Linda, or find my way through the murky shadows of Gino's inconsistency. Keri and I wove our rhythms together seamlessly. Every song we played sounded tighter and more professional.

At 9:00, Frank walked in to put a halt to our fun, collect his money, and rush us out the door to let the next band in. We carried our stuff outside the studio and stood in a slight drizzle.

"That was great Keri," I said. "I guess we'll let you know."

"Let you know, what?" Margo asked. "We won't get better than this. You've got the gig if you want it."

Keri dropped her stick bag and held her hand out to shake our hands.

"Really? Thank you. I love your stuff. Do you have any gigs lined up?"

"We just have to survive one more show with the psycho," Margo said.

We filled Keri in on the show and the problem with Gino, then loaded up our cars. I drove home feeling better than I had for weeks.

CHAPTER

The week flew by uneventfully. In the few short days Nancy had been there, morale had already improved, the work flowed smoothly, and the coffee-break bitching was at a new low. I focused on the pink folders and tried not to think about the show coming up Saturday night, but when it arrived, I was terrified.

I loaded my bass and amp into my car and drove down to The Trocadero at 7:00. The club was in the heart of busy Chinatown, so parking was difficult. I pulled up to an illegal spot in front of the club. Adam was waiting out front.

He came running over to my car when he saw me. Even though the streets were mostly empty, I was embarrassed. There was nothing cool about this guy. His frizzed hair was mashed under a ski hat and his gold-rimmed glasses glinted against the flush of his pink skin. He wore brown corduroys and a tan shirt that looked like his mother had picked them out for his first day of school.

"Hey Kit," he said when I stepped out of the car. "I just talked to the manager and he said you could load your stuff in through the back. Just drive around the corner and there's an alley that runs behind the club."

Great. This dork was representing us.

"Thanks, Adam," I said, trying not to sound annoyed. It was free labor, after all.

"I'll meet you back there to help," he said, starting to walk down the street.

"Just get in the car," I grunted, and climbed back into the car.

"I can't believe you guys are playing with The Venturas," he babbled. "They're like the ultimate riot grrrls, but they can really play and they have, like, really good songs."

"Uh huh," I said.

"I heard the lead singer Paula is like best friends with Bikini Kill. They're total revolutionaries, if you believe some people. I don't know, I prefer more melodic stuff myself, not that they're bad or anything but I think Team Dresch is doing way more interesting things in the whole DIY punk thing."

"Can you stop talking now?" I asked.

"Oh, sorry."

I drove around the building and maneuvered my small car into a narrow gravel street, barely missing the large dumpsters that lined the walls. We parked behind a ramp that led into the building. Two burly guys loaded equipment from a large black truck splashed with a red "Twisted Tours" logo. The Venturas' tour van. I took a deep breath and grabbed my bass out of the back seat. Adam got my amp.

I had seen many bands play this club, and it always seemed slightly touched by magic. The crowd of people, the multi-colored lights painting plumes of smoke into a tapestry of carcinogens, the blanket of noise that unified us. The Trocadero was rock and roll.

The room I stepped into had no magic. I grimaced at the smell of stale beer and B.O. Dreary fluorescent lighting showed a dull plank of a stage, milk crates stuffed with cables piled behind and under it. Big, clunky monitors stood scattered against the wall.

The burly guys dumped their equipment into this chaos and began surveying the room. Roadies, I guessed. Adam was also taking in the scene, his stunned face panning from side to side. The Venturas' roadies could definitely kick our roadie's ass.

"I guess we'll just leave our stuff here," I said, putting my bass under the stage.

"You can't put that there!" one of the burly guys scolded.

"Oh, sorry," I said. "Where should I put it?"

"Who are you with?" the other one asked.

"Broad Street."

He smiled.

"Cute. Like the street."

"Yeah, like the street," I said, then waited for instructions.

"Take your stuff down that hall there," he said. He pointed to an open door at the other end of the room. "There's a room to your right that's for the opening bands."

"Thanks."

Adam and I walked toward the door and around the corner. We found the room, which was not much larger than a closet. It was empty, except for two folding chairs, and had a small mirror on the wall in one corner.

"Our first greenroom," I said, dropping my bass against the wall. "This is an exciting moment for Broad Street."

"This is great, Kit," Adam said, his face glowing redder. "Thanks so much for letting me come backstage with you."

"No problem. Let's go move the car."

When I walked back out, a black van with cheesy orange flames was parked behind me. The flames spelled the owner's identity—The Pussy Willows.

"Great," I muttered.

The first to emerge from the back was Tami. She wore black jeans and a leather jacket. Her hair was again tied tight into a ponytail that pulled her ashen face taut. I got a headache just looking at it. She turned and pulled out a guitar and amp. Caroline followed next. She took out her bass and amp, which seemed to weigh down her tiny frame. Linda was the last to hop out of the back with a handful of equipment.

"Hey, Kit!" Tami said, her yellow twisted teeth exposing a wide grin.

"Hi Tami," I answered, forcing a smile.

She walked next to my car, dropped her equipment, and thrust her hand out. I shook it reluctantly.

"You probably need us to move, huh?" she asked. Before I could answer, she said, "Well, we'll just be a minute."

She turned to Adam.

"Hey, sweet cheeks. Alan, right?"

"Adam."

"Adam, of course. I don't suppose you'd like to help out three damsels in distress?"

He looked at me helplessly.

"I, uh, I guess not," he stammered.

"Great, you're a doll. Grab anything you want out of the van."

Who was she to steal our roadie? Adam was rescued by the crunch of Margo's car pulling up behind the van. Adam and I both walked over to greet her.

"Hi!" she said, hopping out of the car. She wore form-fitting black with her dark hair twisted into a high bun.

"Thank god you're here," I said. "I couldn't take another minute of The Tami Show without you."

"God, spare me. Hi, Adam."

Adam's face darkened to a deep red.

"Hi Margo," he smiled. "Can I help?"

"Sure! Grab anything you want, sweetie. Well, not anything."

His flesh morphed close to purple.

We carried all of Margo's stuff in and I led her to our greenroom. In that short time, The Pussy Willows had already dominated most of the space.

"Oh!" Tami said. "I didn't realize you guys were in here, too. Here, let me move some of our stuff."

She picked up one guitar and moved it approximately six inches.

"Thanks," Margo said, glancing back at me over her shoulder with a smile.

We squashed our equipment into a corner. A cooler also had appeared.

"Can we bring beer in here?" I asked, pointing to the cooler.

"Oh, that's courtesy of the house," Tami said. "Drink up."

I looked at my watch. Almost 8:00. We would be on at 9:00. I popped open three beers and distributed them.

"Where's Gino?" I asked.

"I don't know. He called me around 6:30 and said he was on his way."

Caroline lifted her head up.

"He had to stop by a drum shop and pick up some sticks," she said in her mousy whisper. "He should be here soon."

On cue, Gino walked around the corner.

"Hey," he greeted the room.

I tried to assess his state of mind. He looked sober. His hair was neatly combed back in a pseudo ducktail. He wore a black striped bowling shirt with black jeans. He looked pretty good.

"Hi, Gino," I said.

He put down a bag of sticks and a cymbal bag, walked over to me, and embraced me. I stiffened in surprise.

"Kit," he said softly. "Thank you for giving me a second chance. I am so sorry for the way I acted at our last show."

I glanced at Margo over his shoulder, who looked equally surprised.

"It's okay," I said. "We all make mistakes."

We had to get through this show, I told myself. He did this to himself, I rationalized. But, really, I knew I was just being a shit. He let go of me and walked over to Margo, giving her a hug, too. Then he turned to Caroline.

"Hi sweetie," he nodded to her. She smiled.

He greeted the rest of the room.

"Want a beer, Gino?" Tami asked.

My jaw clenched.

"No, thanks," he said. "I have to get the rest of my stuff. I'll be right back."

Margo and I looked at each other, confused. Who was this guy?

We killed the remaining time parking our cars behind the building, tuning our instruments, trying to ignore The Pussy Willows. I could hear the low rumble of people arriving out front. The heavy red curtain had been pulled shut to hide the stage, and more burly men were putting the final touches on stacking monitors and speakers, connecting microphones and cables, twisting lights into position. Gino was on stage with Linda setting up the drum kit they would share. My palms sweated. A heavy pit rested in my throat that I could not swallow. I had another beer, but it wasn't doing any good. I stood behind the stage, taking it all in, when The Venturas arrived.

I saw the drummer first. She was masculine and stocky, with stringy black hair that hung in her face. She loped up the ramp with sticks in hand, walked directly to a roadie, and started talking. The other two followed. The lead singer was a trashy-attractive blond with thick black eyeliner that contrasted little-girl ponytails. The bass player was a plain but attractive brunette who wore jeans and a black T-shirt. A small diamond glinted from her nose. They walked over to the drummer and the roadie to form a huddle.

I caught myself staring and quickly turned to face the stage, where Linda and Gino were putting the final touches on the kit. I couldn't believe I was less than twenty feet from one of my favorite bands of all time. I had practiced bass lines to their albums, playing their songs over and over in the hope that, through osmosis, I could write a song half as good as one of theirs. Their music was catchy and poetic and brilliant. And they were close enough to spit on.

"Nervous?" Margo asked behind me.

"Completely."

We walked over to the steps that led to the stage; my knees buckled slightly as I climbed up. I walked over to my amp and began setting up. I looked down at The Venturas' huddle, hoping to make eye contact so we could be introduced, but they ignored us. As I was tuning my bass one last time, I saw Tami emerge from the back room and walk over to The Venturas.

"Hey girls!" she called to the group. They turned and smiled.

"Hey, Tami!" Paula, the lead singer said. "What's up?"

They embraced like old friends. I looked over at Margo, who seemed to be about a mile away on this big stage. She rolled her eyes.

Gino was diligently tuning his drums, thumping lightly on the bass drum to check his pedal, lining sticks of various weights neatly on the bass drum. Adam stood behind the stage, smiling up at us like a lost puppy. I hoped The Venturas wouldn't notice him.

I looked down at the crevice beside my side of the stage that housed the sound guy. He was hunched over a mammoth soundboard dotted and sliced with knobs and sliders and needles that defined the right amount of volume in each channel. My heart pumped furiously as I awaited the unveiling of the white noise on the other side of the curtain.

"Ready?" he asked, looking up at me from his chair.

"You guys ready?" I asked Margo and Gino.

Margo nodded.

"Let's do it," Gino said defiantly.

The sound guy held a mike to his mouth.

"Ladies and gentlemen," his voice boomed through the stacks of speakers behind us. "Thanks for coming out to The Trocadero tonight to see the amazing Venturas, all the way from Los Angeles."

The crowd cheered and clapped.

"We're lucky to have a few of our local gals here to warm us up. First up tonight, please put your hands together for Broad Street."

There were just a few claps now, accompanied by a few low "boos." The curtain split, crackling as it slowly revealed the crowded room. The floor was packed with people, mostly kids and the over-21 balcony was filled to capacity. All of the blood rushed from my head and my fingertips. I was sure I would pass out.

It will be over before you know it, I repeated to myself. Just take it one song at a time. Stay calm. One song at a time. One song at a time.

I still couldn't breathe.

Margo stepped to the microphone.

"Thanks for coming out tonight!" she called. "We're Broad Street, and we're here to rock your world."

The audience stared at her blankly.

She turned and nodded to Gino, who started with four solid clicks. We launched into "Priscilla." The toms rumbled furiously as I thudded on the low E string. Margo strummed along, swinging her hips in time with the rhythm. She smiled at me and I started to feel the tips of my fingers again. She sang the verse.

Posing in your platforms and your tattooed smile

Working tavern hours just to say you're wild

You're so different, just like everyone else

You're a cliché…

Gino played along flawlessly, filling instrumental breaks consistently and driving the vocals without stepping on them. When I leaned into the microphone to sing background vocals, my voice echoed in the wall of speakers behind me louder than I had ever heard it. I couldn't believe that just three people could fill a room this size with such volume. Margo's one guitar sounded like five. The stage rumbled beneath my feet with each pluck of my bass string and Gino's drums were perfectly miked so each piece was amplified separately. The energy of the volume set motion to my body and I began to move to the music.

When we got to the end of the song, Margo lifted her guitar high, strumming the strings wildly. Gino rolled on the toms until we all splashed down into a big rock finish. The crowd applauded and a smattering of whistles came from various points in the room. The young female faces closest to the stage seemed to like it the most. They looked about fourteen and all seemed to be wearing the same slutty outfits. They turned and giggled and clapped their red-tipped hands together, pausing between applause to fix their hair.

The second song was just as energetic, and Gino continued to play solidly. I crept behind his rhythm cautiously, wary that he would relapse at any moment, but he continued to lead the way with confidence. Most of the floor crowd bobbed their heads to the music; the balcony crowd paid less attention, distracted by the back bar.

The rest of the set flowed smoothly. Gino grinned as he slammed through the songs better than he ever had before. The young girls seemed entranced by Margo's confidence as she sold each line of the songs like a seasoned Broadway performer. My head swam with the buzz of appreciation. The more the crowd cheered, the braver I became, even daring a few risky runs that I had never attempted before. Each song grew bigger and tighter, and I knew Margo and Gino were high on the audience, too.

By the time we reached our last song, energy was bursting from my pores. I felt like I could play all night. We played "Take That" with fresh fury. After three short minutes, we crescendoed to the end, and once again cymbal-splashed in a big finish. Margo stepped to the microphone.

"Thanks again for coming out! We're Broad Street! Stick around for The Pussy Willows and the fabulous Venturas!"

The high-pitched crowd shrieked—maybe for The Venturas, maybe for us—but I swallowed the adoration like cheap whiskey. The thick red curtain drew closed, slowly muffling the applause.

As we packed up our equipment, Tami was the first to jump to the stage.

"Great job, guys!" she said, slapping Gino hard on the back. "You're gonna be a tough act to follow!"

Can you patronize us a little more? But, I smiled graciously and went back to wrapping up my cords. Adam carried Margo's amp to the greenroom, then came jogging back to help me. I let him carry the heavy stuff, then grabbed my small equipment case and walked over to Gino.

"Great job," I said, genuinely. "That was probably the best you've ever played."

He blushed and looked down at his kit. "Thanks," he said. "You guys sounded good, too."

He looked so helpless and sorry and sad. How could we kick this guy out? Maybe if we eliminated the liquor, we could stay together. Be really good.

Margo and Adam were in the back room. Margo had opened a beer and lit a cigarette; Adam was neatly making a pile of our equipment.

"That was sweet," she said. "Best show yet. I think the crowd really dug us."

"I couldn't believe Gino," I said. "I've never heard him sound better."

Margo stared hard at me.

"Don't even think about it. Tonight was a fluke."

I sighed and opened a beer. Gino walked into the room.

"Hey, Gino!" Margo said over-enthusiastically. "Great job tonight."

"Thanks," he smiled. "You too. You guys sounded great."

The four of us stood in awkward silence. From the main room, we heard the dull clump of a bass drum, then the ascending scales of a guitar being checked for tuning.

"I'm gonna go check out these guys," I said.

"Sounds good," Margo said.

We walked out to the large area behind the stage and found some abandoned speakers to use as seats. The curtain split apart again, but from behind the stage we couldn't see the audience on the floor, only in the balcony, and they were just shadowy figures. Linda pumped her foot in a steady rhythm on her bass drum. Caroline stood like a statue in the corner. They both awaited their commands.

Tami stepped up to the mic.

"How you guys doing tonight?" she yelled.

The crowd responded with a lame cheer.

"We're The Pussy Willows. This first one's off of our last CD, Pussylicious."

She turned and nodded to Linda, who stamped out a four-beat intro on the bass drum. Tami stood up at the mic and sang the first line a cappella—Wait for me baby, cause I just can't stop. She sang the line again and Caroline joined her in harmony—Wait for me baby, cause I just can't stop. They sang the line a third time, and Linda added a third harmony. To my dismay, it sounded really good. After the third line, Linda clicked off four and they exploded into a classic punk structure of simple lyrics, straightforward 4/4 time, and a catchy hook. I hated them.

"Want to go upstairs?" Margo asked.

"Read my mind," I answered.

We slipped through a curtain that divided the back room and the audience. I squeezed past the shrieking teens along a wall that led to a large lobby, where a second set of stairs rose to the over-21 crowd in the balcony. We pushed our way to the bar, where The Pussy Willows were dampened by white noise. On the way to get a drink, a group of three guys blocked our way.

"Hey, you gals were great tonight," the shortest guy said.

"Thanks," Margo said. She was beaming.

"What's your name?" the tall one asked.

"I'm Margo, this is Kit."

"Well, I'm Luddy," the tall one said. He pointed to the shortest one. "This is Jimmy, and this is Slip."

They all looked similar and I wondered if they called each other to plan their outfits. Their cheap cologne overpowered even the thick smoke in the bar area, and gold chains dangled from each of their tan necks.

"Can we buy you ladies a drink?" Slip asked.

"You certainly may," Margo answered. She was a hopeless flirt. "I would love a Cosmopolitan."

"Sounds good," I said, admiring Margo for choosing an expensive drink.

"Be right back," Slip said.

"So, how long you girls been playing?" Jimmy asked.

"Not long," Margo answered, scanning the crowd over Jimmy's shoulder. "Maybe six months."

"Well, you have to let us know next time you play," Luddy said.

"Sure," she said. "Give us your addresses. We'll send out an announcement."

"Better yet," Luddy said, attempting to sound suave. "I can give you my phone number."

Margo looked at him and smiled, but her thoughts were written clearly in her eyes—Dream on, white boy.

"That would be great," she said.

Slip returned with our Cosmopolitans and we suffered through a few more minutes of banal conversation before we were pleasantly interrupted.

"Hi girls!"

Keri came up behind us and slipped into our circle.

"You guys sounded so good tonight," Keri said. "Gino was really on."

"It was a fluke. You have nothing to worry about," Margo said.

"Well, thanks," she said. "Hey, would you guys have a minute to meet someone?"

"Sure," we both agreed quickly.

Margo turned to the boys.

"Thanks for the drinks, guys," she smiled. "Hope to see you next show."

They smiled and grumbled, visibly pissed that two twelve dollar drinks bought them nothing but a tease. We followed Keri through the crowd until we reached a small group of women in a corner.

"You remember Noelle, right, Kit?" Keri said, pulling me through the crowd into her circle of three women.

"Hi!" I said, giving Noelle a hug. "I forgot Keri knew you. How are you?"

"I'm great, thanks," she said.

"And this is my partner, Leah." Keri said.

Partner? Leah was attractive with dark skin and a round face that seemed Native American. Her shiny black hair was cut shaggy short and hip chunky black glasses framed her black eyes. She was petite, like Keri, and my first thought was that these women were too feminine to be lesbians. I was a theoretical liberal, which is all you could be growing up in a white Republican suburb. Even unflappable Margo seemed momentarily taken aback.

"It's great to meet you, Leah," I said, maybe with too much enthusiasm.

Margo looked at Keri, then at Leah, and smiled.

"It's great meeting you. You've got a very talented girlfriend, here."

"I know," Leah said proudly.

We chatted about the stats of our lives—where we worked, lived, grew up—while The Pussy Willows continued lighting up the kids below us. Keri shared the same white suburban background Margo and I had, and worked in an office as a human resources associate. Noelle grew up in Manhattan, where her single mother was the vice president of Deutsche Bank. Leah was from Chicago and had her MBA from Northwestern. Collectively, we were far more likely to organize a political fundraiser than to debate the merits of the current state of music, but we did. We all agreed it pretty much sucked.

From a distance, we heard Tami thanking the crowd and the band winding up with a splashy finish.

"Thanks again!" Tami's muffled voice said. "Stick around for The Venturas!"

"I can't stand that girl," Noelle said. "She's so full of herself."

"You have to admit, their band is pretty good," Keri said.

"Sure," Margo observed. "In a Bananarama sort of way."

"Ouch," Keri said, smiling. "I think I hear the claws sharpening."

Margo smiled coyly.

"Let's see if we can get a seat," I suggested. "I want to check out The Venturas."

I led the group through the bar. The balcony area was packed with people and all the seats looked full. I pushed my way into the aisle so I could get a better look, sweeping my gaze across the sea of heads like the beam of a lighthouse. Generic radicals occupied every seat. And then one head stood out above the rest. Ben. He had his arm wrapped around a voluptuous girl, and he was leaning into her ear to whisper.

A strange buzzing started in my ears, and the movement of the room seemed to slow down, as if the projector clicked into slow motion. I blew him off last time I talked to him, I told myself. What did I expect? But seeing his arm around another girl at my show overshadowed any voice of logic. I turned and walked past Margo, who was standing behind me.

"I have to go to the bathroom," I managed to say. "I'll be right back."

I walked through the crowd with my head down, swallowing hard.

"Hey, you're back!" I heard Slip say as I slid past them, but I pretended not to hear.

The crowd seemed to push in on me from all sides, used cigarette smoke choked me, piercing laughter cut like icicle picks in my ears. When I finally reached the ladies room door, I could barely fit into the packed room. The smoke was even thicker in the non-ventilated area, and tobacco was mixed with the sweet odor of pot. I crammed myself against the wall and tried to remove myself mentally from the room. I closed my eyes and let the rumbling intonations of conversations melt into a calming hum. I focused on my breathing—in, out, slow down, slow down. My racing heart slowed its beat, my breathing grew deeper. I was thankful for the anonymity of the wall. My tears dissipated.

The door squeaked open and Margo squeezed into the crowd next to me.

"Are you all right?" she asked.

"Yeah, fine. I just saw Ben out there and I didn't feel like running into him."

"That asshole? You're not still seeing him, are you?"

"No."

She put her hand on my shoulder.

"Come on," she said. "Let's go backstage and have some free beer."

Margo told Kerri and Leah to follow us downstairs, and we pushed our human chain through the screaming masses as I tried to push Ben's image out of my mind. We finally reached the long hallway that led to backstage. Behind the curtain that separated the bands from the great unwashed, a large roadie sat cross-armed on a stool.

"Hey," Margo smiled, trying to appear nonchalant. "We decided it was a little too much out there."

I waited for him to tell us to leave, that we couldn't bring friends back here, but he simply nodded coldly. I stifled the urge to giggle.

We walked behind the stage, where Adam was still sitting on a monitor. Gino was gone. We walked over to him.

"Hey Adam!" I said loudly to be heard over the music.

He lit up when he saw us.

"Hi guys!" he said. "Isn't this amazing?"

The Venturas were on the dark stage. Their silhouettes stood still, in position, reminding me of an old Charlie's Angels poster.

"Ladies and gentlemen," the sound guy announced. The crowd began to cheer. "From Los Angeles, California, The Trocadero is proud to present, the incomparable, Venturas."

Teenage girls burst into shrill screams. The curtain slowly parted, then a single spotlight illuminated Paula.

"I saw you there," she sang alone. "I saw you there."

Four clicks, and the stage exploded into light.

"In your little red room, with the plastic microphone," Paula sang.

We were all hypnotized, admiring the beauty of complete confidence. Paula was nimbly dancing her fingers around the guitar fretboard, while the drummer, Mandy, slammed around the kit fluidly as if the drumsticks were extensions of her arms. The bass player, Daria, was bopping her head enthusiastically as she climbed through impressive runs on the fretboard. The stage was obviously their second home. Would we ever be this good?

"Where's Gino?" Margo asked Adam.

"Oh, he's with The Pussy Willows. I think they're hanging out in our room."

"Let's not mention Keri to him right now," I suggested.

"Who's Keri?" Adam asked.

"That's Keri," I said, pointing to her and her entourage.

"And why can't you mention her to Gino?" he asked.

"Nobody likes a nosy roadie," I said.

Adam blushed and looked into his lap.

"Sorry."

"I'm just kidding, Adam," I said. "You'll find out soon enough."

He perked up, eyes wide. I resisted the urge to pat him on the head.

"Let's go grab some beers," I said to Margo.

We headed back to the band room. Tami was standing like a teacher in front of the class, as Caroline, Linda and Gino all gazed at her like attentive pupils. Tami stopped talking when she heard us come in, turned and smiled.

"Girls – you're back!" she said. "Good show, huh?"

"Yeah," Margo said. "The Venturas are amazing."

Tami looked stung by the lack of kind words about The Pussy Willows, but her yellow grin only faded for a blink.

"Yeah," she continued. "They're incredible. I've actually known them for a while. They're talking about taking us on the road with them in the spring."

Now it was our turn to be stung. Tami noticed.

"Yeah, it's not definite, but it looks really good," she said. "It would probably be a West Coast thing."

"Great," Margo said. "I know your other West Coast tour fell through. It's good you can finally get out there."

Tami's smile turned into a sneer. Margo turned to me, looking victorious.

"Wanna get some beers?" she asked.

"Sure," I smiled.

I popped open the cooler and pulled out four beers, tucking them between my fingers. Margo grabbed two more and we left the silent room.

We watched the rest of their set for about an hour. They continued to rock hard and inspirationally. We all sat on monitors drinking our beers. I tried not to look at the dim shadow of the balcony, tried not to think of Ben's arm around that girl, tried not to feel like a total loser.

Toward the end of the set, Gino walked around the corner and toward the monitor where Margo and I were sitting. Keri stole a quick glance at him, then quickly looked forward toward the stage. He squeezed onto a small vacant corner of my monitor seat.

"Thanks again for giving me a second chance," he said to me. "This is the first band I really feel good about. I'm totally psyched now. We can be so much better than The Pussy Willows."

I wasn't sure what to say. Did he know our intentions? Was he trying to amp the guilt?

"No problem," I said.

Margo sat next to me, staring straight ahead.

"So, I've been thinking," Gino continued. "I've got this friend in New York who books a small club in the village. I'll give him a call tomorrow and see if I can get us in there."

I looked sideways at Margo, who kept staring straight ahead.

"That sounds good, Gino," I said, hoping he would simply disappear.

"So when should I set something up?" he pressed on. "We don't have any other shows lined up, right?"

"I don't know," I said. "Let's talk about it later."

He watched the band for a few seconds, shaking his foot excitedly. He leaned toward me again.

"I was thinking maybe early next month," he said. "The holidays are coming up, and people are always more in the mood to check out a band around then. I have some friends up there we can crash with."

I kept staring straight ahead, trying to will him away. Margo sighed heavily and leaned over me.

"There won't be a next show, Gino," she said.

"What?" he asked.

"Gino, I'm sorry," she continued. "You're a great drummer, but…"

"But what? We just had an amazing show."

"I'm sorry," she said.

He jumped off the monitor and stared at us angrily.

"You're canning me?"

"I'm sorry," Margo said, "but we just need someone more consistent. You're very talented, but we just can't take any chances."

Shouting this news above the screeching guitar and pounding drums only added to the tension. Gino's eyes narrowed into angry slits.

"You're making a mistake," he said calmly.

"Gino, I'm really sor…" I started to say.

"Kit, please," he said. "You can shove your pathetic apologies. You're a bitch, just like Margo. If you were really sorry, you would have stuck up for me. But you're worse because you don't have the guts to be honest about it."

He looked back and forth between Margo and me.

"Thank you ladies," he said. "I've had very little to look forward to lately. But, now I will take every opportunity to watch this pathetic little Screw Crew of yours run itself into the ground. You think you'll find a drummer half as good as I am in this town? Good fucking luck."

He sauntered away toward the back room. We remained silent as the Venturas' song washed over us. A few seconds later, Gino walked out with Caroline, quickly sailing past us with his jaw clenched.

I was scared. This guy was nuts, and he knew where I lived. Alone. If he was this angry sober, there was no telling what he was capable of with a few drinks in him. How did we get in this mess?

"Asshole," Margo snorted.

Keri looked over, concerned.

"He seemed pretty mad."

"Please," Margo said, "He's all talk. Except for screwing the bass player of The Pussy Willows, he's got no clout in this town. He's a joke."

Tami emerged from around the corner and walked over to us.

"So." She sat down on the same void recently occupied by Gino, "Gino tells me you fired him."

We stared at her.

"That's interesting. Very interesting." She pulled a cigarette from her breast pocket and tapped it against a snakeskin case. "I hope you know what you're doing. He's a great drummer."

"We'll be fine, Tami," Margo said. "We appreciate your concern, but we have a very good replacement. Someone who will stay sober. Someone who isn't a little off the deep end."

"Her?" she said, pointing her thumb toward Keri.

Keri looked back at her, eyes wide. Tami knew she had caught us off guard and smiled.

"Well, she is cute. That's a plus. But, Gino is a very good friend of ours. I really hate to see him hurt like this."

Was she threatening us? Gino didn't have any clout, certainly, but Tami seemed to be the Queen of Darkness.

"Anyway, it will be interesting to see how it all plays out," Tami said. She took her cigarettes and walked out the back door

On stage, The Venturas were winding down. Multicolored lights flashed and strobed against the band, casting psychedelic shadows on the wall behind us, twisting and grabbing and flailing. Paula took off her guitar and held it high over her head.

"Goodnight Philadelphia! We love you!"

Just as I thought she would slam the beautiful instrument against the stage a la Pete Townsend, she plopped it back down around her neck and wailed on the strings. Daria lifted her bass neck high and ran her fingers up and down the fretboard in a busy scale. Feedback built as Mandy splashed the cymbals loudly. Lights flashed, and the curtain closed. The crowd went insane.

Paula returned her guitar to its stand and lifted her T-shirt to wipe her sweaty face, briefly exposing a tiny black bra. Daria rested her bass on its stand as well, while Mandy pulled a towel from the floor to wipe her face. Her hair hung in wet, sweaty strands that clung to her flushed cheeks. The roadies raced up to the stage and handed them bottled water, then went to their guitars to tune them. The crowd chanted for an encore.

Paula walked over to Daria and said something. She nodded and then they walked back to Mandy, who was tuning her heads. They leaned in for a huddle, then stepped back. Mandy pulled a fifth of Jim Beam from under her stool, unscrewed the cap, and took a long swig. She handed the bottle to Paula, who did the same, then to Daria. They resumed their posts and the curtain parted again, escalating the already piercing wail of the crowd. They launched into another big hit from their last album, and once again they sounded amazing.

They played three more songs, and then the curtain closed again. The crowd continued to shout for another song, but this time they were finished. Paula ripped off her shirt and wiped her face and then her underarms. Her thin body was imperfect, a gold belly ring clung to a small but loose stomach. Big, dark freckles dotted her pale skin. Still, her confidence was beautiful.

She walked back to Mandy and held her hand out for the Beam, which Mandy dutifully filled. Mandy grabbed her towel and walked away as the roadies attacked the task of dismantling her kit. Two other roadies began packing away the guitars and amps. They walked down the back steps and toward us. Tami was back from her smoke and the first to attack them.

"Great fucking job, you guys!" she said. "Really, fucking awesome!"

"Thanks," Paula said.

Daria stood quietly next to Paula, then pulled a squashed cigarette pack out of her back pocket. She took one out, but it was broken. I saw my opportunity.

"Need a cigarette?" I asked.

"Yeah," she looked up a smiled. "Desperately, thanks."

"Follow me."

We walked out the back door and stood next to a smelly dumpster. I handed her a cigarette and lit it for her. She sucked deeply, causing the tip to glow.

"Thanks," she said. "I'm Daria."

"I'm Kit. You guys kicked ass tonight, as usual."

"Thanks. You guys played first, right? I was busy getting ready, but what I heard sounded pretty good."

My hero just said my band was pretty good. Not high praise exactly, but a start.

Adam popped his head out of the door. "Hey Kit, need a beer?" he asked.

"Sure. Can you get one for Daria, too?"

"Sure."

Adam disappeared back inside the doorway.

"He's our biggest fan," I said to Daria.

"Yeah. We get all kinds of freaks at our shows, too."

When we got back inside, I introduced everyone and before long we were chatting about our lives and music. Daria was originally from outside of Chicago, so she and Leah bonded over stories about bars and bands. I grew more confident as the conversation progressed and mustered the courage to hand Daria our demo CD with my email address written on it. I saw Margo out of the corner of my eye. She had worked her way into the Paula/Mandy/Tami circle, and they all seemed to be smiling and getting along as if Tami had not just threatened to destroy us. We were all one big happy passive-aggressive family.

By the end of the evening, after the club had thrown out the last of the little girls and sleazy boys, and the harsh fluorescent lights revealed the club in all its true dankness, we said big buzzed emotional goodbyes to Keri's gang. The burly roadies packed up The Venturas' stuff, so the remaining musicians stumbled around gathering various pieces of equipment. As usual, Adam was quick to grab our heaviest stuff, so Margo and I plucked the miscellaneous leftovers. We followed Tami and Linda to the back alley where we had left our cars. Paula and Mandy continued sitting on the edge of the stage, smoking and drinking the near-empty Jim Beam bottle, but Daria picked up a few pieces and followed us out to the car.

"If you ever need an opening band, let us know," I said as we walked out to the back alley to load up our cars. "We're neat and we don't eat much."

"Yeah, keep in touch," Daria said.

Tami, who was walking a few paces ahead of us, snapped her head around, then pretended to ask Linda a question. We walked over to our cars and started to toss in equipment, when I noticed my car was not quite level. I walked around to the driver's side of the car. My tire had been slashed.

"Mother fucker," I said. "Margo!"

Margo walked over quickly.

"What?"

I pointed to the tire.

"That fucking asshole," she said, then walked back to her car. "Fuck!"

Her back tire was slashed, too, and the side of her car had been keyed.

"He's going to pay for this," she mumbled. "That fucking asshole is going to pay."

"What happened?" Daria asked, walking over to our cars. Tami and Linda followed.

"Looks like our little drummer boy wanted to get even," Margo said.

"Gino wouldn't do that," Tami said. "It was probably just some dirt bag. This alley is hardly lit."

"Really?" Margo said angrily. "How are the tires on your van?"

Tami glanced back, but we could see her van was fine.

"We were just lucky, I guess," she said.

Margo sighed heavily.

"How are we going to get home now? We've all been drinking, so we can't call the cops."

"Our bus already left," Daria said. "We were just going to take a cab to our hotel."

"I wish I could help," Tami said. "But we really can't fit much more in our van."

"I'll take you guys home," Adam offered.

"Thanks, Adam," Margo said. "But maybe we should wait for AAA. We can't just leave our cars here."

"Sorry we can't help," Tami said, walking back to the van. "Good luck."

Linda stood for a moment, looking between Tami and us, then followed Tami to the van. I couldn't blame her. It sucked being on Tami's bad side.

"You don't have to wait, Daria," I said.

"Are you sure?" she said.

"Yeah, don't worry about it. We'll be fine."

"Okay. But definitely keep in touch."

"I will. Thanks."

We waited a long hour and a half, with faithful Adam at our side, mumbling hateful words about our ex-drummer and the Wicked Witch of The Pussy Willows. Finally, a lonely AAA driver arrived to twist doughnuts onto our cars and I headed home, exhausted.

CHAPTER

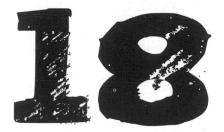

Monday at work, my phone rang.

"Did you see *The Inquirer* today?" Margo asked.

"No, why?"

"They have a review of our show from Saturday. Can you get one?"

"I'll call you back."

I walked quickly out to the lobby.

"I'm going to grab a cup a coffee!" I called to Margie, pushing the door open and stepping into the hallway.

"Could you get me a…" the door closed behind me as I ignored her request. I was too excited to start taking office pastry orders. I pressed the elevator button and went down to the deli next to our building that sold *The Inquirer*. Before purchasing the paper, I opened to the Entertainment section and scanned the contents quickly until I found it.

Local Gals Hold Their Own at Venturas Show

By Dan Dawson

At Saturday night's show at The Trocadero, The Venturas put on their usual terrific show. These gals know how to rock, and they hit every note perfectly with a flawless performance that highlighted the best of their three albums. But the surprise of the evening came from the impressive opening local bands, The Pussy Willows, and the latest addition to the scene, Broad Street.

The Pussy Willows put on a great show, sprinkling their usual solid set with new tunes that put the crackle back in pop…

I skipped to the rest of the paragraph.

…Broad Street, featuring lead singer and guitarist Margo Bevilacqua and bass player Kit Greene, rocked with a punk fury but kept the tongue planted firmly in cheek. Their set alternated between tightly played headbangers and more eccentric fare like a cover of "She" by the Monkees. The effect is something like a B-52s for the new millennium with a decidedly feminist sensibility. Blending an array of influences, the group created a hard yet melodic sound that for all its numerous reference points still seems distinctive.

My head was spinning. This was good. Very good. *The Philadelphia Inquirer* was the biggest paper in the area, read by hundreds of thousands of people from miles away, and they liked us. They really liked us.

I ran back to my office and called Margo. As we read it out loud, the two of us giggled like children.

"I can't believe this," she said. "This is too easy."

She was right. Dale had struggled to promote his band without more than a mention in a paid advertisement. Charlie had been in his band for a couple of years, too, and I'd never seen them mentioned in the paper. Was it our gender that got us this attention? Maybe. But, maybe what we were doing wasn't better, but touched something their male rock did not. After all, did we not have a "decidedly feminist sensibility"? I couldn't wait to show that to my parents. Maybe I was a novelty, but I was going to enjoy it.

I saw an internal call coming in.

"Margo, hang on a second."

I pushed down the hold button, then pressed the second line that was flashing red.

"Kit, good morning," Nancy's soft voice greeted me. I felt my face flush guiltily. "Do you have a second to come back to my office?"

"Sure, I'll be right there."

I told Margo I'd call her back later and walked the much-less-intimidating distance to Jean's old office. After a few knee-jerk anxious reactions to these phone calls from Nancy, I no longer feared them. She called me in on a semi-regular basis now to ask me questions about procedure, speaking to me like a peer rather than an ignorant child.

She had on an elegant lemon yellow suit that complemented her dark hair. She greeted me with a friendly smile.

"Hi Kit," she smiled. "Have a seat."

I sat down in the comfortable chair across from her.

"How was your weekend?" she asked.

"Great, thanks," I said genuinely. "We had a show Saturday night that went really well."

"Actually," she said pulling *The Inquirer* from behind her desk. "I just read your review. That's just great. You should be really proud of yourself."

"Thanks. I just found out about it myself. I'm pretty excited." I then reminded myself that as sweet as this woman is, she was still my boss. "But, I hope you know, this is just a hobby for me. It's not very likely that we'll get swept up by a big label and handed thousands of dollars to tour. I like my job here, and I have no plans of jeopardizing it."

"Kit," she said smiling. "Of course I know that. And if you do get rich and famous, I promise not to hold it against you."

"Well, thanks."

"Now, I do have a concern to bring to your attention." She pulled her chair closer to the desk and crossed her arms in front of her. "And I don't want to alarm you, but it's something we need to discuss."

Flashbacks of Jean's fiery eyes accusing me of mediocrity flashed before me. But Nancy was different. Maybe this time I had finally gone too far with my screw-ups. I had missed a crucial decimal point that had cost a patient her life. My breath quickened.

"What happened?" I asked softly.

She turned around a single sheet of paper so the text would be facing my way and pushed it over to my side of the desk.

"This email came in this morning. Our filters intercepted it because of the profanity."

Filters? Uh oh.

"Do you have any idea from whom this may have been sent?"

I leaned in to read the printed note:

From: davyjones@yahoo.com

To: k_greene@ncburrows.com

Subject: new policy

It's only a matter of time before you pay for what you've done. The troubles you and your cunts have stirred up are going to come around and strike you in the head. I am following you like white on rice. You are going to pay dearly for your transgressions. You are going to get what you deserved for a long time. Have a nice walk home.

Davy

Gino. Holy shit. I felt sick. And scared.

"Kit," Nancy said in a concerned tone. "Is there anyone in this company, maybe someone who used to work here, who might be angry with you?"

"Nancy, I'm sorry," I said. "But I think I know who this is. It sounds ridiculous, but I think this is actually our ex-drummer. He must have gotten my email address from our Web site. I just can't believe..."

I leaned in again to re-read the note.

"I just can't believe he would do this. It seems so... nuts."

Nancy pulled the note back to her side of the desk and looked at it again.

"It's angry, yes." She took a deep breath. "Since it came into our company, I plan to file a police report. I've also talked with a detective to see if we can trace the email. If this guy was just joking around, he's going to be in big trouble. I'm sorry."

"Please, Nancy, don't be sorry. I'm sorry I got the company involved in this. I just can't believe that he would do this." I paused. "It makes me wonder what else he's capable of."

As the words came out of my mouth, I felt a tickle of anxiety. He knew where I lived. He knew I lived alone. Of course he was capable of this. He'd already vandalized my car. What was next?

He was going to kill us.

"Do you have someone who can stay with you for a while?" Nancy asked.

"Yeah. I can ask my sister or my friend Margo. She's in the band, too, but, strength in numbers, right? I'll figure out something."

I looked up at Nancy, who looked genuinely concerned. This made me both grateful and embarrassed.

"I'm so sorry, Nancy. Just as I was telling you that my music life will never interfere with my work life."

"It's all life, Kit. These worlds are never as separate as we think."

I walked back to my desk and called Margo back.

"What is it?" Margo asked upon hearing my shaky voice.

"Have you gotten any weird emails?"

"Not weirder than usual, why?"

"My boss just told me some psycho is sending threatening emails to me."

"Really? Who do you think it is?"

"Uh, isn't it obvious? Do you recall canning a certain unstable drummer recently?"

"I wonder why I haven't gotten anything?"

"Maybe he just wants to kill me."

"Oh, please. He hardly has the balls for that. He's just trying to scare you."

"It worked. He knows where I live, and he knows I live alone."

"Really, Kit. I don't think you have anything to worry about."

"I know." I paused. "I don't suppose you'd like to stay with me tonight?"

There was a silence on the other end that I couldn't interpret.

"Hmm. I don't know. I'm kind of… Well, it could take some juggling."

I was hurt that she wasn't more concerned about me, and that she didn't even seem to respect the fact that I was scared.

"Don't worry about it," I said. "It was just an idea. I thought maybe we could do some writing or something. I'll have Nikki stay with me. No biggie."

But it was a biggie.

"Oh god," Margo said. "Don't ask Nikki. She'll just have that lunkhead Ted over every night to drink all your beer. I'd love to stay with you—and drink all your beer. I have something to do tonight, but I'll be over later, probably around 8:00. Have a hot pizza ready for me."

I worked late to finish a stack of projects, and possibly to procrastinate the walk home. When I got there, I clicked on the living-room light and looked around cautiously. The place was a disaster. When I left my house in the morning I didn't realize I would have a roommate tonight, or my first insane stalker, or a delightful article about my band in the city's paper. Not bad for a Monday.

I stood still for a minute, listening for the creaky footsteps or gurgled breathing of late-night horror movies. The house was still. I carefully laid my bags on the couch, locking the door behind me, and tiptoed over to the phone. There was a message from Charlie.

"Hey, Kit," he said. "I saw the article today. Great job. Give me a call sometime if you feel like it."

He was such a great guy. I never felt uncomfortable with him, even that first embarrassing morning. Why did I chase after the jerks instead of somebody nice? I hated being so cliché.

While I fished for Charlie's number in my bowl of miscellaneous papers, there was a heavy knock on the door. My heart stopped.

"Killer Drummer here, open up!" Margo's voice boomed.

I clicked the deadbolt and opened the door.

"Hi Honey, I'm home!" she said, dragging an enormous leopard suitcase behind her.

"Are you moving in?" I asked.

She looked at the suitcase.

"Oh, this little thing? I'm not a gal who travels lightly."

"I guess not. Anyway, you can have my bed," I offered. "I'll take the couch."

"Nope. That's mine. I like to sleep with the television on."

I was glad to hear that. I had no real desire to give up my bed.

Margo walked to the kitchen and grabbed two beers. She clicked them open and lit a cigarette.

"So." She paused dramatically and stared at me. "I've been waiting until we're settled to give you some good news. Guess what?"

"Columbia Records called."

She furrowed her brow.

"Cute. No, it just so happens that The Philadelphia Music Conference coordinator called me today. He wants us to play the conference. Can you believe it?"

"What? The Philadelphia Music Conference just called you up and invited us to play. No press kit, no blow jobs, nothing?"

"Nope."

I took a swig of my beer and sat at the kitchen table, pulling a cigarette from Margo's pack and lighting it.

"Don't you think it's odd that our ex-boyfriends tried to get into that conference every year, and failed?"

"They obviously weren't good enough."

"Oh, I'm sorry Ms. Santana. I forgot you were such a virtuoso."

"That's not nice."

She pulled up the chair across from me at the table.

"I just mean that it's odd," I said.

She rolled her eyes and sighed heavily.

"Yes, we're a marketable band. I admit that. But so what? That's the nature of the industry. Do you think the Minute Men would have been successful in this generation? They wouldn't. There ain't enough soft lighting in the world to pretty up Mike Watt's ugly mug. Why can't you just enjoy this?"

"I love the Minute Men," I said.

"You're missing the point."

"I know. I guess it's that nagging hippie voice of my parents questioning my commitment to the cause."

"Did you not read the line about our 'decidedly feminist sensibility'?" Margo asked.

"I did like that line."

"We're not strippers. We're musicians. We play our own instruments. We write our own songs. That puts us in the Beethoven category compared to most girl groups."

"You're right. I'm sorry. I don't know why I can't just enjoy this."

"Because you're feeling sorry for yourself. But you shouldn't. We're on a roll here. We have no men helping us out. We're doing this ourselves. Let's have some fun."

"You're right."

"Of course I'm right. Now, they want us to play in three weeks at the Cadillac. There are three other bands, so it will be a short set." She looked at me critically. "So, are you excited?"

"Very."

"I'll pretend to believe you."

Margo held her beer in the air.

"To Broad Street. Feminists for the new millennium."

We clicked bottles.

Margo was right. Why couldn't I enjoy this? Margo and I had done this for ourselves. I should be proud of myself. But beneath it all, a quiet dread nibbled at me.

"Thanks for staying with me," I said. "I know it's lame, but that note really gave me the creeps."

"Are you sure it's Gino?"

"Who else would it be?"

"I don't know. But he knows where I work, too, and I didn't get any email. I know he hates me as much—if not more—than you."

This thought made me even more nervous. At least my fear had a face. I could identify it. If the email wasn't from Gino, then who?

At practice Thursday night, Keri was warming up when Margo and I arrived our usual fifteen minutes late.

"Hey guys!" she said. "How are you?"

"Exhausted," Margo grunted as she dropped her guitar on the floor. "Work was a nightmare today. But, I'm glad to be here."

"Kit, I haven't talked to you since the article," Keri continued. "Pretty nice, huh?"

"Except for the Pussy praise, sure."

"Did they mention them? I didn't even notice," she said, smiling. "Hey, I have some more good news if you can take it."

Margo and I paused from setting up our equipment.

"If you guys are interested," Keri continued. "I have a gig for us in D.C. It's soon—next weekend—but it's at a cool new club called The Ruby Lounge, right down the street from The Black Cat. I have a friend down there and her band is playing. I just happened to be talking to her the other night and mentioned us and she said she'd love to have us open for her band."

"D.C.," Margo said. "That would be great! I haven't been there since I was on an eighth-grade field trip."

"I haven't been there in forever either," I said. "That sounds like a blast."

"Great," Keri said. "I'll set it up. So have I missed any other good gossip?"

Margo and I looked at each other and smiled. We spent almost half an hour filling Keri in on the Music Conference, the slashed tires, the email. As I shared these stories, my anxiety dissipated.

We ran through the set a few times and worked on a new one that I had written. Keri even harmonized some background vocals. Once again, we had pulled ourselves up another rung on the percussive evolutionary scale. I knew in my gut that this was it. This was the lineup that would take Broad Street as far as we could go.

CHAPTER

The emails stopped. Each morning, I logged on with a lump in my stomach, but got only the usual junk, jokes, and business stuff. Still, I looked cautiously over my shoulder every night when I walked home, and was grateful that Margo stayed for a few days. She had been working late most nights, but seemed in better spirits than I had ever seen her. These lionesses now caught and ate their own dinners.

When the D.C. show date arrived, we took two cars. We packed up bass and guitar equipment into Margo's car, and Keri met us around 1:00 with her Civic loaded with drum equipment. The sky was a blanket of gray. The slight aroma of impending snow kissed the chilled air.

I rode with Margo, and we followed Keri closely on I-95 South for the three-hour drive. We had booked a cheap motel slightly south of Washington in a little town called Milling Hill, so we curved beneath the city on the Beltway until we saw the exit. The signs led us onto a dreary little strip of dollar stores, fast food chains, and a low-rent family restaurant called Black Eyed Peas. Most of the parking lots were empty.

"Where are we?" I asked Margo as we drove by a store wallpapered in neon signs for cheap cell phones.

"I think we're in the south."

We followed the directions until we found the motel. We pulled up to the front office and locked the car. Keri parked next to us and we walked into the lobby, which was basically a tiny, unventilated room mostly congested with a desk and an obese woman in a Pepto pink muumuu.

"Can I help y'all?" she asked in a thick drawl, pushing her large body off of a tiny stool and clodding over to the counter.

"Yeah," Margo said. "We made a reservation for a double room."

"Name?" she asked, pulling out a black reservation book and opening to yellowed pages.

"Bevilacqua."

The woman snapped up her eyes and furrowed her brow.

"That's an interesting one," she said snidely, flipping pages and running a chubby finger down a list of names.

"I called a couple days ago," Margo offered.

"Oh, right," she said, then turned and padded to a bookcase piled high with papers. A black tray was balanced on a stack of phone books, from which she pulled out a handful of papers and flipped through them until she found the one she wanted. She waddled back to the counter.

"This has to be you," she said. "Ain't no other foreign names in that pile." She let out a big phlegmy laugh. "You gals are lucky you got a room," she said, revealing a gold tooth. "The Peacekeepers are in town this weekend. This place is completely booked. You probably got the last available room."

She laughed again, which quickly turned into a hacking cough.

"Okay," she said, catching her breath. "I'm gonna need to see a credit card and you gals are gonna have to get parking permits for your cars." She pulled out two bright yellow pieces of paper from under the counter. "Although it won't be hard to find your cars."

The three of us looked at each other. What did that mean?

Margo pulled out her Discover card and the woman squeezed an imprint onto an old-fashioned credit-card slip. She handed us two keys to the same room. We walked out to the cars and drove around the corner toward the room. As our cars crested the turn, I gasped slightly as the intimidating scene struck me. Huge black motorcycles with swollen silver mufflers filled the entire lot like a sea of cockroaches. Their antenna handlebars glinted in the winter sun—skulls dangled from many of them.

"I'll say it again. Where the hell are we?" I asked.

"I think you nailed it on the head," Margo said quietly.

We crept the cars slowly past the bikes, leery of disturbing their sleep, until we found two open parking spots near our room. We got out of our cars and Keri walked over to us.

"What are they?" she whispered.

"I think they're the Peacekeepers," Margo answered. "Let's take our stuff inside and triple lock our doors."

We carried our equipment in quickly. We had a few hours before the gig, so we decided to take showers then head out to get something to eat. Margo showered first while Keri and I sat on our beds and watched a fuzzy rerun of Gilligan's Island.

"It's too bad Leah couldn't come down," I said. "She's missing all the excitement."

"Yeah, well. Her parents are in town, so it's best I'm not around."

"Do they know about you two?"

"They know we're friends and roommates—that's it. Leah thinks they'll freak out, even though she hasn't brought a boyfriend home since college. But, they live in Chicago, so it's easier to lie I guess."

"What about your parents?"

"They finally accepted it. I've pretty much been out since high school."

"Really? That's brave."

"No, it was stupid. I had no idea what I was doing. Teenagers are so threatened by anything different, and maybe they're afraid of some of their own feelings, I don't know. It was a pretty hard time."

"I'll bet."

She sat up and looked over at me.

"Did you know the suicide rates for homosexual teens are higher than any other category?" She looked toward the bathroom door; the shower water was still running, then looked back at me. "I'm actually working on a graphic novel about it."

"Really? I didn't know you were an illustrator."

"Well, sort of. It's always been a hobby of mine. There's nothing really out there for young gay people, no real role models their age. I thought it might be helpful."

"That's really cool, Keri."

I envied Keri's commitment to something so noble. That was the kind of hobby my father would support. As much as I aspired to the ranks of Aretha, demanding respect in my lyrics, I wasn't convinced. I know my father wasn't either.

"Shower's free!" Margo's voice echoed in the bathroom.

"Do you want to go next?" I asked Keri.

Margo flung open the door, billowing steam into the room. She had on a little floral tee-shirt dress and her hair was wrapped in a towel.

"Who's next?"

I took a quick shower and changed into my usual glittery show outfit. Margo wore a tight shimmering black dress. Keri put on black leather pants with a gold blouse and high-heeled boots. Margo opened the door a crack to peek outside.

"Coast is clear," Margo said.

We snuck out to the car with our equipment, tiptoeing carefully around the sleeping motorcycles. I feared the slightest noise might wake their owners. This anxiety quickened my pace to load the car.

"We made it," Margo said, starting the engine and pulling out of the lot. "Now let's find some place to eat."

"I saw a restaurant on the way in called Black Eyed Peas. It looked kind of like a Denny's."

"That's good. Quick, cheap. Let's check it out."

We drove back toward the highway until we saw the restaurant on our right. Margo pulled in and Keri followed.

As soon as we stepped out of the cars, I felt like a Yankee out of water. The parking lot was occupied mainly by rusting pick-up trucks of various hues. Confederate flags hung from antennas and clung to bumpers. Ominous Harleys that must have been sisters to our motel neighbors huddled in a corner of the lot. Our leather and gold shimmered conspicuously like a lit match in the heart of a dark jungle.

"Good lord," Margo said. "Has anyone seen Andy Griffith?"

We chuckled nervously and walked toward the door. Inside, skinny white men with thick tan hides gnawed on their meals. Most of the women were plump, the children well behaved. To the left, I could see the top of a bar area where miscellaneous glasses hung by their bases. A middle-aged woman with tall blonde hair walked over to us, unsmiling.

"May I help you?" she asked in a drawl.

"Yes," Margo said. "Three please."

The woman looked over her shoulder at the half empty room, then back at us.

"Sorry, we don't have any open tables," she said coldly, moving her eyes from our boots to our boobs.

"How about that one?" Margo asked, pointing to a random empty table.

"Sorry, that's reserved."

"And that one?" she said, pointing to another one.

"They're all reserved."

We all looked at each other.

"Do you want to go someplace else?" I asked.

"Where else?" Margo snapped. "There's nowhere else around here."

She turned back to the woman.

"Can we speak to your manager?"

The woman's face sucked into an angry pinch.

"He's at lunch."

"Well, can we wait for a table?" Margo asked.

"It may be a while."

"We'll wait." Margo turned to us. "Let's go wait in the bar area."

The woman sighed heavily and walked back toward the kitchen. We headed toward the bar. When we turned the corner of the wall separating the bar for the restaurant area, we walked straight into the lair of Peacekeepers.

I froze. They were draped across the bar and occupied most of the tables in the small room. Most were big, hairy-knuckled men with spotty beards and thick leather jackets that depicted the Peacekeeper logo—a single white dove speared through the back with a sword. Its soft dead body dropped backwards in an arch, a small trickle of blood slipping down the blade. One large man had a chain connecting his nose ring to his earring. Another man had a shaved head embellished in its center with skull and crossbones. A skinny woman with her back toward us straddled one of them. His tattooed arms wrapped around her worn jeans.

"Let's go somewhere else," I whispered to Margo.

Even she looked a little pale. Keri darted her eyes around the room like a scared rabbit about to be eaten by wolves.

"No," Margo said quietly, and walked into the room.

A large warthog of a man turned from the bar and smiled at us. He had surprisingly white teeth.

"Hello, ladies," He greeted us in a low rumble. "Where's the costume party?"

"I was about to ask you the same question," Margo answered.

Keri and I froze. A few of the Peacekeepers turned from the table to witness our execution. The Warthog stared at us coldly, then burst into a low gurgle that I assumed was laughter.

"A feisty one," Warthog said. "What's your name, sweetheart?"

"My stage name's Aqua Vulva," she said.

"Stage name? You must be a stripper."

Margo smiled snidely.

"Actually," she said. "We're in a band."

The rest of the room turned to watch the festivities. They dissected us with their eyes, seeming to try and place us. Had they seen us on TV? Magazines?

"What're your names?" he asked Keri and me.

"Um, Mary," Keri said softly.

"How about you?" he asked me.

"Kit."

Fuck. Why did I use my real name? I felt my face flush as the eyes bored through me.

"Kit?" a woman's voice asked from a table behind me.

I turned to face the voice. The woman was middle-aged with platinum blonde hair cut very short. She wore a low-cut red T-shirt that was a nice complement to the bleeding dove I assumed was on the back of her jacket. She had piercing steel gray eyes that...

Oh my god.

"Jean?"

My old boss—the one who could not have had a stick more firmly in her uptight ass—sat before me lounging with these animals. She looked at the Warthog, then back at me. All eyes were now on her.

"Who's Jean?" Her leather-clad companion asked.

"That was my stage name," she said.

That voice. Smooth as a knife blade. We stared at each other for what felt like a long time.

"How are you, Kit?" she asked.

"Excuse me, Cupcake," the Warthog grunted. "But I was about to buy these ladies a drink. What can I get for you?"

Margo walked to a clump of empty bar stools. Keri and I followed.

"We have a gig tonight," she said. "So nothing too heavy. I'll have a beer."

"A gig?" he asked. "We may just have to come and see you. What do you think boys?"

The Peacekeepers at The Ruby Lounge. We would be banned from this city for life. I said a silent prayer.

"The Ruby Lounge in D.C.," she said.

Keri visibly stiffened.

"I'll have a beer," she said to the bartender.

"Me too," I said.

I felt Jean's eyes on me as I drank from the cold, frothy mug. It went down smoothly. Keri and I sat quietly as Margo flirted with the beast. As the foam neared the bottom of my glass, I felt a tap on my shoulder. I turned to face steely gray eyes.

"Can I talk to you a minute?" Jean asked.

"Sure."

I swallowed hard and climbed off my stool.

"I'll be right back," I told Keri. Margo was too engrossed to notice my exit.

I followed Jean to the parking lot. When she turned, her gray eyes looked oddly out of place.

"So what have you heard?" she asked.

"I've heard lots of things."

"Try tossing out a few."

"The most popular is that you and Dr. De Medio were having an affair and when he fooled around with that Catholic-school girl, you were so devastated you disappeared."

Her jaw tightened.

"There's also the rumor that you stole money for a sex change operation," I continued. "I'll spare you the details about your drug ring."

Jean shook her head.

"I figured you catty little bitches would just love to hang me out to dry. I knew you all hated me."

"So what did happen?" I asked.

"Let's just say I'd appreciate if you didn't mention that you saw me."

If she was trying to win me over, she wasn't doing it very well.

"No problem," I said.

She stared hard at me, then sighed and leaned against a powder blue pickup truck.

"I know I gave you a hard time," she said. "But you weren't exactly a picnic to manage."

"What do you mean?"

"You and Rachel were always giving me that patronizing fake respect. 'Oh yes, Jean. Right away, Jean.' Then you dashed off and mocked me. Or emailed your sister about what a bitch I was."

The filter. Oh shit. All of those emails I sent about evil Jean. I had called her unfeeling, unsympathetic, frigid, borderline inhuman.

"Why didn't you say something?" I asked.

She looked down at her boots and scuffed the toe against the sidewalk. A tiny stone broke loose and spun forward. She turned her eyes up toward me. They seemed softer now.

"How old do you think I am, Kit?" she asked.

"I have no idea."

"I'm 35. For 35 years I've done the right thing. I went to school, got my MBA, moved quickly up to management."

"Then joined a biker gang."

She smiled.

"Everything was fine in my life, except for the fact that I was miserable. My brother's a Peacekeeper in California. I went out to visit him after everything that happened and, I don't know, maybe I always envied him a little, even though my parents and I had always judged him so self-righteously. I've since learned there's a kind of freedom in living hand-to-mouth."

"There's a dead dove on the back of your jacket."

"I know," she laughed. "Isn't that ridiculous?" She scuffed her boot again. "Maybe I'm in the mood for ridiculous."

I couldn't believe that the woman in front of me was the same one who had made my life so miserable just a few months earlier. She seemed so small now.

"What happened?" I asked.

She looked back down at her boots.

"Well, you girls are partly right. Sam and I—Dr. De Medio—used to work some late nights. We got to be close. I had no idea he could be such a jerk."

I couldn't imagine any woman being attracted to such a cowardly little weasel, let alone two women. But then again, life had been pretty surprising lately.

"So," she continued. "I decided to just disappear. I was too old for the circus, so here I am."

"This is a little circus-like."

"I know. I love it. We just spend our days riding and talking and, well, you know, having a good time. To them, I'm Jade, and they accept me. And I'm not the only one. Bear, the guy who bought your drinks, used to work on Wall Street until he kind of lost it. He realized life was too short to obsess about materials things. Tiny—the guy I'm sitting with—managed a bank. Jugs was in HR. We all just wanted to live a little."

"What are you doing out here?" Margo called from the door of the restaurant. "We're gonna order some food at the bar."

"I'll be right in." I called to her, then turned back to Jean. "I won't mention anything about this to anyone. I promise."

"Thanks."

We walked back in to the bar area, angry eyes glaring at us from the dining room. The noise from the bar had escalated, and I could see the hostess talking to a mustached-man. There were lots of hand-gestures and pointing to the bar area.

Several Peacekeepers surrounded Margo, and Keri had moved her stool over to be in the middle. She was laughing along with the rest of them, which could either be the beer or genuine comfort. Bear was telling a story, and chain guy and the couple who had been making out were listening intently. I tried to picture Bear in a neat Armani suit, and couldn't quite form a believable image. Jean and I stepped into the conversation.

"Oh, Jade," Bear said. "I was just telling these guys how scared you were when you took your first ride." He turned to Margo and Keri. "This woman was so uptight when we first met her, she could crack a walnut with her ass."

"Thanks, Bear," Jean said.

"But now look at her. She's beautiful."

We turned to see Jean blush, and she did look beautiful.

We ordered sandwiches and more beers, and I was feeling a little too buzzed too early to be playing a show that night. I looked at my watch. 7:30.

"I guess we should head out around 8:00," I said to Keri and Margo.

"That's fine," Keri said. "It's okay if we're a little late. The Dildon'ts will sound check first anyway."

"The Dildon'ts?" Bear asked. "Broad Street? Where were these bands when I was a kid?"

"What do you mean?" Margo said, slapping Bear on the shoulder. "You're still a kid."

"I like this girl," Bear said loudly.

Margo's smile dropped as she looked over my shoulder.

"Uh oh," she said.

I turned to see three tall white cops talking to the mustached-man, who was shaking his head and pointing to our crowd. The three walked over.

"I'm afraid I'm going to have to ask you folks to leave," one of them said. He looked young. His clean-shaven face had a slight accent of blond fuzz framing his upper lip.

"I'm sorry officer," Bear said cooly. "What laws are we breaking exactly?"

I wanted to run out of the room, to tell these guys that I was just a kid from Pennsylvania and I had a good job and I paid my taxes and I never hurt a soul. But I couldn't move. Margo and Keri also sat silently. From the corner of my eye, I saw a table of three large Peacekeepers rise and walk in our direction. One of the other officers pulled a billy club slowly from his belt.

"You're disturbing the peace," the young officer replied with a twang, glancing nervously at the men moving closer. "These nice folks here are trying to run a business and you're making too much noise for them to do that. Now, we would all appreciate it if you and your friends would just pay your bill and leave."

Bear rose from his seat, reminding the room how huge he was. He towered over even the tallest officer with intimidating, leather-clad girth. The young cop took a step backward. He tried to keep a harsh expression, but he looked like a kid playing cowboy who had gotten in over his head. The other two cops moved closer to him to form a wall. The mustached manager peered around the dividing wall. The blonde hostess peered around him and I could see the tops of a few farmer hats rising from the dining area and moving our way.

"Now, we don't want any trouble, officer," Bear began. "But we're just here having a drink and some grub. We've paid for everything, so we can't be accused of stealing. We've been having normal conversations that can't be construed as overly disruptive. Now, you wouldn't be biased against us just because we prefer two wheels over four, would you?"

"Sir," the young cop began, then was interrupted by one of the other cops who stepped close to Bear. He looked like an older version of the young cop. His mustache was thick and blonde with wisps of gray.

"Now look," he said in a low, gruff voice. "We're asking you nice one last time. We've had a complaint. Your group is the source of that complaint, and we're asking you to leave. You can leave on your own, or we can take you with us. It's up to you."

This guy had watched too many cop shows.

"You know, we really should get going anyway," Keri said.

I glanced at the clock wall. 8:00. Of course we should leave, but something surged inside me. I was tired of being pushed around by overblown testosterone.

"I haven't gotten my sandwich yet," I said. "And I'm very hungry."

The corners of Bear's mouth turned up slightly. My heart raced as the officer stared at me, then turned and walked back to the manager. He whispered something to him, then the manager whispered something to the hostess, and they both disappeared. Margo elbowed me slightly, but I stared at the officers. A small crowd had gathered by the bar entrance. Men ready to pounce, women wrapping their arms around their offspring. Everyone stood in a trance for a few seconds until the manager and hostess appeared holding big white paper bags.

"On the house," the manager said, handing the bags to Bear, Margo, and me.

"There you go," the older officer said. "Thanks for visiting. Have a nice day." His face remained stone.

Bear stood up and stretched.

"All right gang," he said. "Let's go check out some chick rock."

Some scattered cheers erupted as the group noisily squeaked chairs back into place and clomped loudly out the door. Margo, Keri, and I fell in like dutiful soldiers off to battle the Man. The rush of victory, however unjustified, made me fight the incredible urge to smile.

We climbed in our cars and watched our new friends straddle their bikes and kick start them into a thunderous rumble. Faces peered out of the restaurant glass doors through the shimmer of street lamp reflection. Margo and I looked at each other and burst into laughter.

"Is this rock, or what?" she asked, then squealed her small Toyota out of the parking lot with Keri and The Peacekeepers roaring behind us.

The narrow club stood alone on a small patch of sidewalk, a small red neon sign advertising its name in the window. Next to the club was a pothole laden parking lot attended by a black man who appeared to be homeless. His long army coat pulled his shoulders down and his fuzzy hair was coated with a light dust. We pulled in. Keri and the gang of five cycles wrapped around our cars and lined up neatly toward the back of the lot. The man darted his head between the bikes and us, then walked over to us.

"Hello ladies," he greeted us. I was hit by a powerful stench of urine as he got closer. "Playing the club tonight?"

"Very observant," Margo snapped, pulling her guitar from the back seat.

"Well, I promise to take good care of your cars for you. You gotta be careful in a neighborhood like this."

"I know you'll take good care of these cars," Bear's low voice came up from behind the man. He turned and moved his head up slowly as he took in Bear's ominous build.

"Oh, yes sir," the man cowered.

Bear pulled a fifty from his pocket. "I'd consider it a personal favor if you kept an eye on all of our rides."

"You can count on it," he said bowing. He looked over at Margo gathering her equipment. "Let me help you with that," he said, rounding the car. Bear's hand on his shoulder stopped him.

"We'll help the ladies, thanks," he said.

Bear waved over the bald guy with the tattoo on his head and the chained nose

Peacekeeper. I tried not to think about Altamont, where the Hell's Angels' protection of the Rolling Stones didn't turn out so well. They started grabbing drums and other equipment and carrying it into the club. Keri raced ahead of us, probably to warn her friends about our new fans. I picked up my bass and followed them in.

The club interior glowed with soft red light. It was small, with only a handful of empty tables and a bar. A stairway climbed one wall, where a handwritten sign advertised "Live Music" with an arrow pointing upstairs. Keri was at the bar talking to the bartender, a middle aged guy with a small ponytail at the base of his neck, and an attractive brunette sitting at a stool in front of the bar. All three of them turned when we walked in the door. Keri walked over to us, looking nervous.

"There's been a little bit of a mix-up," she said.

"What kind of mix-up?" Margo asked.

"Apparently my friend had the wrong dates, or maybe I misunderstood her. They have us playing next weekend."

"What?" Margo snapped.

"But it's okay. I just talked to the manager, Bruce, that guy behind the bar. He's letting us play. The only problem is we're not playing with The Dildon'ts tonight. We're playing with a local guy named Dave Walton."

"Well, that's good, I guess," I said. "At least we're playing."

Margo looked skeptical.

"What's this Dave Walton guy like?" she asked.

"Well," Keri hesitated. "He's kind of a singer songwriter-type."

We all looked at our leather-clad fans that had poured into the small room and were ordering pitchers of beer.

"They'll eat him alive," Margo said, then smiled.

We carried our equipment upstairs to another small, red-lit room. The "stage" was really just a void of tables in the front of the room. Keri started setting up her drums, and Margo and I tuned our guitars. The Peacekeepers climbed the stairs and began the occupation. Jean sat with Tiny and the couple we had seen making out. Chain-nose and Baldie sat at another table with Bear.

After a few minutes, a small man walked up the stairs with an acoustic guitar case. He looked to be in his 40s and had a bush of clown-like hair that ringed a bald pate. He had large, thick glasses that made his eyes look unnaturally huge. He looked cautiously at the crowd, then walked over to us.

"Hi," he said in a high, nasal voice. "I'm Dave. I just heard we're both playing tonight."

"Yeah," I said.

Behind his back, Margo raised her eyebrows. I tried not to smile, but couldn't stop myself. His voice had the tonal quality of an air horn.

"Um, yeah," I continued. "When do you want to play?"

"Well," he squeaked. "I was planning on playing two sets, so maybe I could go first and last. My first set's only about 40 minutes."

"Sounds good to me," I said. "What do you think, guys?"

"Perfect," Margo said. "By the way, I'm Margo."

She launched an enthusiastic hand out and Dave shook it fishily. Keri and I introduced ourselves, too.

Once we were set up, we scoped out a table for the three of us near our new pals. We ordered drinks from a waitress whose black lipstick accentuated pale Goth skin. Two aging hippie couples came up the stairs, greeting Dave with quick nods as he set up. They looked suspiciously at our group, but sat at a table close to the stage.

"Good evening," Dave said shyly into the microphone. He sat on a bar stool and balanced his acoustic guitar on his knee.

"Who's this dork?" Bear asked.

Margo turned to him and smiled.

"It ain't The Dildon'ts," she said.

Dave began strumming his guitar soothingly.

"I'm Dave Walton, and I'd like to start out with a little song about my dog, Skip."

"Good lord," Margo said.

Dave strummed through a long solo with minimal chord changes until he finally got to the verse:

Eyes like chocolate, oh so sweet,

They'll melt your heart, and make you weak.

With your little pink nose, and your canine smile,

Why'd you up and leave me for that other child?

"Even his dog can't stand him," Margo said to Bear's table, who burst into loud laughter.

Dave flushed, but kept singing. His table of friends turned and glared at us, then whispered to each other. I was mortified for the guy. He looked so pathetic up there by himself. And yet, he kept singing about his damn dog.

When the painful song finally reached the end, only the small table applauded. I looked around at the stone faces in our crowd, then lifted my hands to clap. Margo looked at me.

"Come on, the guy's pathetic," I said. "At least give him some sympathy applause."

Keri lifted her hands to clap, too, then Margo did the same in an apathetic way. The Peacekeepers remained silent.

"Thanks," Dave said. "Thanks a lot. Now this next one's a little cheerier. It's about my life as a kid on the farm."

"Old McDonald?" Chain-nose called from the back of the room, then they laughed. I noticed Jean did not.

Dave ignored the heckling and launched into a song that sounded like a faster version of the Skip ditty. This tune featured not just a dog, but cattle and sheep as well. At the end, the slight applause trickled through the room.

"We're outta here," Bear said, pushing his chair away from the table.

"Oh, stay!" Margo said. "We're on soon."

"We'll be back," he said. "I just can't take this."

As Dave was starting his next quiet song, The Peacekeepers were loudly gathering their things and making plans for a drink nearby. Dave had almost finished the song by the time they agreed they would go to a dive they saw on the ride in, then dragged their heavy boots loudly through the room. Even Margo looked a little relieved when the last Peacekeeper left.

We sat through the rest of Dave's lame set, and a handful of people joined us in the room. They, too, looked like a gentle singer-songwriter crowd and I wondered how our loud set was going to go over. After another half hour, Dave announced his departure and introduced us. More polite applause as he climbed off his stool and grimly put his guitar back into its case.

"This should be interesting," Margo said.

We walked to the front and checked the P.A., a small head that we had to operate ourselves. After fighting some initial feedback, I strapped on my bass and clicked my amp on. Margo did the same. The small crowd stared at us blankly.

"Hi everybody!" Margo said perkily. "We're Broad Street from Philadelphia. It's great to be here in D.C. tonight." More blank stares. She turned to us and nodded. Keri clicked off into the first song, "Priscilla."

As soon as we hit the first loud note, I noticed faces wince. Keri slammed solidly on the drums and Margo's Fender amp felt piercingly loud. My bass was lost in the muddle. The closest table stuck their fingers in their ears and leaned into talk to each other. They nodded, then got up, and walked down the stairs. Margo looked over at me and rolled her eyes. The only people left were the waitress, who was bouncing her head to the beat, Dave, who sat in a table alone, and two other tables of people. I felt my energy wane. When we reached the end of the song, we were greeted with the same pathetic applause that bookended Dave's performance.

We moved quickly into the second song and another table got up and walked out of the room. We were now playing to four people. I tried to remain enthusiastic, but felt ridiculous. My hips froze, my fingers merely ran through the drill. Keri slowed, too. Her playing was flawless but lifeless as we ran through songs like we were saying the Pledge of Allegiance for the thousandth time. Margo seemed to keep her energy up, but I could tell she was annoyed. As we wound down the fourth song, we heard loud voices from downstairs. We stopped to stare. So did Dave, the waitress, and the sole surviving couple. The wall of noise came up the stairs. I felt surprised relief when I saw Bear's head appear.

A potpourri of people had joined them. There were three rockabilly guys with long sideburns and denim jackets, two heavily-painted women who looked like prostitutes (but who was I to judge?), and two young bikers wearing leather jackets. The crowd filled the room, hailing the waitress enthusiastically.

"Let's start again," Margo said.

I smiled.

"Definitely."

"Thanks for coming out tonight," Margo said happily in the microphone. "We're Broad Street from Philadelphia, and we're here to rock your world."

The Peacekeepers and their band of cretins cheered wildly. Keri clicked off four, and we sang "Priscilla" again. This time, my hips swayed, my lips locked into a permanent smile, and energy pulsed through my veins like mother's milk.

After the set, the party began. Shots of Jagermeister were washed down with big pints of cheap beer. Our gang took up most of the room and drowned out poor Dave attempting a second set. Margo sat with Bear and the two young—and not that bad looking—bikers. I sat with the two rockabilly guys, whose names were Paul and T.J. They weren't bad looking, either. Keri sat with Jean and two Peacekeepers. We swapped facts about our lives. Paul and T.J were also in a band and we made plans to help each other get gigs in our respective cities. As closing time approached, my buzz was proportionate to my flirtation ratio, and I leaned close to the cuter of the two, Paul, whose slicked back brown hair and matching chocolate eyes (just like the dog Skip!) were looking pretty good. He responded by moving his cowboy boot next to me, touching my leg just enough to make it tingle.

The lights flicked on and off.

"Last call!" the Goth waitress announced to resounding boos.

I looked over at Margo, who seemed to be forming a nice little pact herself with one of the young bikers, a dark-skinned cutey with black eyes that looked temptingly dangerous.

"Party back at our place!" Bear announced.

The bribe of more booze got everyone to respond to the waitress's request to get the hell out.

"Where's the party?" Paul asked.

"Back at our motel in Milling Hill. Wanna come?" I slurred.

"Milling Hell? Why are you staying at that dump?"

I laughed.

"Hey Margo!" I called over to her.

She was doubled-over laughing, falling into her young biker's embrace. She looked up, her eyes heavy with alcohol.

"Apparently they call that dump we're staying in 'Milling Hell'!" I said.

She looked at me, squinted her eyes as if to process this information, then burst out into laughter again.

Neither of us were in any condition to drive. I scanned the room for some semblance of sobriety, and paused at Keri and Jean. I walked over to them.

The lights clicked on and off again.

"All right, folks, let's go!"

This time it was the manager. He had tolerated us long enough.

"Hey, Jean," I said as I approached the group. "Would you be all right to drive? I don't think Margo or I should be behind a wheel."

She cocked her head and smiled.

"That's not going to look very good on your annual review," she said.

Jean was a biker and had a sense of humor? I wasn't sure I could handle this.

"Sure," she continued.

"Keri, are you all right?" I asked.

"I'm fine," she said. "I only had a couple beers."

"Perfect," I said. "Let's go."

We grabbed our equipment and headed back to Milling Hell. Jean drove Tiny, Margo and biker boy. I rode with Paul and T.J., my head peeking between the two front seats. Keri's car was too full of drums to take more than the other young biker.

The drive back was hazy, and the evening got hazier. There was more beer at The Peacekeeper Plaza, and the last thing I remembered was sitting on one of their beds with my legs wrapped around Paul, my skirt riding up to my waist. I leaned my head back for just a minute. My eyelids were so heavy.

I woke up the next morning with a pounding headache. I was under the covers, boots and all. I felt a body next to mine, but I was afraid to turn and identify it. This was the last time, I promised myself again. From this day forward I would never overindulge, never be in another compromising position. I prayed the warm flesh beside me wasn't Bear, or worse. The body stirred.

"Oh shit," Keri said. "We were supposed to check out at 11:00."

I turned to see Keri, also fully clothed, with a deep sleep wrinkle creasing her pink cheek. Somehow I had made it back to our room. I smiled.

"Morning," I said trying to spare her the wrath of my morning breath.

I peeled my body from the bed to peek over at the two lumps in the bed next to ours: Margo and the young biker. They did not look as fully clothed.

"Time to get up!" I said. My head was still fuzzy. I still felt drunk.

The lump stirred, and Margo turned to face us. Her one eyelid opened to stare at us, then snapped shut again.

"Someone kill me now," she said.

Keri pulled herself out of bed.

"Come on," she said. "Let's get a nice greasy breakfast. I know a great restaurant."

"Funny," I said, twisting out of the sheets.

"Kh," Margo said. "Can you throw me that T-shirt?"

I picked up the floral T-shirt that was draped over a chair and tossed it her way. Margo wriggled under the sheets, groaned, and pulled herself up. She looked over her shoulder at the body next to her, then smacked it with the back of her hand.

"Get up," she said, then looked at us and shrugged.

The lump stirred and turned around. The guy still looked pretty good this morning. His black shiny hair was crumpled into a sexy disarray; his bronze skin was stubbled with morning beard. Margo got up and walked around the bed, retrieving his clothes from the floor and plopping them next to his head.

There was a loud rap at the door.

"Housekeeping!" a muffled woman's voice called.

"We'll be right out!" I called back.

We all took turns in the bathroom, washing our faces, brushing the night off our teeth and replacing our smoky clothes with clean ones. The biker clothed himself under the covers and rose to sleepily greet the three girls who stared at him quizzically.

"Well," he said, standing and stretching. He walked over to Margo, picked up her hand, and kissed it. "I guess I better get going. Keep in touch."

"Definitely," Margo whispered.

The biker turned toward Keri and me. "You gals were awesome last night."

"Thanks," we said.

"See you around."

He walked to the door and opened it, flooding the room with sunlight, then pulled it shut.

"That was one sexy guy," I said. "What was his name?"

"Beats me," Margo answered.

A few minutes later, we went outside to pack up our cars. The lot was empty. Even the young biker had disappeared. The sun warmed the morning chill, and the only sound was the faint whoosh of cars speeding down a distant highway.

CHAPTER

" We identified the source of the emails."

Nancy stood in the doorway of my office, arms crossed. I turned slowly, my heart pounding. Who would my future killer be?

"Do you know a Dale Burkhardt?"

Dale? I had barely thought of him since the day in Clark Park. That seemed like an eternity ago. Why would he threaten me like that?

"Yes," I answered. "That's my ex-boyfriend."

Nancy squeezed into my office and closed the door behind her.

"Kit, this could be serious. You might want to think about pressing charges."

I took a deep breath. This wasn't what I expected.

"I don't know, Nancy. I think he's just really mad at me. He's kind of a jerk, but I don't think he's dangerous."

I knew I sounded like a stereotypical abused spouse, but I didn't think I was being naïve. Dale cheated on me, yes, but he was never violent. Clark Park was the first time he even raised his voice toward me.

"I'll trust your judgment, Kit," Nancy said. "The emails do seem to have stopped. But if you change your mind, let me know."

"Thanks, Nancy."

After she left, I picked up the phone and dialed a work number I had called a million times before.

"Retro Records," a female voice answered.

"Is Dale there?"

A pause. "Kit?"

"Yeah."

"Hi, it's Maria. I haven't heard your voice in a while. How've you been?"

I thought about this question. She had asked me how I was doing many times before, and I had always answered with my rote—"fine, thanks." But this time, her question highlighted a new lightness in my life. Was this happiness?

"I'm really great, Maria. Thanks."

"Hold on, I'll get Dale."

The phone clunked down on a counter, and Maria called for Dale.

"Yello!"

"Hi, it's me."

There was silence on the other end of the phone.

"How are you?" I asked.

"Shitty. You?"

"Listen, Dale. I want to know why you sent me that email."

"What email?"

"They traced it back to you."

More silence.

"If you're trying to make a point," I said, "I don't get it." I felt surprisingly calm.

"I just worry about you being by yourself," he finally said.

"So you want to scare me into being worried, too?"

"I know. It was stupid. I was a little drunk when I sent it. I just keep seeing your name in the paper, and I guess it kept reminding me of you when I spend most of my time trying to forget. "

I smiled. How many times had I sat alone, drinking myself into a stupor? I pictured Dale with a whiskey bottle and computer mouse, convincing himself that he could prove I needed protection by creating a stalker. Did this mean I'd won? The band that I had started, to make Dale miserable, had actually made Dale miserable. But Broad Street had become something else, too.

"I know what you're going through," I said. "And it sucks. But you'll get through it."

"What?"

"Give it time. Find a friend. Believe me, it helps."

I floated through the rest of the week. Time that had once dragged by as a constant reminder of my solitude now passed more quickly. Maybe I would buy a motorcycle.

We had two rehearsals to prepare for the music conference show, and Keri continued to get stronger every time. She even brought in two song ideas that we perfected and added to our set.

I got to the Middle East club Saturday night a little after 8:00. The club had three levels—the first floor was a bar with a jukebox, the second floor was for live music, and the third floor was an occasional comedy club. On cue, Adam was waiting on the first floor, ready to help with the equipment. He looked as disheveled as always, his thick hair and wardrobe rumpled.

"Hey Adam," I said.

"Hey Kit!" he said, leaning down to pick up my equipment. "Looks like a good bill tonight."

"Go ahead – give me the poop on all the bands."

"Well, I don't want to bore you."

"Knock your socks off."

"Okay, well, since you asked, I'm sure you know Zen Guerilla will put on an awesome show. They just got signed by Subpop and you know they're from Newark but they moved out to San Francisco recently, and they put on a crazy live show. EDO is, like, insane, and this band Mothra has like a pop sound but it's a mix of good humor. And this other girl band, Mae Pang, is getting some buzz…"

I could concentrate no more. How many bands were playing tonight? Good lord.

I ignored Adam's rambling trivia as I followed him up the stairs into a large empty room dripping with dark wall tapestries. I waved to Keri, who was on the stage talking to a skinny guy with glasses. Most of the scattered musicians were average-looking rockers, but there was a small group of two men and two women who looked ready for Halloween. One guy wore a silver suit with a matching silver hat and thick black glasses. The other guy had a green plaid suit and a yellow fedora. The two girls were dressed in harem-like sheer pink and orange silks, their hair tied in ponytails at the tops of their heads. I couldn't decide if they looked cool, or ridiculous.

"I'm going to go down to wait for Margo," Adam said.

"Okay."

I walked over to Keri, who smiled when she saw.

"That guy's the drummer for the headlining band, Teaser," she said excitedly. "He said they expect a few labels here tonight."

My chest tightened.

"Really? I wish I didn't know that."

"Why? You'll be great, as always. We're gonna totally kick ass." She looked over my shoulder. "Oh, there's Margo."

Margo and Adam dragged equipment behind the stage, then we began the arduous waiting process. We were third on a five-band bill, so it would be about three hours before we would play. I sucked down Diet Cokes to keep my energy up.

I thought the first band, Sleepy Lagoo, was painfully ordinary. Their songs melded together like one big hookless mess. The costumed band took the stage next.

"Thanks for coming out tonight," the silver man said into the microphone. "We're Fruity Too Shoes."

The harem girls stood to either side of Mr. Silver, palms pressed together above their heads in genie pose. Mr. Plaid was on keyboards, and started a Middle Eastern melody using a distorted clarinet voice. The girls started shifting their heads back and forth between their raised arms. They looked ridiculous. I looked at Margo and Keri, and the three of us burst into laughter. Mr. Silver stepped to the microphone, glancing angrily at our table, and Margo quickly snapped to a straight face. The girls began to sway their arms as if in a breeze. They stole awkward glances at each other to make sure they were in synch.

"Until I ate your cracker I just couldn't see," he spoke/sang. "The twisted little gnome that's inside of me. I'll give you all my money if you just don't cry. I'd rather eat my organs than to see you lie."

The song droned on. I glanced around the room to see a common expression—confusion. But as the song reached the end, a group of girls walked up from the bar, set their drinks on a table by the stage, then began to follow the genie dance with waving arms and warbling heads. These freaks had groupies.

The three of us stifled laughs and rolled our eyes through the rest of their set. Adam squirmed uncomfortably as members of the band shot angry looks our way. I felt bad, but I couldn't help myself. When they finally reached the end, I was convinced they were ready to kill us. I'd also sucked down five diet cokes, so the caffeine wasn't helping my anxiety

Fruity Too Shoes packed up their few pieces of equipment. I waited to approach the stage until they were safely away from the area and being praised by their small huddle of adoring fans. I felt their angry eyes on me as I pulled my equipment around from the back of the stage and started setting it up. I glanced up to see the floor filling with what seemed to be an older crowd than usual. Adam stood grinning off to the side. In the back corner, I saw the shadowed figure of Laura Cook from the City Paper.

Keri was tuning and tightening and adjusting the stool nervously. Margo chatted over-confidently, always a sign that she was anxious. I tried not to think that how we were about to perform would be written about and judged and criticized. Just have fun with it, I kept repeating. It's just another show.

"Ready?" Margo mouthed to us both. We nodded and I turned to Keri and smiled. She responded with a stiff grin, then clicked four counts.

"Take That" exploded to life. I concentrated so hard on hitting the right notes, that I felt my fingers occasionally slip to the wrong ones. I saw the Fruity gang huddled near the bar, glancing in our direction and whispering.

It's just another show. Keep calm.

I sang the background chorus stiffly, then stumbled my way to the end of the song. As we hit the crescendo note, Adam applauded alone as the crowd took the moment of quiet to squeeze in some dialog.

"Thank you," Margo said overzealously. "This next one's a little song about a local musician who shall remain nameless. It's called 'Poser.'"

A few people chuckled as I ran through my introductory bass line. I flubbed one note, but not too badly. Margo smiled and swung her hips and Keri splashed around the kit confidently. When I looked up at the audience, I saw that Charlie had joined Adam. He glanced over at me and smiled. When I smiled back at him, I realized I felt lighter, the notes came easier. The music oozed out of my fingers and lips and body until I could almost taste its sweetness.

When we reached the end of the set, most of the audience ignored us, but our group cheered and whistled.

"One more!" Leah called, but the sound guy immediately resumed the house music to let us know there was no time for an encore.

We packed our things quickly and pulled the equipment behind the stage. After I was finished, I walked over to Charlie, who was talking to Leah.

"Hi stranger," I said, giving him a friendly peck on the cheek. "Thanks for coming out."

"You were great," he said.

I wanted to tell him how much his being there meant to me, how my mood improved because he was there to support me. Not because he wanted to get laid, but because he liked me.

But Leah was there, so I smiled at him and hoped he understood.

I chatted with the three of them about our adventures in D.C., and Margo came back with drinks. As she handed one to me, I saw over Margo's shoulder that a stocky man was walking toward us. His white hair was tied in a ponytail.

"I really enjoyed your set," he said, his big rosy cheeks pushed up into a grin as he moved into our conversation circle; his strong cologne stung my nose.

"Thanks," Margo and I said in unison.

"I'm Jackie Rose." He plunged his chubby hand toward me to shake it, then worked the rest of circle as we each made introductions. "I'm with a studio in Center City. And I would love to record you girls. I'm always looking for new projects for a collaboration I have with Dynamic Records. Have you recorded before?"

I was stunned. Dynamic Records? Is this how it worked? You just play a club at the right time in front of the right guy, and your career is officially launched? It seemed too easy, but visions of tour busses and platinum albums and music documentaries flashed before my eyes.

"We have a demo CD," I answered.

"Yeah, I have one with me," Margo said. "I'll give you a copy."

"Great," he continued. "I think you girls have a kind of raw energy that would be interesting to record. Can you come down to the studio next week sometime?"

"Sure," I said quickly. "When?"

He pulled a calendar from his back pocket and flipped through the pages.

"How about Tuesday?" he said.

"Um," Margo hesitated. "I actually can't do Tuesday."

Keri and I shot her angry glares.

"I'm sorry, any other night would be good for me."

"No problem," Jackie said. "How about Thursday, about 8:00?"

"Perfect," I answered quickly. The other two agreed.

"All right," he said, stuffing the small calendar back into his pocket. "I'm off. It was good meeting you girls. I'll see you Thursday night."

He shook our hands and walked out of the room. We waited until he was safely out of earshot before squealing.

"Dynamic Records?" I said. "Oh my god!"

Charlie hugged me. I caught his eyes when we parted and for a brief moment I thought I might be falling in love. I just wasn't completely sure who or what I was falling in love with.

I sailed through my work week, numb. When Thursday night finally came, Keri,

Margo and I carpooled to Jackie's studio, which was in a large brownstone in Center City. We struggled to find parking, then settled for a spot four blocks away. We hurried to make the meeting time.

We stepped up to the deep mahogany door of the building and I rang the doorbell. As the door slowly creaked open, I half expected Lurch from The Addams Family to greet us. Instead, it was a small woman with long graying hair that blanketed a colorful dress.

"You must be Broad Street," she said sweetly. "Please, come in. I'm Ruth, Jackie's partner."

We walked through the vestibule and into an incredible old mansion. My eyes were drawn to the painted tin ceiling that loomed high above me, then down to a dark wooden staircase. On my right was an enormous living room. Portraits thick with oil paint lined the walls and intricate Oriental rugs covered the hardwood floors. Overstuffed cranberry chairs and sofas nestled by the marble fireplace that was ablaze with a warm glow.

"Is this your house?" Margo asked.

"Yes," Ruth answered. "It was left to me by my great grandmother. Our family's been here for years. It's a big job to keep up with and always needs a lot of work, but it's worth it. I would hate to see it chopped up into apartments like most of the old places in Philadelphia."

We followed her into the living room.

"Have a seat," she said. "I'll get Jackie."

We walked over to the fireplace and sank into the plush velour furniture.

"I could get used to this," Keri said.

The fire crackled and hissed soothingly.

"It's Broad Street!" Jackie's voice interrupted the quiet room. "Welcome!"

He was wearing a red silk kimono that wrapped around the ball of his stomach. A gold chain hung from his neck, strangled by thick gray chest hair that popped from the neck of his wrap. His white hair was still tied into a ponytail at the base of his neck, and his cheeks were aglow. As we stood to greet him; he shook each of our hands enthusiastically. I felt like we were greeting the Wizard of Oz.

"Come on down to the studio," he said.

We followed him down a long red hallway. I glanced at the small oil paintings that lined the wall. Each one was surely worth more than my entire salary. Jackie led us down a long narrow staircase that ended in a large carpeted room filled with recording equipment. I scanned the room, my eyes stopping on a wall of Platinum and Gold records. I caught Keri's eyes and nodded toward the wall. She glanced over at them, then looked back at me with eyebrows raised.

We turned back to face two computers that glowed from each corner of the room; between them stretched immense soundboards checkered with dozens of knobs and sliders. A young stocky blond guy sat in front of one of the boards with headphones on, his head bent forward in concentration. We walked closer, causing him to jump slightly. He pulled the headphones off.

"Jimmy, I want you to meet Broad Street," Jackie said.

Jimmy smiled and rose, shaking each of our hands in introduction.

"This is my son," Jackie said proudly. "As if you couldn't tell. We're lucky we can keep this business all in the family."

He turned to us, and his voice became serious.

"You never know what fucking slimeballs are out there to stab you in the back." His eyes locked with each of ours briefly, and then he burst into a jovial grin again.

"So let me give you the tour."

He reviewed the equipment in the recording room first. I smiled and nodded, hoping he wouldn't notice I had no clue what he was talking about. We then went into smaller rooms adjacent to the recording room, each of which had a musical niche. The small vocal room had an impressive microphone dangling from the ceiling. The drum room had a sparkling Yamaha kit; the guitar rooms had walls of Fender, Hartke, and Marshall amps. Margo, Keri, and I oohed and ahed and smiled and nodded, and I could tell they were just as overwhelmed as I was.

When we were back in the main room and Jackie was rambling on about the latest computer software that did practically everything except write the song, I stole another glance at the gold and silver records shimmering from the wall. This was serious.

"Can we get you ladies something to drink?" Jackie asked. "Beer? Wine?"

"Sure," Margo said. "I'll have a glass of wine, red if you have it."

"That sounds good," I said.

"Yeah, I'll have one, too," Keri said. "Thanks."

"Great," Jackie said, then turned toward his son. "Jimmy, would you go grab us some drinks?"

His son clicked something on the soundboard, spun his chair around and headed up the stairs.

"Have a seat," Jackie said, pointing to a leather couch against the back wall.

We sat down. Jackie pulled one of the engineer chairs over to us.

"You can see by the evidence behind you that I know a little something about this industry. I've been in the business a long time," he said, leaning forward on his elbows, "and I know how tough it can be. For every album on this wall there are a million bands that will never come close to that kind of success. Most bands start because they watch a video or listen to a song on the radio and think all it takes is a guitar and some balls to make it. Some actually have a little talent, but most don't. And those that do have no clue how to go about marketing themselves."

He paused dramatically.

"I think you girls have a little talent. But, I have to be honest with you, I listened to your demo the other day, and it's crap."

I felt myself flush, ashamed to have had the audacity to even hand this obvious professional our primitive demo.

"The recording is muddy and distorted. The levels are completely off. The guitar is out of tune and the drums speed up and slow down a dozen times in a three minute song."

"That was our old drummer," I said softly.

Jackie nodded his head and smiled at Keri.

"I didn't think you could have been so bad so recently. You were a metronome the other night. Anyway, I thought the bass playing was pretty solid, the vocals were okay. Overall, the songs weren't bad."

He was interrupted by Jimmy padding down the steps with a bottle of wine in one hand and four wine glasses pinched between the fingers of his other hand.

"Oh, great," Jackie said. "Jimmy, would you mind pouring?"

Jimmy put the glasses down on a small table at the end of the couch and poured four glasses of red wine and distributed them. He started to walk back to the board, but his father interrupted him.

"Son, would you mind giving us a few minutes?"

His lips pursed slightly before he sighed and walked back up the stairs.

"He's a good kid," Jackie continued. "He just never knows when to take a break. Anyway, as I was saying, the songs weren't bad. The arrangement is a little primitive, and the vocals could use some work, but I think there's something there."

I drank the bitter red wine, feeling lighter with Jackie's borderline praise. He took a big swallow of his wine before continuing.

"Now what we can offer in this studio is a chance. Here's my idea. There were a few songs you played the other night that I really liked. I'd like to work on those songs with you – as well as hear what else you have. The songs on the demo could also be possibilities, but they'll need some work. Once we get about four good songs perfected, we record them. By the time we're finished, I guarantee you won't recognize yourselves. We can turn this band into something really special. I'll take it to my rep at Dynamic, and we'll see if we can get a nibble."

I glanced over at Margo and Keri. They each sat wide-eyed, their wine glasses nestled in their laps. We would be famous. Somewhere in the near future, I might join the ranks of my heroes—Chrissy Hynde, Debbie Harry, Kim Gordan. I took another sip of my wine as fantasies of money and fame flooded through me.

"So what do you think?" Jackie asked.

"Sounds like a great opportunity," I said quickly.

"It's an excellent opportunity," he said sternly, "and not one that many bands get. Now, this studio normally charges $200 an hour for recording time, but because I'm going to take a personal interest in this project, I'm going to lower that price to just $75 an hour."

I felt myself deflate.

"We have to pay for this?" Margo asked.

Jackie looked at her and wrinkled his brow.

"Margo," he began patronizingly. "Do you have any idea how much it costs to put out a record? Thousands and thousands of dollars. Some bands spend $10,000 on demo CDs. And that money doesn't guarantee that record will even be heard. I'm guaranteeing you that if you can produce a decent record, it will be heard. I also think we can do it for less than five."

"Thousand?" I asked.

It was my turn for the look.

"I know you girls are new to the industry," he said. "But ask around. This is a very good chance for you. Of course, it's up to you. You can continue playing the same local clubs in front of the same audience over and over. But, this crowd will grow tired of you and they will stop coming to see you. Or, you can take a minimal risk, and have your music played around the country. You might get to play in Europe or Japan or Iceland. But, music is a tough business and, to be honest, it's an ageist business. Now you're all young and cute and that's great…but it won't last forever."

"So what would we need to do?" Keri asked.

"First, think of this as an investment. Once you get signed, you'll get every penny back. I would take $2,500 up front, and then we'll see how far that takes us."

"We don't have $2,500," Margo said.

Keri and I nodded; the three of us looked helplessly to our new guru for some guidance.

"Do you have anyone that might lend you the money?" he asked.

The three of us looked at each other for answers.

"Maybe my parents could lend me some money," I suggested.

"Yeah, mine might be able to do that, too," Keri said.

Margo looked at the two of us, then looked back at Jackie. He raised his eyebrows in anticipation.

"Can we get back to you?" she asked.

"Of course!" he said. "I would just need to know fairly soon, because I'd have to work you into our spring schedule. We've got Stitch in 9 coming in to cut a new record in a few weeks, and we're putting the final touches on working with The Venturas."

"The Venturas are coming here?" I asked.

"Well," Jackie raised his palm to the air. "Nothing is official, but we're close."

"So when would you need to know?" Keri asked.

"I'll tell you what," he said. "Let me know by next Monday."

"No problem," I said, my mind already spinning with ways to approach my parents.

As he walked us back upstairs and to the front door, I glanced in the living room where we had been just about an hour before. The fire was out and the room was dark. Only a small wall sconce lit our way down the dim hallway. He opened the door to the bitter cold night.

"Remember girls," he said as he shook each of our hands. "You are a good investment. Believe in yourselves."

The door creaked closed behind us.

Once back in the car, Keri and I could hardly contain our enthusiasm. I twisted myself around to see her in the back seat.

"Did you see those records?" I asked. "There were some huge names on that wall."

Margo remained silent as we chirped away. I turned to see her staring stonefaced out the front car window as she navigated her way back home.

"What is it, Margo?" I asked.

"I don't know," she said. "I think it's kind of creepy that he didn't mention the money right away."

"I guess that's how it works," I said. "He's giving us a break."

"So he says. Don't you think it's odd that all of the albums on his wall are from the 80s? I didn't see anything current on that wall."

"Maybe he just hasn't had a hit in a while," Keri said. "That still doesn't change the fact that he worked on all those gold records."

"Tell you what," I said, "Jackie said The Venturas were recording with him. I have Daria's email address. I'll send her a note and see what she thinks."

Margo stared silently at the road before us, which irritated me. Wasn't this what we had all hoped for?

The next day at work, I was still buzzing from the evening. Decimal points and medical terms and doctor's egos became mere stepping-stones on my ascension to the fame that surely awaited me. But every time I saw Nancy's kind face or Rachel's friendly smile, or heard the banter of the office gossipers, or smelled the fresh coffee brewed in the lunch room, I felt a strange sensation that I couldn't quite identify. Oddly, it seemed to border sadness. I knew what to expect from this place, which lent a certain comfort. There were friends here who genuinely cared about me. I wasn't sure what awaited my life post-Jackie. But I knew I wanted to make music, and he would hand me that opportunity.

I decided to call Nikki to fill her in. Her machine picked up.

"Hey, it's me," I began. "I wanted to let you know the latest with the…"

"Kit?" Nikki's tired voice answered the phone.

"Are you sleeping? It's 3:00 in the afternoon."

No, I'm just, tired," she paused. "I broke up with Ted last night."

"What? What happened?"

"You were right."

"Right about what?"

"He never planned to leave his wife. We had a long talk last night and he told me for the eight thousandth time that it just wasn't the right time, blah blah blah." I could hear her softly crying. "I have totally fucked up my life. I have no job. I'm alone. You hate me for being so stupid."

"You know that's not true."

"Why can't I just be normal? Why do I continually pick the wrong guys?"

"That is normal. Believe me, you're not alone."

"Kit, you can't understand. You have a great job and a band and interesting friends and a great place. What do I have?"

"Nikki, you have a family who cares about you. You're beautiful and smart and a talented artist. Maybe you should focus on that for a while." I paused. "Look, I got mixed up with the wrong guy many times. Dale never treated me with any respect. Then there was this other guy who was a total asshole. But being alone has really taught me a lot. I'm not saying it's easy, but overall I feel better. When I was with these guys, I just felt like shit about myself all the time. Now, I only feel like shit some of the time. But, even that's gotten better."

There was a silence on the other end.

"Maybe you're right," she said. "But right now I want to feel sorry for myself."

"Fair enough. Want to come over for pizza tonight?"

"Thanks, Kit, but not tonight. I'll call you tomorrow."

When I hung up the phone, I was worried. She sounded so defeated. I could hardly tell her the good band news now.

Keri called me at home that night.

"I got the money!" she said. "My parents said they'd lend me $1,000. They're actually pretty excited about it."

"You're kidding! I haven't even gotten up the nerve to talk to my parents yet."

"I told them about Jackie and how he's produced so many big names and they think it's a great opportunity." She paused. "When do you think you might talk to your parents? We have to get back to him by early next week."

"I know. I'll call them tonight."

"How about Margo?"

"She hasn't said anything about it."

Keri was quiet on the other end and I suspected she was pissed.

"Look," I said. "Don't worry. We'll get the money."

"Okay," she said skeptically. "Call me later and let me know how you make out."

"No problem."

But of course it was a problem. I was sure my parents thought pursuing a dream of rock fame was equivalent to pursuing a job as an actress or a painter. While creativity is certainly noble, it must be grounded with a solid profession. Like teaching about creativity.

Then again, I could lie.

This was an interesting idea. It certainly wouldn't be the first time I'd lied to my parents. In high school I could hardly be expected to tell them I'd attended a liquor-soaked party. I was sparing their unnecessary concern by telling them I was actually off to see a wholesome film with my friends. And when my college grades plummeted my freshmen year, I couldn't tell them it was because I was sleeping through morning classes. It was for their own good that I invented an intestinal disorder. These little white lies never hurt anyone. I survived and they didn't have to worry.

But this was different. In the business world, I believe this would be called fraud.

It wasn't like I wouldn't pay them back. I'd definitely pay them back.

Why would I need $1,000? Car repairs? That would have the protective parental clause attached. They certainly wouldn't want their daughter to be without a car. School? My father always approved anything academic. But these were too far from the truth. Maybe I could weave music into these lies.

My car broke down on the way to a gig after taking a class about Chaucer.

No, sloppy. Music lessons. That might work. I would tell them I needed $1,000 to take music lessons. The Curtis Institute of Music just started a new program for beginners and I could learn the acoustic bass and how to read music. Perfect. Curtis was one of the best music academies in the country. My plan had an academic twist that wasn't too far from the truth. I did need the money to learn how to be a better musician. I would just be taught by a pop teacher instead of a classically trained one.

I pulled the phone from its cradle and paced the room. The clock pecked at the silent room like a bird tapping on a window. I took a deep breath and dialed. My father answered.

"Hi Dad," I said cheerfully.

"Hello," he said, his voice gravelly.

"What's wrong? You sound like you have a cold."

"Ah, just allergies."

"There's nothing to be allergic to this time of year."

"I'm allergic to old age. How are you? We haven't heard from you in a while."

"Oh, I'm okay. Work's good. My new boss is nice. Band is good."

"So what's up? It sounds like you have to tell me something."

I inhaled deeply to calm myself. It's for his own protection that I need to enhance the truth. Okay, alter the truth. But this is the chance of a lifetime, and when we get signed and our album joins the wall of gold and platinum, it will all be worth it.

But the words that came out of my mouth were, "I need to borrow a thousand dollars to make a record."

What happened? I had told the truth. That was it. I had hit the end of my dream.

I pulled a corner of the blanket from the back of my couch, and wrapped it slightly around me as I waited for his reply. I heard the crackle of a cigarette pack on the other end of the phone, the click of a lighter, the hiss of inhaled tobacco. He knew I was in no position to criticize him.

"A thousand dollars," he said slowly, pensively. "To make a record."

I had to sell this, and quickly. I exhaled one long breathless summation of Jackie's credentials and proposal, sounding crazed and desperate. My father remained silent.

Finally, he said, "And if you don't get signed?"

"I will still pay you back every cent. I promise."

"Like the car? Like your Spring Break vacation to Florida? Like…"

"Dad, you've made your point. But this is different. This is an investment. I was hoping you would believe in me enough to take this chance."

My father chuckled.

"Looks like I trained you well. It was only a matter of time before my guilt trips came back to bite me on the ass."

I let a moment pass. I was out of ammo and my future was in my father's hands.

"My concern is that this sounds a little too good to be true. This guy sees three young girls with stars in their eyes, and I'm worried he may take advantage of the situation."

My hope drained away.

"Why is this so important to you?" he asked.

This was a valid question, and I struggled for an answer.

"Dad, I know this isn't the life you envisioned for me. But this band has connected me to things in a way I've never experienced. There have been so many women in music that have influenced me in a positive way. I guess I want to do that for other people."

"Aren't you doing that now?"

"I don't know, maybe in a small way. I guess I just feel like this recording opportunity will give me a bigger voice."

He was silent. I took a deep breath.

"I'm sorry I'm such a disappointment."

"There's no need to be dramatic."

"I'm not. I just feel like I always let you down."

I heard the crackle of his inhaled cigarette.

"You are not a disappointment, and I'm sorry if I've made you feel that way." He exhaled. "You remind me of myself at your age. Maybe sometimes I wish I had taken a few more chances. That takes a lot of courage. But as your father I also want to protect you. Things don't always work out the way we hope they might."

It had been a long time since my father surprised me.

"What didn't work out for you?"

"Oh, I don't know. I just ran out of time."

"What do you mean? You taught thousands of students, you fought for the rights of underprivileged people. As much as I complained, I always admired that. You made me want to make a difference."

"You will. I'm not sure a band is the answer, but I'll help you out. I just want you to be careful. You don't need to be a famous rock star to make me proud of you."

"Thank you, Dad. Thank you. You won't be sorry, I promise."

"We'll see."

I stared at the quiet phone, back in its receiver. I had just upped the ante. I had to make this work.

I took another deep breath, and called Margo.

"So," she said, "What's happening? Has Dynamic called yet?"

"Well, I do have some good news. Keri and I got the money from our parents. A grand a piece."

"Already? Don't you think we're moving a little fast? We don't even know this guy."

"We have to move fast. He needs to know what we're going to do."

"I don't know, Kit," she said. "My parents don't have that kind of money. They don't live in Swarthmore, and Wal-Mart doesn't exactly offer tenure."

I sat down, embarrassed by my ignorance. That was why Margo had been so hesitant about the studio. I liked to think I was paying my dues, living hand to mouth with my own paycheck and feeling independence creep into my life after college. But I always had the safety net of my parents. I didn't have to pay for my own college, like Margo did, or work through high school to help pay the bills. I had naively assumed that the rest of the world could easily pick up the phone and solve a problem.

"I'm sorry, Margo," I said. "That was stupid of me."

She was silent for a moment.

"I have a little money saved," she began. "I was going to use it for something else, but I could put that into the pot."

"What were you saving it for?"

"Nothing important. Don't worry about it."

"Well, like Jackie told us, we have to think of this as an investment. You'll get your money back. We all will."

She paused, then echoed my father's skepticism.

"We'll see."

That Monday night, the three of us went to Jackie's house. I had called him over the weekend to let him know we had the money to get started. When we rang the bell, Jackie's son answered the door.

"Hi Jimmy," Margo greeted him. Keri and I smiled enthusiastically.

"Hey," he said glumly. "Come on in."

We followed the somber boy down the same dark hallway. Despite the chilly evening, the fireplace remained dark and the air in the house was damp and cool. We descended the stairs to the basement studio, where Jackie was waiting. He had on a different kimono tonight. This one was embroidered with white herons choked by a blue sash.

"Good evening girls," Jackie said, standing up to shake our hands. "Ready to get started?"

"Definitely," I said.

"Great. Tonight we'll just get the business end of things straightened out."

He turned to his son.

"Jimmy, why don't you bring us some wine?"

He clomped slowly up the stairs. I realized my initial assumptions were true. Lurch did live in this household.

"Okay, then. Have a seat and we'll get started."

We once again sat on the couch beneath his wall of fame. This is it. This is how it all starts. A glass of wine, an eccentric guy in a kimono, a click of an amp, and my new life begins.

Jackie reviewed the schedule. We would come into the studio three times a week. We would take the CD song by song, beginning with a list of our best 15 songs. We would start with the arrangements, then we would record the basic tracks. To embellish these tracks, he might hire some additional musicians—horns, lead guitar, percussion. The resulting project would be fabulous. We drank our wine and listened to Jackie's monologue. I was hypnotized.

"How does that sound?" Jackie asked.

"Expensive," Margo said.

I shot Margo a look, and she shrugged her shoulders.

"I'm sorry, Jackie," she continued. "Of course it sounds great. But now we're talking about hiring musicians, which would not only take more money, but totally alter our sound. I'm just worried that we'll get in over our heads."

Jackie smiled at Margo.

"Margo," he began. "I can see you're the voice of reason in this band."

"Not usually," she said, and we chuckled.

"You're a smart girl," he continued. "It's good to question these things. Here's what I'm going to do for you."

He pulled his chair a little closer to the couch. I winced at the amplification of his strong aftershave.

"I promise you I will keep you posted on our costs. We'll have a running tally as we move along, which will be used against the credit you're giving me tonight. If we run much over, we'll start a tab. I have such confidence in this project that I will keep this tab unpaid until after the project is done. Once we're finished, and we get a label to back the CD, we'll have the label take care of the entire amount."

"And if we don't get signed?" Margo asked.

"You will get signed," Jackie said.

He looked at each of us carefully.

"So do we have a deal?"

"I think it sounds great," I said.

"Me too," Keri agreed.

We all looked at Margo.

"Well, I certainly wouldn't want to be the dissenting voice here," she said. "These girls know that's not my style."

"So is it a deal?" Keri asked.

"Sure," Margo said. "What the hell."

"Great!" Jackie said, pushing his wheeled chair back toward the sound board as he stood up. "I'll just get the paperwork and we'll be done."

We watched quietly as Jackie went upstairs.

"Paperwork?" Margo said. "Look, if he gives us something to sign, I say we take it to someone. I've heard horror stories about bands getting stuck in lousy contracts."

As much as my impulse shopper called to me, I had to agree on this point. A contract was pretty scary.

"No problem," I said.

The ceiling quivered as footsteps walked down the upstairs hallway and then came down the stairs. He held a brown folder in his hand.

"Okay," he said sitting down. "Now this is just a formality. It protects you as much as it does me."

He pulled a legal-sized stack of papers from the folder. The front page alone looked like it had thousands of words in illegibly tiny print.

"This contract just says that you are hiring my services. That you are giving me a deposit for those services, and I am legally bound to deliver those services."

He handed the papers to Margo. Keri and I bent over her shoulders to look at it. Dozens of "herewiths" and "party tos" and "waivers" littered the page. A corner staple appeared to hold together at least a dozen similar pages.

"Now I know this looks intimidating," Jackie said. "But it's really just a standard contract that any band has when they first get started. I just need you to sign a few pages, initial a few things, and we're set to go. But, of course, take your time to review it."

He stood and picked up the wine bottle, refilling each of our glasses.

Even without a law degree, I could tell this contract looked pretty binding. It appeared that we were legally obligated to repay all expenses incurred at the studio. A third party could pay this expense, but if we weren't signed, we would herewith be screwed.

"I would feel more comfortable having a lawyer look at this," Margo said. "Not that we don't trust you, Jackie. I just think we need to make sure we know what we're getting into."

"Of course, that's fine," he said. "But there really isn't anything in there that I haven't reviewed with you. But I certainly want you to feel comfortable with this agreement. It's hardly the first time a lawyer has been involved in one of my deals. Go ahead and take that copy with you."

He stood up, clicked something on the soundboard, then turned back to us

"I do need to get some sort of deposit tonight, though. As I mentioned, I am holding the studio space for you, so I just need a good faith payment."

He turned back to the board. I leaned in toward Margo.

"I haven't gotten my dad's check yet," I whispered. "He was mailing it this weekend. Have you, Keri?"

"Not yet."

Margo looked at us both and shook her head.

"I can give him a thousand tonight," she said.

I grabbed Margo's knee excitedly.

"You won't regret this," I said. "This is the chance of lifetime."

She looked at me like a mother about to hand her child a forbidden piece of gooey candy, then pulled her checkbook out of her purse, and opened it up.

"Who do I make this out to?" she asked Jackie.

The next morning at work, I began my morning routine—click on my computer, log onto my email, sip my coffee, try to wake up. After reviewing the long list of interoffice memos regarding updates on proofreading procedure, I switched to Web mail to check my personal account. There were eight messages, most of which were jokes that I deleted immediately. Then I clicked on an unfamiliar return address. The message opened.

Hey Kit –

Great to hear from you! We had fun playing with you guys at The Trocadero, too. We've been pretty busy touring the past few week. I'm definitely looking forward to sleeping in my own bed.

It's funny you asked about Jackie Rose. He was trying to scam us into coming to his studio, but we found out he's a total washup. He did a bunch of big names in the 80s, but he hasn't had a hit in a long time. Sounds like he's trying to find the next big thing in Philly, but his reputation in the industry is shit. I'm sure he knows what he's doing, but I'd be leery of the guy.

Also, some maybe good news—we might be playing the Lollapalooza tour this summer and there is a chance we might be able to get you guys on the bill in Philly. They asked us to recommend a band that would be a good fit and I suggested you. I'll keep you posted. It would be fun to play another gig with you guys.

Daria

I stared at the note for a long time, reading and re-reading—Jackie's reputation in the industry is shit—but we might be playing the biggest tour going. The emotional roller coaster of this band thing was going to kill me. How was I going to break this to Margo? Hey, great news—we might be playing Lollapalooza but, oh, you just scraped together a thousand dollars you don't have and we plan to spend it all on a wash-up. Crap.

When I got back home, I decided to call the one person who might understand. The phone rang a long time before Charlie picked it up.

"Hey Charlie. It's Kit."

"Hey there. How are you?"

"I might be really great, but I'm not sure."

"That sounds intriguing."

"I need your opinion on something."

I explained the whole Jackie situation—the upfront money, the pressure to sign a contract. As the details spilled from my mouth, even before I mentioned Daria's email, I heard the same information Charlie heard—the facts added up to a con.

"You think this is a scam, right?" I asked.

"Well…" he began.

"Go ahead, you can say it. I'm an idiot."

"No, that's not true. The guy's done some impressive things. And I know that a band is liable for expenses incurred in a studio, even if they're signed by a label, but usually these expenses are seen as a loan. Once the band starts touring and selling albums, that revenue is used to pay off the loan. It just seems a little odd that he's not just selling you the idea of studio time, which at $75 an hour is not bad for a decent studio. It sounds like he's trying to lock you into his studio by dangling his former label connection in front of you with the promise of getting you signed. I guess that's the part I find odd."

"That's true, I didn't really look at it that way. Why wouldn't he just ask us to record at his studio?

"Would you if he hadn't promised other things?"

"Probably not."

"So what are you going to do?"

There was a knock on the door. I opened it to see Margo's face, pale and stunned.

"Charlie, let me call you back. Margo's here."

I hung up the phone.

"What happened?" I asked.

"Did you hear?" she said. "Kurt Cobain killed himself."

CHAPTER

Margo and I sat at my kitchen table staring at the CD cover of a baby floating in a pool, chasing an elusive dollar bill. We let the music of Nirvana wash over us, Cobain's pained voice made harsh by a fast-paced life. He was a stranger, a god, beautiful, and frightening, and raw. He was my voice and Margo's voice and Nikki's voice, and he decided he would rather blow his head off than take responsibility for how he made us all feel. What the fuck? I felt numb.

"I can't believe it," Margo said, tugging another drag from her cigarette. "Why would he kill himself?"

"Who knows? He's been a mess since he hooked up with Courtney. I remember seeing Hole at The Khyber. She was totally wasted."

"You can't blame her," Margo said. "He was pretty fucked up before that. I feel bad for that poor little baby."

I shook my head, took a long drag of my cigarette and exhaled. The room filled with a bluish haze.

"Oh shit," I said.

"What?"

"Nirvana was supposed to headline Lollapalooza this summer."

"So?"

I took a deep breath and crushed my cigarette into the ashtray.

"Okay, I have good news and bad news," I began.

"I hate when things start like that."

I took another big breath. "I heard back from Daria and I'm sure this is just a rumor and we can get the money back from Jackie. We didn't sign anything. I'm sorry.

I know it's your money on the line."

"What did she say?"

"She said that even though Jackie had some hits in the eighties, he hasn't done much since then, he doesn't have much of a reputation anymore, that kind of thing."

Margo squashed a cigarette into the ashtray, pulled another one from her pack and lit it.

"That's okay," she said finally.

"What?"

"What the fuck. You only live once, right?"

I smiled. "Yeah. Thanks." I exhaled for what felt like the first time in a while. "Really, thanks. I know it wasn't easy to get the money."

Margo shrugged.

"I did get some very good news in the same email," I said.

"Hit me."

"Daria also said she recommended us to play the Philly Lollapalooza show."

"Holy shit."

"Yep."

"The Pussy Willows are going to be pissed."

"I know. Isn't that awesome?"

"Meow."

The last Nirvana song on the CD ended and the room fell silent.

"I still can't believe he's gone," I said finally. "What a weird morning."

Margo was quiet.

"Are you okay?" I asked.

"I haven't always been a very good friend to you," she said. "I don't know what I would do if anything happened to you."

"Don't worry, you're stuck with me."

"I have to tell you something, but I don't want you to be mad at me."

"Why would I be mad at you?"

"Well," she hesitated, "Because I started taking night classes. It's a landscape architecture program. I think that visit to your parents' house really made up my mind. I forgot there were normal moms who like normal things like gardens." She paused. "Anyway, that's why I was saving money and that's why I've been busy at night. I haven't told anyone, not even my parents. It shouldn't take much time away from the band, but it will take some, and so I just thought I should tell you."

"That's great," I said.

"You're mad."

"No, well, yes, a little. I thought we were going to try to take the band as far as we could?"

"I'm not going anywhere. I just need a change. I hate my job, and I'm tired of doing what everyone else wants me to do. The band is fun, but I just want a career that's a little more, I don't know, predictable."

I felt her stare burn toward me, but I refused to turn to look at her.

"You know, you were the one who gave me courage to try this," she said. "It's weird, I've always been interested in gardens. They're just so opposite everything in my crazy family life. Controlled, quiet, calm. There's just something really appealing about that.

"I guess the grass is always greener. So to speak."

Margo sighed.

"Kit, this is not a big deal. I'm not giving up on our band. I love playing with you, and lord knows I can't pull weeds in my tight stage dresses. Plus, I'm far too vain to step off a stage. It's just something else in my life. And, anyway, you're the real balls of the group. You've always been the one to make anything happen, not me."

I never thought of it that way, but she was right. I had done some things I didn't think I had the courage to do. I had discovered a new side to myself, and this side was perfectly capable of taking on whatever challenges might head my direction. And ultimately, did it really matter if we got signed? Was the idea of success with the band more significant than the few smaller moments with the important people in my life? Look where it got Kurt Cobain. All that money and fame and the guy was miserable.

I remembered Nancy's words. It's all life, Kit. These worlds are never as separate as we think.

"So…" I hesitated. "You can make a record and take your classes?"

"We'll work it out."

"I guess I can accept that."

"You better, or I'll kick your ass with a garden weasel."

"Fair enough."

Margo sighed again. "I'm exhausted. Do you mind driving me home? I don't feel like schlepping on the subway."

"Sure."

On the drive to her apartment, we listened to KDU's tribute to Nirvana.

"It really feels like the end of something," Margo said. "It's more than Cobain. It's the end of, I don't know, like, being young or something. Like we can't just keep fooling around."

"I don't think growing up has to be boring," I said. "It's just figuring out how to balance it all. I love my band, and I'm lucky enough to have good friends and a decent job. Obviously, Cobain couldn't do that."

We listened quietly to the music as I pulled up to Margo's apartment.

"Thanks for driving," she said, then turned and kissed my cheek. "See you next practice."

She climbed out of the car and walked toward the tall old brownstone, the place where it all began. She unlocked the glass door, then turned to smile and wave at me before disappearing into the building.

On the silent ride home, back down Broad Street, I watched the fading sky sail above me and listened to Nirvana. Blues melted into shades of pinks and oranges, broken by the clean black line of telephone wire that connected families and friends and unsolicited phone calls and wrong numbers and tapping computer keystrokes. I thought about the pulse of the thousands of signals bound together by this single black coil. How small it seemed to carry so much information. Each of these tiny heartbeats seemed heavier than this thin black wire could hold. My race to make a CD no longer seemed so important. Fragile new melodies rang in my ears like delicate lullabies. I wanted to call Charlie. I wanted to call my sister and my parents. The people in my life were what really mattered. I hoped never to mute them again.

EPILOGUE

This year's Lollapalooza was a continual reminder of the loss of Kurt Cobain this past April. Nirvana was to headline this year's tour, but the band seemed very present at the event. First, his widow Courtney Love surprised everyone by performing before headliners, Smashing Pumpkins. Just before The Breeders' set, the P.A. played Nirvana's "All Apologies" and the cheers were louder than for some of the live acts. Another nice surprise was the performance from Philly's own Broad Street, who released their debut CD, Broad Strokes, this summer. Sure, the band's music is a derivative, but Broad Street captures the energy of a great party, where the cocktails are flowing, the dance floor is grinding, and your hosts always know how to have a good time.

— Laura Cook, *City Paper*

Christine Weiser is a professional writer and editor and the one-time bass player for the Philly girl band, Mae Pang. Her current band, The Tights, can be heard in clubs in and around the Philadelphia area. In her other life, she is the co-author of *Ask Mr. Technology, Get Answers* (Linworth 2007), copublisher of *Philadelphia Stories*, and managing editor of *Tech & Learning*. Broad Street is her first novel.

ACKNOWLEDGEMENTS

Broad Street would not have been possible were it not for my friendship with the original bodacious siren, Lynette Byrnes. Lynette and I met through our boyfriends, clicked, and eventually had the crazy idea we could start a rock band. The fact that neither of us really knew how to play seemed incidental. We'd figure it out.

And we did. We formed *Mae Pang*, a mainly chick rock garage band. We went through the requisite drummer turnover (including my future husband), until we found Elisa "Chi Chi Boom" Chiusano. We had a blast being a part of the Philly rock scene, commiserating with our peers over empty clubs, no pay, crappy sound systems, and the eternal wait between sound check and performance. It was exhausting and fun, and inspired many scenes for this book. We're still at it today, now as *The Tights*, with our fab keyboard player and chart-maker extraordinaire, John "Uncle Boogie" Byrnes. Thanks for the rock, guys.

No less important to the birth of this book is the inspiration and motivation I received from my friend and business partner, Carla Spataro. When we met at a local writers' group, Carla and I were struggling to get our first novels finished. We often commiserated over the ups and downs of the writing process, and Carla kept pushing me forward, first through the writers' group and then by suggesting the fabulous Iowa Summer Writing Festival. These experiences helped me write past those first three chapters (which I'd rewritten roughly 1,200 times), find a voice for Kit, and finish the book. Since then, Carla and I have started *Philadelphia Stories*, the free literary magazine featuring local authors that we hope inspires other writers. It's way more work than we ever dreamed it would be, but I love it and am proud of it. Thank you, Carla.

Of course, none of this would be possible without the incredible support of my husband, Rob Giglio. Rob is always there to keep me balanced with the perfect encouraging words, and has been a good friend even back when he was our pain-in-the-ass drummer. We're also lucky to have one very cool kid, Dexter. Love you guys.

Thanks, too, to all of my friends and family, especially my dad, who helped me search for my muse very early on.

QUESTIONS FOR DISCUSSION

1. This novel is set in the 1990s and addresses themes of female empowerment. Both Margo and Kit say that they want to be as good, or better than, their male counterparts, but their behavior doesn't always support this claim. In what ways to you think women undercut their own power? Do you think young women's attitudes about feminism or female empowerment have changed significantly over the last ten years? Twenty years?

2. Do you think Kit considers herself a feminist? Why or why not?

3. What do you think is the central theme of Broad Street? How was this theme reflected through the characters' actions and development?

4. How did your impressions of Kit shift throughout the novel? What changes did her character make that most impressed you? What do you think she could have done differently or better?

5. Kit always seems to make the wrong choices when it comes to men. Do you think these unhealthy choices are typical of young women? Why or why not? What might influence this decision-making in a positive or negative way?

6. Kit and Margo become close friends who, by the end of the novel, have very different agendas. Do you think they will remain friends? Have you been able to maintain relationships with friends even after the things that first brought you together changed?

7. At the beginning of the novel, Kit's boyfriend Dale cheats on her, but once Broad Street begins to have some success, Dale wants her back. What do you think this says about his character?

8. Throughout the course of the novel, we see both Kit and Margo change. How do you think music helps them to achieve confidence?

9. Both Kit and Margo struggle in their relationships with their parents. Kit feels like she can never live up to her father's intellectual expectations, and Margo is consistently embarrassed by her parents wildly inappropriate behavior. What influence do you think these parent-child relationships have on the characters' behavior and decision-making? Why do you think this is a central theme in so many novels? Did it remind you of the way you and your parents relate to each other?

10. Kit engages in some risky sexual behavior and experiments quite a bit with drugs. Did this disturb you or did you find this to be a common theme in coming-of-age novels and real-life experience?

11. Towards the end of the novel, Kit and Margo sign a questionable contract with a record producer. Would you have done the same thing in their situation? Do you think this was a good decision on their part? Why or why not?

12. Have you ever known anyone like Kit and Margo who march to the beat of their own drums? What do you admire about these people? What do you disapprove of? Have they had an effect on your life?

13. Where do you see Kit and Margo in five or ten years? Still with Broad Street? Still in the music business? Or do you see their lives taking them away from music?

Become a Member of
Philadelphia Stories and Support Local Arts!

Philadelphia Stories is a nonprofit literary magazine and companion website that includes writing and art from the PA-DE-NJ area and is provided to the general public free of charge. *Philadelphia Stories* is a 501c3. Every contribution you make is tax deductible. The magazine has no salaried employees. The majority of the magazine's operating expenses come solely from members and fundraisers. Please consider becoming a member today.

Become a member of Philadelphia Stories and enjoy these great benefits while helping to ensure the magazine's on-going viability

Michener ($20-$49)
Free One Year Subscription

Buck ($50-$99)
Free One Year Subscription, plus your choice of a Philadelphia Stories coffee mug or t-shirt

Whitman ($100-$499)
Free One Year Subscription, plus your choice of a Philadelphia Stories coffee mug or t-shirt plus free admission to ONE fundraiser/event per year

Potok ($500-$999)
Free One Year Subscription, plus your choice of a Philadelphia Stories coffee mug or t-shirt plus free admission to ALL fundraisers/events per year

W.C. Williams ($1,000+)
Free One Year Subscription, plus your choice of a Philadelphia Stories coffee mug or t-shirt plus free admission to ALL fundraisers/events per year plus exclusive VIP dinner with noted local author and other Williams level donors

I would like to become a Philadelphia Stories Member at the following level:

- ☐ Michener($20-$49)
- ☐ Buck ($50-$99)
- ☐ Whitman ($100-$499)
- ☐ Potok ($500-$999)
- ☐ W. C. Williams ($1,000+)
- ☐ Other _____

Name:_____

Address:_____

City:_____ State:_____ Zip:____ Email:_____

Phone: (   ) _____

Amount:_____

☐ **Please keep my gift anonymous**

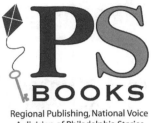

BOOKS

Regional Publishing, National Voice
A division of Philadelphia Stories

PS Books publishes literary and commercial fiction, nonfiction, and anthologies with a preference for, but not limited to, the Delaware Valley. *PS Books* is a division of *Philadelphia Stories* (www.philadelphiastories.org), a nonprofit literary magazine and companion website that publishes literary fiction, poetry, and art from PA-NJ-DE and provides it to the general public free of charge. *PS Books* distributes their titles nationally.

Coming Spring 2009 from PS Books:

The Singular Exploits of Wonder Mom and Party Girl by Marc Schuster: Audrey Corcoran never dreamed she'd try cocaine, but a year after a bitter divorce, she meets a man named Owen Little who convinces her that a little buzz might be exactly what she needs to lift her spirits. And why not? He's already turned her on to jazz, and no one in his circle of hip, sophisticated friends ever thinks twice about getting high. Soon, however, her escalating drug use puts a strain on Audrey's relationship with her daughters, and she begins to sell cocaine from her home in order to subsidize her habit. At turns horrifying and hilarious, *The Singular Exploits of Wonder Mom and Party Girl* offers a scathing indictment of American consumer culture and the wildly conflicting demands it makes upon women.

BROAD STREET

Order your gift copy of Broad Street – or any PS Books titles – using the handy order form below. Your purchase will help support Philadelphia Stories magazine – a nonprofit that publishes established and emerging writers from the PA-NJ-DE area.

YES! I want to order a copy of _____ for just $13.95!

Name_____

Address _____

City, State _____

Phone _____

E-mail _____

Please Charge my order to:

☐ MasterCard   ☐ VISA   ☐ Discover   ☐ AMEX

Account # _____ Exp. _____

Signature _____